A PLUME BOOK

MISSING PERSONS

CLARE O'DONOHUE is a freelance television writer and producer. She has worked worldwide on a variety of shows for the Food Network, the History Channel, and truTV, among others. She is also the author of the Someday Quilts mystery series.

ALSO BY CLARE O'DONOHUE

The Lover's Knot
A Drunkard's Path
The Double Cross

MISSING PERSONS

A KATE CONWAY MYSTERY

Clare O'Donohue

A PLUME BOOK

PLUME
Published by Penguin Group
Penguin Group (USA) Inc., 375 Hudson Street, New York, New York 10014, U.S.A. •
Penguin Group (Canada), 90 Eglinton Avenue East, Suite 700, Toronto, Ontario, Canada
M4P 2Y3 (a division of Pearson Penguin Canada Inc.) • Penguin Books Ltd., 80 Strand,
London WC2R 0RL, England • Penguin Ireland, 25 St. Stephen's Green, Dublin 2, Ire-
land (a division of Penguin Books Ltd.) • Penguin Group (Australia), 250 Camberwell
Road, Camberwell, Victoria 3124, Australia (a division of Pearson Australia Group Pty.
Ltd.) • Penguin Books India Pvt. Ltd., 11 Community Centre, Panchsheel Park, New
Delhi – 110 017, India • Penguin Books (NZ), 67 Apollo Drive, Rosedale, North Shore
0632, New Zealand (a division of Pearson New Zealand Ltd.) • Penguin Books (South
Africa) (Pty.) Ltd., 24 Sturdee Avenue, Rosebank, Johannesburg 2196, South Africa

Penguin Books Ltd., Registered Offices: 80 Strand, London WC2R 0RL, England

First published by Plume, a member of Penguin Group (USA) Inc.

First Printing, June 2011
10   9   8   7   6   5   4   3   2   1

Ⓟ REGISTERED TRADEMARK—MARCA REGISTRADA

LIBRARY OF CONGRESS CATALOGING-IN-PUBLICATION DATA
O'Donohue, Clare.
    Missing persons : a Kate Conway mystery / Clare O'Donohue.
      p. cm.
    ISBN 978-0-452-29706-7
    1. Women television producers and directors—Fiction. 2. Missing persons—
Investigation—Fiction. 3. Chicago (Ill.)—Fiction. I. Title.
    PS3615.D665M57 2011
    813'.6—dc22

                                                              2010044984

Printed in the United States of America
Set in Adobe Garamond Pro
Designed by Eve L. Kirch

*To my sister, Mary, who stole my clothes in high school
but has since made up for it with friendship, love, loyalty,
and the occasional gift of great earrings*

ACKNOWLEDGMENTS

This mystery series is based, sort of, on my years as a television producer. The frustration, annoyance, craziness, and profanity is from my actual experience, but the rest of it is pure fiction. Over my years as a producer, I had a chance to meet people from all walks of life. So many of them welcomed me into their homes, shared their stories, and, in some cases, became my friends. Thanks for your kindness, and the occasional free pie even when I made you cry. (I'm talking to you, Anise "Yam Good" Morrison.) And to all my friends in television, I hope you feel I've done a good job with this book. Of course, it wouldn't even be a book without my agent, Sharon Bowers of the Miller Agency, who has talked me off a few ledges and helped me move forward as a writer. And thanks to my editor, Becky Cole, who championed this series at Plume, for letting me go where my imagination was taking me. To Nadia Kashper, Mary Pomponio, the men and women in sales and marketing, and everyone at Plume who put this together, thanks, once again, for all the hard work. To my first readers, Karen Meier, Alessandra Ascoli, Peggy McIntyre, and Tom Carroll, your feedback was invaluable. To Dr. Brian Peterson, chief medical examiner for Milwaukee County, thank you for never letting on how tired you must be of all my questions. To my mother, Sheila O'Donohue, for reading through each manuscript. To my family, V, Kevin, and my many friends, your support has meant the world to me. And to the faithful readers of the Someday Quilts mystery series, thanks for all the kind words and e-mails. Though Nell's story continues to unfold, I hope you also enjoy spending time with Kate.

One

"I want you to tell me about the day your husband was murdered."
The woman glanced toward the camera before returning her
eyes to me. Then, in a quiet tone, she launched into the story. It
was one she must have told a hundred times in the last three years—to
police, family, friends, prosecutors, and now, to me.

Her husband had managed one of those excessively cheerful chain
restaurants in the northwest suburbs of Chicago. He'd recently started
putting in a lot of hours because the couple was saving for their first
home and planning a family. He'd wanted, as the woman now told
me, to give them a secure future. But it wasn't to be. One night, after
he'd closed the restaurant and let the rest of the employees go home, he
stayed to send some e-mails to the corporate office. While he worked,
two men broke into the restaurant, one of them an ex-employee. Fear-
ing identification, the men shot the husband in the face. His last words,
apparently, were, "Tell my wife I love her." The killers were caught six
hours later, having stolen only forty dollars. The rest of the day's take
had already been deposited at the bank by the assistant manager.

"Forty dollars," the woman repeated, still struggling to believe that
her husband had been murdered, and her future shattered, for so paltry
a sum.

She told the story beautifully, and with remarkable composure. But
as I listened, nodding my head empathetically, my eyes glistening as
if on the verge of tears, all I could think was—this would be so much
better if she cried.

When she finished, she leaned back and looked, as they all do, for
my approval. I gave it. I was her friend, after all. Though we'd only
spoken once before today and I'd met her only two hours ago, I was
now her best friend. That was what I needed her to feel so that she
would trust me, tell me things in confidence, forget that a cameraman
and audio guy were just a few feet away, recording everything she said

for the cable television show I worked for. *Caught!* was one of dozens of true-crime shows littering up television and yet we never ran out of new murders to profile.

I leaned forward in my chair. We were sitting with our knees only inches apart, but I needed to get even closer to block out everything but me.

"You did a great job with that," I said. "It was really hard, I know, but you did better than anyone I've interviewed."

I could hear the sincerity in my voice. I could imitate sincerity so well that even I believed it. I glanced toward the photo of her husband, strategically placed behind her left shoulder.

"Doug was a very special man."

As they all do, she turned to see what I was looking at and saw the photo of her husband on their wedding day. She kept her eyes there, reluctant to turn her back on him.

"He had such wonderful dreams for you both," I continued. "I can imagine it was something you talked about a lot."

"It was." Her voice cracked.

"He must have wanted to give you everything."

"He did."

"I guess that's why he was working so late."

That was it. Tears came down her face. She began to shake. I reached over and placed my hand on hers. She turned her eyes back to me. She was so vulnerable, in so much pain. It would look great on camera.

I leaned back and spoke gently. "I want to go over the last question one more time. I know this is difficult, but tell me again about the day your husband was murdered."

She barely got through the story.

Two

"Sometimes I don't like you." Andres Pena, my cameraman, loaded the last of the equipment in his van. I waited by my car, parked in front of his.

"That's okay," I said. "I'm not that fond of myself right now."

"The way she thanked you for helping her. It's like being thanked by a cow right before you bring down the hammer on its skull."

"You forgot the hug."

Like so many interview subjects, she wanted me to stay afterward to chat, to keep in touch, to really become friends. It's interview euphoria, and since I rarely share it, I like to get out as quickly as possible. Even waiting outside the house for the crew to pack up, as I was doing now, made me a little jumpy.

"Nobody has to do the show and nobody has to watch," I said, repeating what had become my mantra. "But they do."

"You don't have to be so good at it."

"Yes, I do," I argued. "If I don't bring back what the network wants, I don't get hired for the next job. And neither do you."

Andres nodded. "It's going to look great. The way she chokes up when she says his last words. I pushed in a little. You'll really see the tears." So much for his conscience.

I've been working as a freelance television producer for nearly twelve years. The title "producer" can mean a lot of different things depending on what area of entertainment you work in—from the person who spends ten years trying to get a film made to the lead in a sitcom who wants to feel more important. In my tiny little corner of the basic cable television world, a producer actually produces an episode of a show. That is, a production company creates a show, like *Caught!*, and hires people like me to conduct the interviews and write the episode. The episode airs on some network, in this case Crime TV, and my name appears in small print that goes by too fast for anyone to see. Assuming, of course, that anyone watches credits, which they don't.

I prefer to work in the field. I go to the interview subjects rather than have them come to a studio. It's typically easier, cheaper, and more interesting to shoot people where they actually live or work, so it's done a lot. In my career I've interviewed CEOs and prison inmates, celebrities and coroners, gardeners, beauty queens, UFO nuts, orphans, and even a monkey. When you watch a documentary and the interview subjects are looking slightly off camera while they talk, they're talking to someone like me. My face and my voice never end up in the finished product, so there's no glory in it. But there is money. And as long as you don't worry too much about who gets hurt, it's an interesting job.

I always tell myself that no one is forced to tell their story to a television crew. Like a drunk sorority sister in a *Girls Gone Wild* video, they might eventually regret their actions—but while it's happening, they want it to happen.

Yeah, I know how that sounds.

"Did you hear about a new doc that Ripper is producing?" Andres lit a cigarette and leaned against my car. Andres was nearly forty, three years my senior, and he shared my weary acceptance of our profession. But he justified his actions differently—no drunken sorority analogies for him. He had three kids, two mortgages, and a dog with arthritis.

"Mike mentioned something."

"I hear it's about unsolved cases," Andres said. "Sounds depressing as hell."

"It's going to be episode after episode of kids on milk cartons, crying parents, and earnest cops who will never give up."

He laughed. "Who wants to watch that crap?"

"Are you kidding? It'll be a huge hit. People love other people's misery. It makes them feel superior. It's just no fun being on the other side of it."

He nodded but said nothing. Andres was like that. He knew when it was better to keep his mouth shut. But our sound guy, a musician who called himself Victor Pilot, wasn't so discreet.

"How's the divorce coming, Kate? Has the old man completely fucked you over?"

"Not completely, Victor."

Not yet anyway.

"If you're lonely at home, you can always hang out at my place."

Victor was in his midtwenties, a decade younger than me. And while I still had my figure, my long red hair, and the unmistakable scent of a woman who hasn't had sex in a while, I couldn't figure out why he continually hit on me. Whatever his reason, I wasn't interested. I was in the process of getting rid of one dreamer with more confidence than common sense. I didn't need to take on another.

"Thanks anyway," I told him.

"You need to get out there, lady," Victor prompted.

"Papers aren't even signed yet. We're still, believe it or not, arguing over the four hundred dollars in our savings account. The lawyers charged six hundred dollars to fight for that."

"Then why not sit down with Frank and figure it out without lawyers?" Andres asked.

It was a reasonable question, but then Andres has never been divorced. Divorce, and the subsequent dividing of the assets, isn't about reason. It's about revenge.

"It's my money," I answered. "If I'm going to give it to some man who has never done anything for me, I'll give it to the lawyer."

"Better than giving it to Frank's new squeeze," Victor offered.

Though the mention of my husband's girlfriend made bile rise into my throat, I just smiled. Unlike my interview subjects, I wasn't dumb enough to offer up my private hell for the enjoyment of the general public.

"The good news is that with all the true-crime shows you've done, you probably know eight ways to kill him and get away with it," Victor continued.

I took the shot tapes from Andres and opened my car door. "Problem is, I've done enough shows to know that if Frank ends up dead, I'll be the number one suspect."

Within twenty-four hours, I'd find out I was right. Who says you can't learn anything from television?

Three

Frank and I had met in high school. I was smart, bored, and anxious to get out of the middle-class Chicago suburbs I grew up in. I wanted to be a writer and travel the world, which made me odd in a school full of kids who didn't think beyond Friday night. I was also too skinny, more Olive Oyl than Kate Moss. And I was taller than a lot of my classmates, with red hair and glasses. Not exactly prom queen material.

Frank shouldn't have been interested in me. He played basketball. He was popular, sensitive, and handsome, from a family with more money than mine, and he wanted to be a painter.

If there is something more romantic than a seventeen-year-old guy turning his back on the easy life that seems almost his birthright so he can struggle for his art, I don't know what it is.

And if there is something more annoying than a thirty-seven-year-old man turning his back on his responsibilities as he continues to struggle, I don't know what that is either.

We married right after college. I had a degree in journalism, Frank in accounting. I immediately found a bad-paying job as an associate producer at a local news station and Frank went to work in the office of his father's construction firm. Things were good for a while. When our friends were single and complaining about their love lives, we would feel smug. But when one friend took a job in London because nothing was holding her in Chicago and another had a passionate affair with a famous musician, the smugness began to melt. Our friends were free to make crazy, interesting, wild choices, and it suddenly felt as though all our choices were already made.

It's not that I'm against meeting your life partner on the playground. It's worked out for a lot of people, and I'd hoped it would work out for us too. But Frank and I didn't turn out to be the people we said we would be. In the twenty years since high school, I've only used my passport once, and that was to show identification on a flight to Pittsburgh. I write cable television informational programs. Despite having my name in the credits of dozens of shows, nobody thinks that makes me a writer. Including me.

Frank went even further off course. His father fired him from the construction firm after he failed to show up thirty days in a row. His painting career never took off, unless you count the summer he painted our bedroom a soft blue. For a while he put painting aside and sought new passions, new outlets for his creative energy. First it was gardening, then cooking, then ceramics, and then I stopped keeping track. The interest would start off high and gradually melt away. The books and supplies he'd bought would find their way into the basement without ever having turned into something that paid for itself, let alone supported us. For a while he made big plans and promises, but in the last few years he didn't even look guilty when the bills arrived and he had to hand them over to me.

Instead of looking for a job, Frank spent most of his time watching TV, hanging out with his friends from high school, and reliving the glory days of his basketball victories. I would come home after a fourteen-hour shoot to a sink full of dishes and a lecture about how I was working too hard. After months of my pleading to help out a little, Frank did one thing for me. He went to the grocery store to pick up milk.

And somewhere in the dairy aisle he met Vera. And had an affair. And fell in love. And filed for divorce.

I should have been thrilled to have the deadbeat husband land on someone else's doorstep. And when my sister, my mother, our friends, coworkers, neighbors, or the UPS guy asked me, that's what I said. (The UPS guy was, technically, just dropping off a package for Frank, so he may not have been asking, but he heard anyway.)

But, as often as I said I was glad to be rid of him, I didn't know what I really felt. All right, maybe I had some idea. I felt angry, betrayed, humiliated, and slightly embarrassed that while I spent my days surrounded by male cameramen, male audio guys, and often male interview subjects, Frank stayed home and watched ESPN—and yet he was the one who had an affair. Not once, not even once, had someone hit on me in all the years I'd been working. Not that I would have cheated, but that's hardly the point.

One thing was for sure, I was alone in our tiny two-bedroom bungalow with an upside-down mortgage and a leaky roof, and he was happy with someone else.

When I got home from the shoot, I dropped the tapes on the kitchen table next to a note from Frank. "Picked up some stuff. Brought in your mail." He'd doodled a mailbox with a face, arms, and legs in the corner of the paper. It was a cheery little note, flaunting his happiness, it seemed to me, making it a mean little note.

It also didn't make sense. What *stuff* had he picked up? I walked around the house but I couldn't see what was missing. His clothes had been gone for months. He'd taken his paints and easel from the garage a week after he'd moved out. And I'd removed our wedding photos from the bookcase. There was no sign that Frank had ever lived in this house, so I couldn't figure out what there was left to take.

I made myself a turkey sandwich and grabbed a pop. I sat in the kitchen, reading the paper and going through the mail. It was only when I walked into the living room a second time that I realized the space above the fireplace was empty. The painting was gone. Frank had done an oil painting of a couple walking hand in hand down Michigan Avenue and given it to me when we bought the house ten years ago. It had decorated that wall ever since. I'd gotten so used to it, and in the last few years, so used to not looking at it, that its loss had escaped my notice for nearly an hour.

I didn't want the painting. And after everything that had happened, I didn't even like it anymore. But it was technically mine. It had been a gift from Frank. Before I could stop myself, I'd dialed his cell phone, ready to demand it back. It was my painting, something I had treasured since the day he gave it to me. That's what I was going to say. Even as I dialed, I knew how pathetic I would sound.

But it got worse.

"Hello?" The voice was female.

I hung up.

"Oh, my God," I yelled to an empty house. "She's answering his cell phone. What kind of person answers another person's cell phone!"

I knew what kind of person. The "we're so in love we have no secrets from each other" kind of person. I momentarily comforted myself with the notion that the hang-up might make her think there was *another* other woman. Then I remembered caller ID and just felt stupid.

Do you ever have a moment in your life when you think, "This is not what I signed up for?" And then you look around for someone to blame and there is no one, just you. I guess you could go see a shrink and blame your mother, but that wouldn't work for me. She hadn't wanted me to marry Frank in the first place.

After all the years of being unhappy in my marriage, after Frank's announcement that he was leaving me, after months of lawyers and divorce filings and angry phone calls with the man who had once promised to love me forever, it was finally real. A real person on the other end of the phone. All I knew about her was her first name, Vera, not even enough to Google her. But hearing her voice, I knew she was real. Everything that had once been real for me, every happy memory with Frank, was reduced to dust.

At eight o'clock I went to bed and watched the last half of a bad romantic comedy where two characters survive supposedly hilarious misunderstandings before realizing they belong together. In real life, couples like that wouldn't last five minutes, but in TV movies we're led to believe it's the real thing. Watching the couple kiss and the screen fade to credits, all I could think about was that woman from the interview. "Tell my wife I love her," her husband said as his last words. That was the real thing.

Is it wrong to envy a woman whose husband was shot in the face? Probably.

Four

What is that?

I had fallen asleep with the television on, but the buzzing wasn't coming from an infomercial about a device that will save hundreds of hours in the kitchen. It was something else.

I looked over at my dresser and saw my cell phone moving around on my nightstand. I'd put the phone on vibrate for the interview and forgotten to return it to ring. It was nearly midnight, never a good time to get a call. And it was Frank's cell. This wasn't going to be fun.

"What?"

"Kate?" It was a woman's voice. The same woman's voice.

"Who is this?" I decided to play dumb.

"My name is Vera Bingham. I'm Frank's . . . friend." Nice. Hesitation. Means she's a little embarrassed. And should be.

"He's not here." I don't know why I said that. It sounded tough.

"I know, Kate. He's . . . well, something's wrong. He's sick or something. I've called an ambulance."

"What do you mean, something's wrong? Is he throwing up or something? Can I talk to him?"

"No. I thought you might want to meet us at the hospital. St. Anthony's. It's on Division and . . ."

"I know where it is."

Twenty minutes later I walked through the doors of St. Anthony's looking for my husband's mistress. There was a grandmother type with a younger man, probably her son, holding her hand, and a twenty-something blonde wearing a short skirt and four-inch heels. It had to be her. She looked like a midlife crisis.

"Vera?" I asked.

The blonde looked up at me and blinked.

"Are you Vera?"

Behind me, I heard a woman clear her throat. "I'm Vera."

I spun around. A third option I hadn't seen before, a woman who looked in her early forties, with short, stylish but graying hair.

"You're Vera?"

She smiled. "You're Kate. I would have picked you out anywhere."

She was waiting for the doctor, she told me, so there was no news yet. She gestured toward a seat and offered to get coffee, which I accepted mostly because I needed time to think. She was older than me. She was shorter, and probably twenty pounds heavier. Not to be shallow, but I'd just assumed he'd left for perkier breasts and a smaller waistline. In what midlife crisis does a man leave his wife for an older woman?

When Vera returned, we sat and drank the bitter coffee and stared, in exaggerated ways, down the hall, hoping for a doctor, hoping for something that would prevent us from having to chat. No one came.

"What happened exactly?" I asked once I'd run out of coffee.

"I don't know. He was fine. There's a reunion of his basketball buddies this weekend and he'd been playing at the park all afternoon. He's been trying to get back in shape, so he's been playing a lot. Plus, he wanted to practice for the reunion. This evening he wasn't feeling well. Nothing serious, just a little stomachache. And, I guess, he was acting odd."

"What do you mean, odd?"

"He asked me why I'd gotten yellow sheets. I hadn't. The sheets were white."

"So he was having some problems with his vision."

"I thought maybe he was tired."

"Then what?"

"We went to bed. I thought he'd fallen asleep, but after a while, I realized he wasn't breathing. I couldn't wake him so I called an ambulance."

"He wasn't breathing?"

"He didn't seem to be. I couldn't tell."

"But you couldn't wake him?"

She shook her head. "The paramedic said it could be a heart attack."

"He's thirty-seven. You don't have a heart attack at thirty-seven."

"You can," Vera said.

"But he's in good shape. Maybe he needed to lose ten or fifteen pounds, but he doesn't smoke or do drugs." Unless, I thought, he does those things with you.

"He's under a lot of stress," she said quietly. "The divorce has been hard on him. All the anger."

So she was saying this was my fault. I took a deep breath, considered slamming her head into a wall, realized it wasn't the most productive solution, plus there were witnesses, and just nodded.

"Well, you don't die of a heart attack at thirty-seven," I said.

And she agreed. The two of us, with our nonexistent medical training, discussed the best way for Frank to make a full recovery and the odds that he would be home (her home, I assumed) in days. By the time an hour had passed, I was half convinced it wasn't a heart attack at all, but something more like indigestion. I was starting to feel annoyed I was losing a night's sleep over it.

A tall man, African American, wearing a doctor's coat and a worried expression came toward us. "Mrs. Conway," he said to Vera.

"I'm Mrs. Conway," I said.

I could see the confusion and embarrassment in his eyes. Though I was the wife, I was clearly not the woman who had brought Frank to the hospital in the middle of the night.

"How's Frank?" Vera asked.

He grabbed an empty chair and pulled it toward us, positioning himself so he was facing us both equally.

"I'm Dr. Milton. I have some bad news. We did everything we could but it was too late. Frank didn't respond to our treatments. He didn't make it. I'm very sorry."

I could feel myself blinking. I could hear the blonde tapping the toe of her boot on the floor. But the doctor's words had entered some kind of echo chamber. They were vague and didn't make sense. He was saying Frank was dead. But that couldn't be true.

Vera gasped and grabbed my hand.

"Was it a heart attack?" I asked.

"Probably," the doctor said. "We'll know more after the autopsy."

"No." Vera sounded suddenly emphatic. "Frank wouldn't want that."

The doctor shifted uncomfortably. "Are you a relative?" he asked, as if he were about to suggest this wasn't any of her business.

"I'm his fiancée."

I looked at her. First I was hearing of it. "Well, I'm his wife," I said as coldly as I could. "I want to know what Frank died from, so, as his next of kin, I'm authorizing the autopsy."

The doctor patted my knee. "Mrs. Conway," he said, "I'm glad you feel that way, but I want you to understand, I want you both to understand, that I wasn't asking for permission. When we have sudden, unexpected death in a relatively young, otherwise healthy person, an autopsy is essential."

"But not required," Vera said.

The doctor took a deep, calming breath that was, I'm sure, supposed to inspire Vera and me to do the same. "Not always," he said.

Because of a documentary I'd done about the death industry in the United States, I knew that autopsies were rare and getting rarer. People who die in accidents or from possible homicides get an autopsy, but people who die in the hospital, older people, and those with known diseases rarely do. In some states the number is as low as five percent. It costs money to perform the procedure, there are fewer people interested in the specialty, and many people can't stomach the idea of their loved one being cut up, so doctors rarely press for them. Unless the police are involved, they mostly don't happen. I knew that. Obviously the doctor knew that. But what was interesting was that Vera seemed to know it as well.

I let go of Vera's hand. "I want an autopsy. I want to know why Frank died, and I'm sure his parents will as well."

The doctor nodded. "I'm sorry for your loss," he said in the general direction of both of us.

We sat there for a while, each in our own thoughts. I watched as a small boy with a cast on his arm walked over to the blonde, who hugged him tightly. As they left, I got up.

"I guess we should start planning the service," Vera said.

I ignored the comment. I wanted to point out that whoever she thought she was in Frank's life, I was legally his wife. I didn't need my husband's mistress to help me plan his funeral. I wanted to point it out, but I didn't.

"I have to call his family," I said.

"I'm sorry." She looked up at me, tears filling her eyes.

"Me too."

As I walked away, I could hear her sobbing behind me.

Five

Frank's mother wouldn't believe me. His father asked for the name of the doctor. His best friend since high school, Neal, just kept saying "shit" over and over. After spending twenty minutes convincing my parents I didn't need them to come to my house, I decided to leave the rest of the calls for the morning.

I crawled into bed and hugged the pillow. Neither tears nor sleep would come. I just lay there remembering the night we met.

I'd seen him walking the halls of our high school, though I doubt he'd seen me. He was hard to miss. Tall, with dark-brown hair and caramel eyes, he had more confidence than I'd ever seen in anyone not running for political office. We didn't speak in freshman or sophomore years, though we were always in several classes together. High school is not exactly a place where athletes and geeks mingle.

At the beginning of junior year, I was invited to the sixteenth birthday party of one of the most popular girls in school. She'd invited the entire junior class to witness the middle-class Chicago version of a coming-out party. It started with her parents giving her a car and ended when the birthday girl vomited a combination of scotch and sausage pizza on her mother's living room carpet.

In between, Frank introduced himself to me. He told me he liked my book report on *The Crucible*. I told him I liked the way he drew pictures for his report, rather than just giving an oral presentation—a viewpoint the teacher didn't share. That's when he told me he loved to paint and I said I wanted to travel. Before I knew it he had walked me home and kissed me good night.

It was my first kiss. It was a perfect kiss, though in all honesty I have nothing to compare it to. I would never admit this to anyone who hadn't known me for twenty years, but Frank is the only man I have ever kissed. We started dating after that night and had never been apart again, until, well, I guess until four months ago.

On that first night, as he walked me home, he quoted Keats, gave a fairly convincing argument as to why it would be the year the Cubs made it to the World Series (they didn't), and shared with me his secret for the perfect French toast (orange juice in the batter). He was a sixteen-year-old Renaissance man.

And he looked at me as if I were the first person in the world to really get him. I don't think it was an act. I think a lot of people only saw the star athlete or the best-looking guy in school. But he had all this promise in him. All this potential. He was smart and curious. He could install anything, fix anything, create anything.

What he lacked was persistence.

I'd fallen in love with all he could be and found myself married to what he was. But I guess he could have said the same about me. He once said he loved introducing me to people and watching as they realized how cool I was. It remains the nicest compliment I've ever received, even though I'm absolutely certain the last thing I am is cool. Maybe, eventually, he realized that too.

"How did we get from that night to this, Frank?" I asked the empty place on his side of the bed.

There was a slight breeze in the bedroom, and I thought for a moment that he might be haunting me, but I realized I'd left the window open. I don't believe in ghosts, and I don't think the dead come back to spend time with their loved ones. But even if Frank was a ghost, I knew he wouldn't be coming to me. He would be haunting Vera.

Six

"Crap, crap, crap." I got louder with each repetition as I ran from room to room. "Where did I put it?"

On the night Frank had left, after he'd calmly told me he was in love with someone else and would prefer—that was his phrase—not to be married to me anymore, I'd taken off my wedding ring and thrown it at him. I'd never bothered to go in search of it until now. I was heading to meet his parents at the funeral home and I knew his mother would look at my hand to see if it was there. I knew everyone would look. I stood in the kitchen and relived every humiliating moment of that conversation, trying to remember where he had been standing when I finally had my turn to speak.

I wish I'd said something pithy and sophisticated, like a character in some movie from the 1930s where divorce was the plot of a screwball comedy, the husband was Cary Grant, and everyone drank constantly. I could have used a drink that night.

What I actually said was both incomprehensible and slightly crazy, and something I would prefer never to repeat. It was also the last time Frank and I had ever been alone in a room together. He'd made sure of that. The coward.

"The refrigerator," I suddenly remembered.

I lay on the floor, which desperately needed sweeping, and reached my hand into gunk and crumbs and whatever evil things live under a refrigerator, until my fingers reached a hard, round object. I pulled it out, rinsed it off, and put it back on my finger. It felt a little tight.

By the time I got to the funeral home, I was late. And just as I was about to walk in, my phone rang. I almost didn't answer, but it was Ripper Productions, my best client. They produced mostly true crime and some medical mystery shows. The money they offered was nothing special, but they paid within two weeks. Getting paid quickly, sometimes getting paid at all, is something of a battle for freelancers like myself, so I always worked for Ripper whenever they could use me.

"Kate, it's Mike. You are going to love me."

"I already do," I said. I was lying. Mike was slimy and annoying, and he thought he was creating a masterpiece with each half hour of his sensation-heavy shows. He was based in New York, so we'd never actually met, but even with eight hundred miles between us, he made my skin crawl.

"Remember the last time we talked, I told you about this new show I was pitching? I just sold it to Crime TV. It's called *Missing Persons*. Each episode centers on some ordinary idiot, just living his life, when—for no reason—he just vanishes. Police can't figure it out, family is beside themselves, his life seemed perfect but maybe it wasn't. That kind of thing. We talk to the police, the families, the friends. It's all about their frustration and how they just want to know what happened. It's a mystery show but the drama is still playing out. We end each episode with a voice-over asking for the public's help in solving the case. Great stuff."

"It sounds interesting. Can we talk about it next week?"

"I need you to start Monday."

I hesitated. I work mainly the cable television circuit—documentaries and informational programs—so it's anything from an exposé on gang violence to a food contest. I'm contracted to work for a day or a week or whatever it takes to make one episode, but rarely longer. I might work twenty days one month and none the next. I never know. Which means if I get called for jobs, I do them. Mostly no questions asked, because if you ask too many questions, the job goes to someone else. I imagine it's the same for hit men.

I took a deep breath. "I'm sorry, Mike. My husband died Wednesday."

"I thought you were divorced."

"I was in the process of getting a divorce."

"Lucky you. Now you get out of paying the lawyers. My last divorce cost me a bundle," he said. "Was he insured?"

"Excuse me?"

"Life insurance?"

"Yeah. We both had it."

"Ka-ching."

I started to explain that I couldn't remember if I'd even kept up the payments, but I was beginning to feel a little sick. "I'm on my way into the funeral home," I said.

"Right. Bad time. I'll call you later."

"I don't think I can start Monday."

That was painful. I needed the work to make the mortgage.

"We'll figure something out," Mike said. "It's a great story: missing girl just out of college, brokenhearted family. It's in Chicago, so no travel for you. Plus, the family will love talking to someone who just lost her husband. It'll make them feel like you get their pain. They'll spill their guts."

I hung up, tried not to vomit on my shoes, and went inside.

"Hey, sweetie." My sister, Ellen, wrapped her arms around me just inside the doors of the funeral home. Ellen was only two years older than me but had always treated me like a child. Like me, she had spent her entire life in the Chicago area, gotten married young, and never left the country, but somehow she saw herself as more worldly than I was. Tougher and more cynical. Even my job didn't win me points for being a hard ass. Ellen taught seventh grade, a job, she frequently pointed out, I would never be able to handle.

"What are you doing here?" I asked.

"You can't go through this alone."

"Frank's parents are supposed to be here."

"They're in the director's office," she whispered. "Have you seen them since the separation?"

I shook my head. "They were paying Frank's legal fees, so that pretty much cut off all contact between us."

"His mother is practically hysterical. She blames you, I think."

I took a deep breath and headed toward the director's office. "This just keeps getting better and better, doesn't it?"

Seven

Frank's mother, Lynette Conway, had never been a big fan of mine. She thought her son was meant for better things than an ordinary girl from his high school. She had had visions that Frank would go on to Harvard, maybe run for Senate someday. It was like she had never met her own son, who was so disinterested in politics that he'd never even registered to vote. It didn't matter. In her mind, I'd kept him from a life of influence and glory.

His father, Alex Conway, on the other hand, had seen firsthand that Frank had the ambition of a well-fed cat. Though he'd never directly said it, I'd felt he understood my frustrations and was a little embarrassed that his son hadn't done more with his life.

"Hi," I said as Ellen and I entered the office. "I'm Mrs. Conway," I told the director. I heard a disparaging sigh from Frank's mother.

"I'm so sorry for your loss," the director said. He looked like a man who spent his days with the dead. His slight, almost skeletal, body was covered by an expensive three-piece suit in a somber gray. What hair he had was slicked back, and a pair of bifocals was perched dangerously close to the end of his nose.

"We've been making the plans while we waited for you," Alex said.

"I'm sorry about that." I smiled apologetically. "I've been getting a lot of phone calls from Frank's friends."

"He had so many friends." Lynette buried her head in her tissue and cried. I wanted to go over and comfort her, but I knew I wouldn't be welcome.

"I'm so sorry, Alex." I hugged his dad. "It's not supposed to happen this way, is it? A parent isn't supposed to bury his child."

"These last few months have been surreal. How are you holding up, kiddo?"

I shrugged. "I don't know what to feel, it's just so unbelievable."

So was standing with my in-laws, or ex-in-laws, or whatever they were, making polite conversation. Alex moved toward his wife. Ellen took my hand. We all stood awkwardly for a minute.

"If I might suggest some options for you, Mrs. Conway." The director broke the silence.

"*I'm* Mrs. Conway," Lynette said.

"So is Kate," Ellen told her.

The director nodded patiently. It was clear from his demeanor this wasn't the first long-standing family argument to play out its final scene in his office. "Every one of Mr. Conway's loved ones is to be included in the decisions, obviously."

"We're paying for it, so we're *making* the decisions," Lynette said.

For a moment I considered arguing the point, but I had less than a thousand dollars in my bank account so I couldn't fight them even if I wanted to. And did I want to? Was it really my responsibility anymore? I sat quietly while Frank's parents picked the most expensive package there was and made arrangements for his burial in a plot they already owned.

When they bought the plots, there were three adjoining ones available, and Lynette suggested they get a fourth for me "nearby." We turned them down, but Frank and I used to joke that his mother would figure out a way to spend eternity next to her favorite child. Sitting there, I realized she'd gotten what she wanted.

"All that's left now," the director said, "is for the next of kin to sign the papers allowing for the transfer of his body to our custody." He held up a pen and, after a moment's hesitation, Alex leaned forward.

Ellen grabbed it. "She's the next of kin," she said and gave the pen to me.

"Only legally," Lynette said.

"Legally is what counts," Ellen told her.

"He died of stress." Lynette spat the words at her. "Stress caused by the divorce."

"Frank cheated on Kate. Frank left Kate." Ellen was barely containing her anger. "If Frank died of stress, it's stress he caused."

"Men don't cheat if they're getting what they need at home," Lynette shouted.

"That's enough." Frank's father jumped out of his seat. "We're all emotional. We're not thinking. Lynette and I will handle the rest of the arrangements. Kate will, of course, be presented as Frank's wife at the wake and funeral. Most of our friends didn't even know they were separated. There's no point in bringing up that ugliness now and dragging our family name through the mud."

I suppressed a laugh. There's nothing like a death in the family to make everyone realize what's truly important, is there?

"Are we done?" I asked the director.

"As soon as you sign this form."

I signed.

"I'll see you at the wake," I said and walked out of the room without looking at any of them.

Eight

The next morning I took a bath, stared at my wedding ring, took it off because I felt like a fraud wearing it, then put it on again, and stayed in the tub until the water turned cold. My sister had left me a message about how I needed to stand up to "those people" who had raised "a good-for-nothing son" who had "ruined" my life. I didn't know which part was more offensive: that I should yell at people who had lost their oldest child or that, in my sister's eyes, my life was ruined.

At about noon, the doorbell rang. News had begun to trickle out to the neighbors, and I'd already received two casseroles, an apple pie, and something unidentifiable that combined noodles and blueberries. I assumed this was another well-intentioned dish I didn't feel like eating.

Instead, I opened the door to a large man holding a package. He was dressed in an ill-fitting dark-brown suit, with a yellowing, but once white, shirt and a blue tie. I'm not much for fashion, but he looked to be wearing something the Salvation Army would reject. Behind him was another man, younger and dressed better. Neither of them looked all that happy to be there.

"You Kathleen Conway?" the large man asked.

"Yes."

He handed me the package. "This is for you. It was on your doorstep. Can we come in?"

"I don't know you."

He wearily reached into his pocket and pulled out a badge. "Detective Scott Podeski." With that he pushed past me into the house. His friend followed in his footsteps, leaving me at the front door wondering if I should run. Probably not, but I knew I didn't want to hear whatever bad news these guys had obviously brought with them.

"This isn't a good time," I said.

"We're with homicide."

"Seriously?" It was a stupid comment, but I couldn't imagine why homicide detectives would show up at my door.

Podeski didn't care for my surprise. "You were married to Francis John Conway."

"Yes."

"How long?"

"Fifteen years."

"When's the last time you saw him?"

"I don't understand. Why are you asking about Frank?"

"Ma'am, if you could just answer the question. The last time you saw him?"

"It was three weeks ago, at my lawyer's office."

As we spoke I noticed the other man, the younger one, was taking notes.

"Is this about Frank's death? It wasn't a homicide. He died of a heart attack," I told them.

"Maybe, ma'am. A Dr. Milton requested an autopsy."

"I requested one," I corrected him.

That surprised him. "Why?" he asked.

"Frank was only thirty-seven and he was in good health."

"His death seemed suspicious to you?"

"Not suspicious, just unexpected. What's this about?"

I wanted to get control of the conversation, but Podeski eyeballed me, making it clear he wasn't interested in letting go.

"Detective, do you have information I don't have?"

"You weren't the one who brought him to the hospital."

"No."

"Who was?"

"Vera . . . something. I don't remember her last name."

"Bingham."

"If you knew, why ask me?" I was sounding defensive. I tried to calm down and change the tone of the conversation. I hadn't done anything, but homicide detectives questioning me about the death of my husband made me *feel* guilty. "Would you like to sit down?"

"No, ma'am. We won't take up any more of your time. Are you sure you hadn't been in contact with your husband since the meeting at your lawyer's office?"

"I didn't say I wasn't in contact with him. I said I hadn't seen him. He came by the house the other day . . ."

"The day he died?"

"I suppose so, yes. He left me a note."

"Do you have it?"

"No."

"You got rid of it?"

"I wouldn't put it that way. It's just, why would I keep a note from my estranged husband?"

"What did it say?"

"That he stopped by to pick up some of his things."

"The divorce, was it amicable?"

"Are they ever amicable?"

He smiled a little at that. "No, I guess not," he conceded. "You weren't home?"

"That's why he left me a note."

"Which you don't have."

"No."

"But you admit he was here."

"Admit? No. I'm *telling* you he was here. There's nothing to admit." I was arguing semantics with a homicide detective. That would look good to a jury.

Podeski looked around the living room. "Nice little house. Just the two of you?"

"We don't have children."

"But you had insurance."

"Are you asking me if I killed Frank?"

"I didn't say that," he said.

"You're a homicide detective. You must think someone killed Frank or you wouldn't be here."

"Not true, actually. The doctor had some concerns. We were called in to ask some questions."

"What kind of concerns?"

Podeski handed me a business card with his name and a phone number imprinted under the logo of the Chicago Police Department. "We're sorry for your loss, Mrs. Conway."

Then he and his silent note-taking partner left.

I stood at the door, taking it all in. Frank wasn't just dead. Possibly someone had murdered him. It didn't make sense. Everyone loved Frank. The only person with even the slightest motive to kill him was me.

Nine

After they left I thought about calling a criminal lawyer, just in case, but I didn't know one, and anyway, it seemed an over-reaction. They had to be wrong. No one had killed Frank. I knew that sometimes the police investigated deaths like Frank's, ones that were sudden and unexpected. I'd done stories about it. It was routine. I wasn't going to drive myself crazy imagining otherwise.

After about ten minutes of standing in my living room, I noticed that I was still holding the package. I went into the kitchen, sat at the small Formica table we had inherited from Frank's grandmother, and opened it. It was something to do, something that would keep me from thinking about Detective Podeski.

The package was from Mike, or rather the associate producer who worked for Mike. The associate producer, or A.P., did all the initial legwork: finding stories, conducting pre-interviews, and sending out information to the field producer.

I was supposed to read through everything and come up with a list of questions for each interview subject. The interviews weren't designed to find out the truth about the missing woman or get any answers as to why she had disappeared. That really didn't matter. What mattered was what story we wanted to tell: the one that would interest the viewers. She was a good girl who crossed paths with a killer or a bad girl who brought it on herself. She was a saint or a con artist or a whore. And the people around her were either heartbroken because of her disappearance or they were the cause of it—or, most likely, a combination of both.

Once I had the story, I would write the questions that would be most likely to get me the answers I needed. Sometimes I wrote questions that could take me in two directions—she was good, she was bad—so I could change my mind in editing.

I hadn't accepted the job, but I guess Mike knew I would. He'd included hard copies of e-mail correspondence he and the A.P. had had with each potential interview subject, giving them my name and cell-phone number as the person to contact and making ridiculous statements about how we hoped that the show would uncover the truth and lead to some resolution in the case.

The rest of the package had the usual stuff: a list of interview subjects, a summary of the case, and photos of the victim. Everything I needed to come up with a story good enough to kick off a new show and get it the media attention, and thus the ratings, the network needed.

The only unusual thing was the police report. Normally in cases for *Caught!* I would receive a full report, with everything from the initial statements to the arrest. But *Caught!* dealt with solved crimes, and this was most definitely an open investigation. Someone had taken a black marker and marked out some of the information on my copy of the report. It made sense that they weren't willing to reveal everything they knew, but I did wonder what the police were holding back.

As I went through the file, I started to relax. It was one of the things that I really enjoyed about producing: the chance to dig deep into something I knew nothing about. Whether it was a documentary on World War II or a missing girl, I could immerse myself in the subject and forget everything else, including my crappy, mixed-up life.

I took out a blank notepad and began making notes.

Her name was Theresa Moretti. She was twenty-two when she disappeared just over a year ago. She'd graduated from college three weeks before and was looking for a nursing job. She lived with her mother and a younger brother in the Bridgeport neighborhood on the city's South Side. She spent her spare time doing volunteer work at a local hospital, even becoming the recipient of the mayor's Volunteer of the Year Award. And when she wasn't being the community do-gooder, she hung out with friends, including her best friend, a woman named Julia Kenny.

The Saturday of last year's Memorial Day weekend, she'd told her mother she was going out to meet Julia at Hank's Restaurant, a local coffee shop. But, according to police statements, Julia had no plans to meet her and hadn't seen her that day. Where Theresa actually went, and what she did that day, was anyone's guess. After she walked out of her front door, she was never seen again.

About four months before she disappeared, she'd begun dating a man named Wyatt Brooks, a twenty-five-year-old aspiring actor she'd met at a bar. He'd agreed to be interviewed for our story, as had her mother, her friend Julia, and the police detective who worked the case. The A.P. included a note saying that an interview was tentatively set up with the mother for Tuesday and the detective Wednesday, and she was still pursuing a former assistant state's attorney and Theresa's ex-boyfriend Jason Ryder for potential interviews.

I spread out the photos on the table. There is a term in television—camera friendly—which means that someone is attractive enough to be watchable on TV. Being camera friendly is usually the minimum required for the home buyers on real estate shows or the chefs on cooking shows.

But the standard for true crime is higher. As Mike once told me, "Ugly girls may get murdered, but they don't get featured on *Caught!*" Watch any true-crime show and I guarantee you the vast majority of women featured will be young and beautiful, a bias that probably gives the viewing public the mistaken impression that attractiveness is a risk factor for murder.

Theresa was no exception. She was very pretty with light-brown hair, brown eyes, and an open, relaxed way about her. The A.P. had scribbled a note that said Theresa had been beauty queen at fifteen. Miss Bridgeport, whatever that was. There was even a photo of a teen-age Theresa wearing a crown.

The rest were all the typical photos to describe a happy, wholesome life—Theresa with her family, all wearing Santa hats; another with a good-looking young man I assumed to be her boyfriend; a third taken when she would have been maybe ten years old.

There were a dozen pictures all telling the same story. A beautiful, happy girl, the light of her family, a bright future, a career helping others, in love and perhaps ready to marry (we'd push that even if it wasn't true), had vanished into thin air.

Could she have run away from their smothering attention, into the arms of an unknown lover? Or met her fate at the hands of a stranger?

Or, worse, could she have been murdered by one of the people in these photos—someone she loved and trusted? Stay tuned through the commercial break and find out.

Or I guess in this case, don't find out. We would end the show with no answers, just a lot of desperate people whose lives had stopped the day Theresa vanished. I knew Mike was drooling at the follow-up shows that would inevitably be ordered by Crime TV—the ones showing the missing person found somewhere, and claiming that the show somehow had a hand in solving the case. We weren't just making television, we were helping people. That would be the network's press release.

Although I always enjoyed certain aspects of true-crime shows— the interviews with cops and forensic experts, the walks through the crime scene, the speculation about the murder itself—I never enjoyed dealing with the family. It was raw pain, up close. But, for the moment at least, it had an odd attraction. Sure, it was grief and confusion and anger. But it was someone else's. Someone else's life torn up. And right now that was about all I could handle.

I e-mailed Mike and told him that after reviewing the materials, I felt close to the story and wanted to help this family find answers. It was bullshit, and he'd know it was bullshit, but he wouldn't call me on it. Twenty minutes later, he wrote back saying he felt better knowing that someone with my talent and sensitivity would handle the episode, also bullshit, and we agreed I'd start on Tuesday—the day after Frank's funeral.

It was only two o'clock, but I was done for the day. I had Chinese food delivered, grabbed some candy from the kitchen, and crawled into bed. I watched the first two seasons of *Gilmore Girls* on DVD, while eating fried wontons and chocolate-covered raisins, a surprisingly delicious combination. I tried not to think about Frank, Detective Podeski, Theresa Moretti, or creepy Mike of Ripper Productions. Instead, I relived Lorelei Gilmore's anguish over borrowing money from her parents, the wackiness of her friends and neighbors, and the delights of raising a nearly perfect daughter.

What I didn't do was cry.

Ten

When I got up the next day, I watered the grass, cut away the dead flowers that had wilted under the July heat, and tried to pretend everything was normal. Then I went to bed again and stayed there until it was time to get up for Frank's wake.

By then I'd lost my wedding ring again. I'd taken it off and put it on so many times I couldn't remember where it was. I promised myself that the next time I took it off, it would be forever. Kind of a reverse wedding ceremony. I'd light candles and say a few words and make an evening of it.

It took me nearly a half hour to find the ring, next to the book *Travels with Charley*, on the desk in the tiny office that also served as our guest room. It had been my favorite book in high school. John Steinbeck and the call of the open road. Frank didn't think much of the book. Or, I should say, he never bothered to read it. I'd written his paper for English class, taking away what little incentive there was for him to discover it for himself.

When we were first married, I tried once to get him to read it, and to learn about other things I liked. He smiled, made some comment that he already knew exactly what I liked, and before I knew it we were both naked. Those were good days.

Once I had the ring on my finger again, I dressed in black, pinned my hair into a French twist, and drove to the funeral home. I was early. I wanted to be the first to arrive, or I guess I knew I was supposed to be. When I walked in the door, though, the director met me, breathless and nervous.

"We have a small situation," he whispered. "My absolute apologies but Mr. Conway's . . . fiancée has insisted on spending some time with him. I thought it was best not to make a scene. We have another service going on across the hall."

He seemed on the verge of a breakdown. He was probably already nervous about a rematch of wife vs. the in-laws. Now he was getting the full-on soap opera that was my life, and he wasn't any happier about it than I was.

"It's fine," I said. "She's welcome here." That was nonsense, of course, but I didn't want the man to collapse on me.

"You might want to suggest she conclude her time with the deceased before his mother arrives."

I smiled. I felt for the first time that I had someone on my side. Someone who realized just how really nuts this all was.

"Don't worry. We're all one big happy family," I told him.

Vera was kneeling at the coffin, talking softly to Frank, or Frank's body, I guess. But she wasn't alone. At the back of the room, sitting off in the corner, was another woman about Vera's age. If this was another "fiancée" I was going pull Frank's corpse of out his coffin and throw him out the window. It would probably kill the director to have a fuss like that in his funeral home, but at least it was a handy location to die.

"Can I help you?" I asked the woman.

She looked up. Her face turned red. "Are you, um, the wife?"

I nodded.

"I'm so sorry about this," she said. "I'm a friend of Vera's. She insisted on coming. She wanted to say good-bye."

She looked so distressed and embarrassed, I felt sorry for her. I sat down next to the woman. "I'm Kate."

"I'm Susan. And I really am sorry about all of this. It must be hell for you. Vera is a good person. She sees the best in people. She just doesn't always see what's obvious to other people. She really needed to be here and I don't think she's really thought about how his family would view her."

"Has she met any of them yet?"

"Just Neal."

"Frank's best friend."

I felt a stab of betrayal, as if by meeting Vera, Neal had taken Frank's side. But then why wouldn't he? Neal wasn't my friend. Not really. We'd just known each other for over twenty years. He was best man at my wedding and I babysat his daughter when his wife was in the hospital having their twins. But he had been Frank's friend first.

Vera got up from the kneeler by the casket and leaned over to Frank, kissing him on the cheek. Then she saw me. I was expecting her to turn white and flee the room. I think common decency required it. Instead she rushed toward me, pulled me from my seat, and hugged me tightly, while my arms flailed about, unwilling to return the gesture.

"Neither one of us is alone," she whispered to me. "We'll always be tied to each other because of our love for Frank."

"Okay." I pulled myself from her, a move that took considerable force.

As I did, I noticed my sister and her husband walk into the room. It wouldn't be long before the place was filled with lots of people who were tied together because of Frank. I wondered if she planned to hug them all.

"Maybe we should go." Susan stood up and put her arm around Vera.

Vera seemed confused. "But I thought . . . It's too early. I can't leave yet."

Susan looked at me, an apology in her eyes. "What do you think?"

I wanted to laugh. The wife and mistress arm in arm at the husband's wake. What did I think? That it's ridiculous. That we're not French. That it would kill his mother.

"I think you should do whatever you feel Frank would want," I said.

As I walked away I saw Frank's parents come into the room. "Let the fun begin," I muttered.

Eleven

"He was such a wonderful man, and you were such a great couple," my friend Lucy said to me.

"Thank you." I gave her a hug.

I'd been standing by the coffin with Frank's parents for more than two hours, greeting person after person, many of whom knew that Frank and I had been at each other's throats for months.

"This is just so horrible for you," she said. "You must feel so bad about all the things you said about him."

"I wouldn't say that."

"Don't be like that, Kate. Frank was a great guy. He was just going through a weird time. An early midlife crisis. You guys would have worked things out. We all thought so."

There it was—the rewrite I'd been hearing variations of all evening. Just two weeks ago, Lucy had described Frank as the most pathetic waste of space she'd ever seen. It was such a harsh statement that I'd actually come to his defense. And now Frank was a great guy, and this pesky divorce was just a bump in the road that he and I would have laughed about on our fiftieth wedding anniversary.

Nearly every one of my female friends made some statement to that effect. Frank was great, and we had been great together. Always looking to be unique, Frank's sister took a different route. She told me that in a way I was lucky. I was already used to his being gone, so his death wouldn't be as hard on me as it would have been if we'd stayed together.

Frank's male friends skipped the whole affair/separation issue. Instead, they were obsessed with finding out about Frank's medical history, wondering who would be next. I told each one in turn that as far as I knew he had been healthy, but if they were looking for recent information, I wasn't the one to ask.

About halfway through the evening, it spread around our friends that "she" was there. Everyone looked, but no one, not even Neal, went over to talk to her. If his parents had noticed her, they didn't acknowledge it. They just stood next to me telling each mourner that Frank was a great artist and how proud they were of his talent. If Frank had been alive to hear his parents, the shock probably would have killed him.

"Which one is she?" my sister, Ellen, whispered to me, pointing a less than discreet finger toward Vera and Susan.

"The one with the short hair."

"She's old."

"I don't think so. I think she just doesn't dye her hair."

"You are way prettier."

"And yet he chose to be with her," I reminded Ellen. "I guess he wasn't superficial."

"I'm going to tell her to go. She's upsetting you."

I grabbed her arm. "Ellen, she's sitting at the back of the room, not speaking to anyone. Leave her alone. I don't want to draw attention to her or to this whole mess."

"You are much nicer than I am."

It was a typical Ellen insult. By wrapping it in a compliment, she had deniability in case I got upset. But I knew what she meant. She meant I was weak. I had let my husband walk all over me, and my in-laws, and now his mistress. I'd heard all of it from her before. She meant well, but she didn't get it.

It wasn't just that I didn't want to draw attention to Vera. I also kind of respected what she was doing. She sat quietly in the back corner of the room, talking to Susan and glancing miserably toward Frank's coffin. It had to be hard being in a room full of people who knew Frank in a way she never would. People who didn't want to know her, who didn't see her loss, just the makings of an awkward social situation. She wasn't wanted and she didn't belong. But she stayed. And probably Frank hadn't yet screwed up, hadn't disappointed, hadn't lied or broken a promise or shut down emotionally. The Frank she knew was perfect, and he'd always be perfect. Looking over at her I did sort of admire her. But since I knew the real Frank, mostly I thought she was an idiot.

"Hey, there." Andres was suddenly at my side. He hugged me tightly, and I leaned into his shoulder. "This sucks, doesn't it?"

"I don't know where to start."

"Mike told me you are doing the *Missing Persons* shoot. Are you up for it?"

I shrugged. "A sudden and unexplainable tragedy. Looks like that's becoming my specialty."

"This probably isn't the time, but the police called me today. They were asking where you were the day Frank died."

"They were what?" My voice had gotten an octave higher and a tad too loud, so I pulled Andres out of the room and into a side area where people had brought food and coffee.

"It was some detective," Andres told me as he poured me a coffee. "He said he was just looking into some concerns there were about Frank's death. He asked me, you know, what you said about Frank since the separation."

"What did you tell him?"

"I told him that we worked together sometimes. When we worked, we talked about the shoot and where we would eat lunch, that's it. I told him I never heard you say an ill word about Frank."

I smiled. "So you lied."

"You said a few things, okay. But you didn't kill the guy."

"Did the detective say Frank was murdered?"

"No. He wouldn't answer any of my questions, just kept asking me what I knew. A real-life *Dragnet* episode." Andres looked around. There were two people in the room, both Frank's cousins, but they were engaged in a serious conversation about the stock market and weren't paying attention to us. "Do you think he was murdered?" he asked me.

"Of course not," I said. "The doctor got this all started. The wife and the mistress were hanging out together in the emergency room. I guess we looked suspicious, a little too cozy. But the paramedics said it was a heart attack."

"They told you that?"

"They told Vera."

Andres nodded, deep in thought. "Man, if he was murdered, Mike's going to want to feature it on an episode of *Caught!*"

An hour later, friends and relatives had begun to say their good-byes. Everyone offered a comforting squeeze of the hand, but no one knew what to say. Under normal circumstances it's tough to know what words to offer a grieving widow. In my case, the not-quite-ex-wife, not-really-widow situation, few managed to look anything other than embarrassed.

Vera outlasted even Frank's parents. Then she and Susan quietly left. As they were leaving, Susan promised me Vera would not attend the funeral and thanked me for being so understanding.

"How that guy managed to get two such wonderful women, I'll never know," she said. It broke my heart a little to realize that even in his new life, he wasn't fooling anyone but the woman who loved him.

Once I was alone I did what I had managed to avoid all night. I went to the casket and saw Frank's body lying there. It didn't look like him. They never do. His chin was pushed into his chest, making him look far heavier than he actually was. His normally tousled hair was swept back and gelled, and he was wearing a suit. His parents must have bought it, since Frank didn't own a suit. It looked expensive and serious, the kind a prosperous banker might wear. In death his parents finally got the control over Frank's image they'd always wanted.

I knelt at the casket and started a prayer, but I didn't know what to pray for. Finally I gave up.

"I hate you," I said to Frank. "I just thought you should know that."

He didn't answer, which wasn't entirely unexpected.

"Your girlfriend wasn't what I pictured. Well, she is a little wacky but she'd have to be to fall in love with you. I would know."

I smiled, wanting to make it clear to him, to what was left of him, that I was only kidding. I wanted to touch his hand, but I couldn't work up the nerve.

"This is so stupid. I don't know what you did to put yourself here.

I don't even want to think what you've been doing that strained your heart so much."

I wanted to shake him or hit him, somehow wake him up. But I just knelt there and stared at his waxy face.

"Now your life is just one more thing you've left unfinished."

I heard a cough. I jumped up and spun around. The director was at the door to the room.

"I'm so sorry to disturb you, Mrs. Conway, but we're closing. Are you finished mourning for the evening?"

I smiled a little. "I guess so."

Twelve

The funeral went smoothly. Neal gave him a lovely eulogy that managed to avoid any mention of the last four months. My sister and parents sat beside me at the service offering their support, without the usual advice on how to handle the in-laws. Frank's parents introduced me as their son's widow to their friends. And as promised, Vera didn't show up. All in all, it wasn't as bad as I thought it would be.

As I was leaving the graveyard after the burial, I noticed a message on my phone. It might have been a little impolite to listen to it while standing among headstones, but I knew who it was, and if I didn't get back to him, I'd get calls all day.

"Kate, it's Mike. We've got an interview with the ex–assistant state's attorney for Thursday, but we're running into a problem with the ex-boyfriend. He thinks we're going to make him look like a suspect, which I assured him we won't. He's turned me down. I think if you called him, you could work your charm. We need him. He's going to be our suspect. I know it's your ex's funeral today, so I don't want to disturb you. Just send me a text to let me know you'll call the guy this afternoon. I'll e-mail you his number. And, you know, sorry about your loss."

I texted him two words, "will call," and headed for home.

I had barely changed out of my widow clothes and into a pair of old sweats when I dialed Jason's number.

"Is this Jason Ryder?"

"Yeah, who's this?"

"My name is Kate Conway. I'm working on a show called *Missing Persons*, and we're doing an episode on Theresa Moretti."

Doing something work related made me feel normal, which really it shouldn't have. There's nothing normal about talking some poor guy into looking like a killer for the sake of a television show.

"I talked to someone from your show," Jason said. "I told him I wasn't interested."

"He told me. I guess I just wanted to explain . . ."

"I know what these shows are like."

"We're trying to help the police find Theresa."

"No, you're not."

He wasn't stupid. I went another way. "Look, the whole way these shows are set up is that we present the facts of the case and the opinions of the participants, and that sometimes leads the audience toward a possible solution."

"Meaning you make someone like me look guilty even when we're not."

"It sometimes happens that way. If, for example, Theresa's mother or her friends have bad things to say about someone from Theresa's life, then obviously we're going to want to include those comments."

"But if they're lies, then I'll sue you."

"We're pretty smart about protecting ourselves from charges of slander, Jason. We will not say bad things about you in voice-over, but we may include sound bites of other people saying bad things. As long as we don't have evidence that these people are lying, and we've done our best to get your side of the story, the show is in the clear."

"But they'll make stuff up. You don't know those people."

"And I don't know you. But I want to be fair and warn you how these things work. I don't want you to have any regrets later." My voice was firm and ominous. I wanted to scare him, but I also wanted him to think I was on his side. "The people watching the show are going to wonder why you didn't want to talk. They're going to think you have something to hide. If Theresa's family does have something to say about you, and you don't defend yourself, well, the audience will draw their own conclusions."

"But you'll let me tell what happened, so people won't think I hurt Theresa."

"That's what I want."

I could hear grunting on his side of the phone. He didn't want to do it, but he felt he had to. Whatever Theresa's family planned to say about him had to be pretty serious.

Finally he spoke. "Okay, I guess I can do it Thursday afternoon, but I'm not going to go into a lot of personal stuff. I'll just say we dated and we broke up, and let people see that I'm a good guy."

"Absolutely. This is your opportunity to say whatever you want."

And then it will be edited to say whatever Crime TV wants.

Thirteen

I felt a little sleazy after the phone call. I usually do, but I also felt like I'd accomplished something. It might seem odd to take pride in being good at a profession you don't respect, but I did.

Jason Ryder wanted to do the interview or else he wouldn't have agreed to it. To misquote Eleanor Roosevelt, you can't manipulate someone without their consent. He wanted to be heard. And if he really had nothing to do with Theresa's disappearance, which he probably didn't, then being on television might actually help him clear his name. So, in a way, I was doing a public good. Or, at the very least, I wasn't really hurting anyone.

I still had the photos of Theresa spread out on my kitchen table, but I pushed them aside. The haunted images from the past I was interested in were from my own. I opened up the first of several photo albums I had fished out of a box in the garage and started slowly leafing through them.

They were the typical pictures: awkward teenagers in Christmas sweaters posing by the tree, prom photos with Frank making goofy faces because he hated being in a tuxedo, pictures of us in college looking lovingly at each other though we broke up every other week during that time, and finally about a dozen photos of my hand showing off a sparkling new engagement ring.

The second album was all wedding photos. The official ones were staged, with smiles that were too wide to be real. After the ceremony the photographer posed us all on the altar, my family on my side, his family on his. If we were really becoming one big family, then the photographer should have mixed us all up and put his sister next to my dad and my sister next to his younger brother. Maybe the photographer knew that despite the niceties it would never really work out that way.

Just like in the photo, for the rest of our marriage, most of my family aligned with me, and most of his with him.

Still, as I looked at the photos from the reception, I saw genuine happiness. There was love in Frank's eyes, and in mine. I'd forgotten how much in love we really were.

Once we got back to the honeymoon suite, he called me his wife for the first time, and I stared at the gold ring on his left hand. I couldn't believe this beautiful man belonged with me for the rest of my life.

"You're my next of kin now," he said as we were lying in bed that night. "If I'm ever on life support, you get to decide whether to pull the plug."

"Looking forward to it." I leaned over and kissed him. "But it better be a long time from now because I have big plans for our seventy-fifth wedding anniversary."

"That's the night you'll leave me for a younger man. Someone who can still get it up long after I've outlived my usefulness to you."

I laughed. "That's when I'll know it's time to pull the plug."

Sitting in my kitchen fifteen years later, I could still feel my happiness from that night and I wanted to find a way to crawl back into it and stay there. But the phone rang. It was Alex. I hesitated. I was pretty sure he was calling to check up on me, and I didn't think I could provide the appropriate mix of grief and shoulder to cry on. But I couldn't just let it go to voice mail. He was still my father-in-law, kind of.

"Hello," I said.

"Kate, it's Alex." He paused. "How you doing, kiddo?"

"Okay. Just remembering."

"Yeah, me too. Lots of good memories."

"Yes, lots."

The conversation stalled for a minute.

"Listen, Kate, I didn't want to bring this up at the funeral, but we have to talk about something important."

I couldn't imagine what was left to say. "Really? What?"

"Frank's insurance."

He was the second person to bring up the insurance policy. It was one thing coming from Mike, but I never expected Alex to be so concerned with my coming into a little money.

"We had a ten-thousand-dollar insurance policy," I told him. "To be honest with you, I think I missed the last few payments. With the way things were, and money being so tight, I guess I didn't think it was much of a priority."

"That's not what I'm talking about. I mean the work one."

"What work one?"

"When Frank came to work for me after college, I made him a partner. I'd hoped it would make him feel like he was building something for himself, instead of just a kid working for his dad. I took out an insurance policy on him. It was for two hundred and fifty thousand dollars. You're the beneficiary."

"Of two hundred and fifty thousand dollars?" The idea of so much money should have made me feel giddy, but it only made me uncomfortable. "Did Frank know any of this?"

"Of course. Didn't he tell you?"

"No."

Frank had part ownership in his father's construction firm and he didn't bother to tell me. I guess Frank had secrets that predated Vera.

"I haven't filed a claim yet," Alex continued, "but I'll do that for you in the next few days. The thing is . . ." He stopped. I could feel his tension from the other end of the phone. "The thing is, kiddo, it's better not to discuss this with Frank's mom."

"Of course, Alex. Whatever you want."

What I thought was, why would I talk to Lynette? We went through fifteen Thanksgivings and Christmases without exchanging more than a few words. I wasn't about to change a family tradition now.

Alex, I could hear, had relaxed. "Thanks, Kate. I just want you to know that I've always loved having you as my daughter. And I know Frank loved you too. Right up until the end."

Tears formed just behind my eyes but refused to go anywhere. My voice, though, quivered. "Thanks, Dad."

I wasn't in the mood to go back to the photographs after the call. When Frank went to work for his dad after graduation, he hated it.

He'd gotten an accounting degree under pressure and had no intention of spending his life adding numbers, as he frequently used to tell me. When he quit, or was fired, or just stopped showing up—it depended on whose version of the story was true—I was kind of proud of him. But what he'd told me at the time, and since, was that his dad cut him out completely. We weren't to expect anything in the will, he would say. His parents were so bitterly disappointed that he was wasting his education, they'd told him they wouldn't throw away another penny of their hard-earned money on him.

But it was a lie. Alex kept him on as a partner, knowing Frank would inherit a significant sum, and he'd kept up an insurance policy so I would be taken care of just in case his son hadn't been able to. And Frank knew it.

I shut the wedding album and dropped it and the other albums onto the floor. Tomorrow they would go back into the box in the garage.

The photos of Theresa that had been covered up by the albums were now facing me again. I looked at her beautiful face and the genuine happiness in her eyes.

"I wonder what lies you've told, Theresa," I said to the photos.

The girl in the photos just kept smiling, as if she had nothing to hide.

Fourteen

The Moretti house was a typical Chicago bungalow, brown brick, with a postage-stamp lawn and neat rows of flowers. A small statue of the Virgin Mary was placed among the flowers. It looked like most of the houses on the block in this very Catholic neighborhood. Until I got to the front door.

There was a poster taped to the door, a photo of Theresa, with the words "Have you seen our daughter?" above the photo. I couldn't imagine being reminded of a lost child every time I walked in or out of my house, but then, the Morettis probably didn't need the poster to remind them. They needed it to remind everyone else.

Theresa's mom, Linda Moretti, welcomed me as if I were an old friend. She even had coffee and a dozen or so pastries waiting on the kitchen table.

"You shouldn't have gone to so much trouble," I said as I grabbed a cheese Danish.

"No trouble. I own a bakery. My son works with me. He made these. He's a genius with pastry."

He was. The Danish was flaky and just sweet enough to be a perfect complement to coffee. While I was eating, Andres and Victor arrived. I asked them to set up the lights and camera in the Morettis' living room, and while they did that, Linda and I sat in the kitchen. Since I'm usually meeting the interview subject for the first time on the day of the interview, it's important we establish a relationship right away. Sitting in front of a camera can be very intimidating and people tend to clam up. I need whoever I'm interviewing to feel they have an ally in the room. And since it usually takes about an hour for the crew to be ready anyway, it's the perfect opportunity to create that bond.

"My husband died about six years ago," Linda told me. "There are times when I wish he were here to go through this with me, and other times when I'm just grateful he didn't live to see this."

"I can understand that. This has to be a nightmare for you."

She nodded and turned her attention to more than two dozen photos and home movies she had collected for me. That was more than I could have hoped for. We love using home movies when there's a show on a murdered or missing person. It's haunting to watch a happy person open presents on Christmas morning, knowing they didn't make it to Easter.

Linda had made a copy of each of the movies and put the photos on a disc, but she wanted to show me anyway, so I would know her daughter. I dutifully sat and listened to each story, asking easy questions and offering sympathetic smiles. Theresa's life, at least in the photos, did seem as ideal as they come. Loving family, big group of friends, close-knit community. There was nothing in smiling image after image to suggest what cruel turn her life would take. Sitting there, I found myself caught up in the same question Linda was asking. Why?

"This is the last photo of all of the three of us together." She held up a picture of Theresa flanked by her mother and a young man. The man, who I assumed to be her brother, was in his early twenties and had a tired, almost angry expression. The women were smiling. They were all dressed up, with presents in their hands, maybe guests at a wedding or a similar celebration.

"This must be so hard on you and your son."

She sighed. "You know, in a way, it's brought us closer. We understand how precious life is, and we just want to spend as much time together as we can. My son came to work with me after Theresa disappeared. He was going to move to the North Side, but when it all happened, he decided it was more important to stay close to home."

She put the picture down and went on to the next one. As she showed me each photo, she told me a little bit about her daughter's life. I listened and asked questions. I could see that it was the first time in a long time that Linda had indulged herself this way, and she was a little hesitant.

As I've learned since the separation, friends and family are all ears for the initial few weeks. The person in pain can call at odd hours, burst into tears at dinner, cancel social plans at a moment's notice, or just talk on and on about their loss. But too much emotion makes people uncomfortable. Little by little, friends and family begin backing away. They start saying things like, "You need to move on," or "It's time to let go." And they're probably right. It's easy for grief to go from a temporary condition to a lifestyle choice.

But in most cases I think what happens is that the people don't move on; they just shut up. I knew at the one-month mark that none of my friends were interested in another retread of my relationship, so unless there was news, I said nothing. They all thought I was healing, and it made them feel better. And maybe it helped me feel better too, since I was forced to find a subject other than Frank to talk about.

It was something I also understood from the many times I'd sat with families being interviewed for *Caught!* They had all lost loved ones to murder and, sometimes years later, were still in the center of their grief. They had all heard "Time to let go" from their families and friends and had learned to keep the memories to themselves. But the pain was still there.

When I came to their door, I was a welcome relief. I hadn't heard the story a thousand times. I hadn't been there for the death, the funeral, the trial. It was all new to me. And not only was I willing to hear their story, I was eager. I wanted all the details. I wanted the pain on display. It didn't matter that I was just using them for a television show; I could always see the gratitude and comfort they got from knowing I would never ask them to move on.

But sitting here with Linda I was in unfamiliar territory. She had the same appreciation for the chance to tell her story, only this time her story wasn't finished. Her daughter wasn't in a grave. She was out there somewhere, and Linda might never know where. How could she "move on," I wondered. Even when her friends were sick of hearing the details, even when the yellow ribbons had been taken down and the "Help Find Her" posters had faded, there were no answers.

"This is from her graduation. It was just weeks before . . ." She left the statement unfinished. She handed me a photo of herself with Theresa. Theresa was holding a small silver charm. "It's a nurse's cap," Linda explained. "She's planning to be a nurse."

I noticed the way she spoke of Theresa in the present tense. "Wonderful profession," I said.

"This was when she was eight." Linda showed me another photo. In this one a young Theresa stood by a church in a white dress and veil.

I recognized the occasion. "Her First Communion."

"The dress was more than I wanted to spend, but Theresa was so insistent." She smiled at the memory. "She said she'd save it and wear it for a wedding dress. I explained to her that it probably wouldn't fit when she was old enough to get married, but she wouldn't budge. I gave in. I told her we'd get this dress for her Communion and we'd get her a whole new beautiful dress when she got married."

She started to cry. I put my hand on hers and we sat silently. I looked at her with all the compassion I could, but then I got to wondering if Andres was almost ready with the lights.

The first episode of *Caught!* I'd ever done was about a high school senior, a star athlete, who'd been murdered by his stepfather. The boy's mother was so full of pain and guilt I cried with her. I did a terrible job with the interview and a worse job with the script. The crime scene photos, of that boy with a gunshot wound through his heart, stayed with me for weeks.

It didn't help anybody for me to care, but it was crucial to the interview that I seemed to, so I sat and held Linda's hand while she cried, until Andres walked into the room.

"We're ready," he said.

I turned to Linda. "Why don't we just get this interview finished, so we can talk again afterwards?"

"You're so kind," she said. "It makes such a difference to talk to someone who really wants to help."

Fifteen

After a few adjustments of microphones and lights, we started the interview. Linda and I were seated facing each other. I began with easy questions, things about Theresa's childhood, to get Linda relaxed and over the initial discomfort of being in front of a camera.

Theresa was a wonderful child, her mother told me: playful, smart, curious, and good in school. She was every parent's dream. I've interviewed the parents of murderers, drug addicts, and gang members. It's always the same—they were perfect children. I guess when all you have are memories, you want them to be sweet.

In Theresa's case, though, it seemed to be true.

"She was named Volunteer of the Year . . . ," I said.

Linda immediately smiled. "Yes. And it was well deserved. Theresa's always been a volunteer. When she was about six, she went around the neighborhood collecting change to send to starving children. She'd seen one of those 'sponsor a child' commercials and she wanted to do it," she said. "She was upset that someone her own age was going hungry when she had so much. At six!" She laughed. "And then it was one thing after another. In high school, she organized a group of students to send letters to soldiers fighting overseas, and in college she volunteered at a hospice for cancer patients and organized the school blood drive."

"That's amazing," I said. And a little annoying. My most recent act of altruism was buying a sandwich for the homeless man on my corner. And I spent a week patting myself on the back over that.

"She got the mayor's award for raising funds for a local clinic that was about to shut its doors," Linda said. "They were waiting on grant money, but it was slow in coming and in the meantime they had a budget deficit of a hundred thousand dollars. When Theresa heard about it, she just knocked on doors until she'd raised the money." Her pride was evident.

"She must have knocked on a lot of doors to get a hundred grand."

"That's Theresa. She never gives up. Not on people, not on causes." Her lip quivered. "That's how I know she's alive. I know she'd never give up."

"You weren't very fond of her boyfriend, Jason." I switched the subject. After ten minutes of listening to Theresa as Linda remembered her, it was time to get to the real person.

Linda took a deep breath. "Jason wasn't Theresa's type. They dated for a short while, a few months, but when she realized he wasn't right for her, she didn't want to waste his time and she broke it off."

"What type is Jason?"

She shrugged. "He's a nice kid. He comes from a good family. They don't live far from here. It's just that Theresa wanted what her father and I had. She wanted a home and a family. Jason was a bit wild for her. She didn't see him settling down."

"Is that what she told you?"

"She didn't have to tell me. A mother knows."

"When Theresa broke it off with him, how did Jason take it?"

"He called the house a few times and left angry messages. He came to the door about a week before Theresa went missing. My son, Tom, told him that Theresa wasn't interested in talking to him and he'd have to go. They got into it on the front lawn."

"Shouting?"

"There was lots of shouting."

"Did it get physical?"

"No. My son isn't the violent type. He just said that Jason wasn't welcome anymore. Tom was upset, though, for days afterward."

"What did your son and Jason say to each other?"

"I don't know. I heard Jason say something about Theresa not being the good girl we thought she was. Mean things like that. They got quiet for a minute, then it started up again. I went into the kitchen so I didn't have to hear it."

"That's a pretty awful thing to say to someone's brother, that Theresa wasn't a good girl. What do you think he meant?"

"I think he was upset. People say things when they're upset. He didn't mean it, obviously. Jason was madly in love with Theresa. He was obsessed with her."

"Obsessed? That's a pretty strong word."

"She told me he used to show up at the hospital where she was doing some volunteer work. I think he wanted to check on her, see if she was where she said she would be."

"That would scare me. Was Theresa scared of him?"

"She didn't use those words. But she was glad when Tom had that talk with him. I think it put an end to it. Theresa was already dating Wyatt, and they were happy together. She didn't want to get back with Jason, and I guess after he talked with my son, he finally understood that."

"What's Wyatt like?"

She smiled. "He's a dream. I'd be so happy to have him as my son-in-law. Theresa and Wyatt were so in love with each other. They looked like the top of a wedding cake. He keeps her picture next to his bed. Even now."

"He's still in touch with you?"

"We talk every week. Wyatt has become like a second son."

"And the day she disappeared . . ." I only had to start the question. This was familiar territory for Linda.

"It was a great day. A summer day, like now. We were going to have a Memorial Day picnic on Monday, and Theresa and I were going to make potato salad and all the fixings. Only we didn't because on Saturday Theresa disappeared." She took a deep breath. "She left about eleven o'clock that morning to meet up with Julia, her best friend since grade school. They were going to have coffee. Julia had just gotten engaged and Theresa was helping her with the wedding. She was going to be the maid of honor."

Linda stopped. I could see that she was backing away from the story. She didn't want to go to the next part and I couldn't blame her, but it was the whole reason I was here.

"When did you realize Theresa was missing?"

"When she didn't come home for dinner, I called her cell phone but she didn't answer. I started to get worried. Theresa used to say I was overprotective. I waited. I shouldn't have waited, but I didn't want her accusing me of treating her like a child. When it was almost midnight and she still wasn't answering her phone, I called Julia." Linda's voice shook. "She said that Theresa hadn't met her for coffee. She hadn't seen her all day. I don't know why Julia didn't call me when Theresa didn't show up at the coffee shop."

"Julia told the police they didn't have plans to meet that day, is that right?"

"She was mixed up. They had plans. Theresa told me they had plans."

Linda was waving her arms around; her voice was getting louder. At some point someone must have suggested that Theresa might have lied to her mother, and it was pretty clear that there was no way Linda would accept that explanation.

"What do you think happened?"

"I think she got taken by a stranger." She was getting more insistent with each syllable. "I think she's out there doing something against her will, trying to escape, trying to come home."

"Any possibility she ran away from home, maybe decided to start a new life?"

"Why? Her life was perfect. We're a very close family, Theresa, her brother, and me. We used to joke that Theresa wouldn't buy a pair of shoes without talking it over with me. We were best friends. She would never have gone willingly."

"And you don't think she's dead." I said it gently, but it didn't matter what my tone was. That's not a gentle question.

She bit her lip. "No. I'd know if she were dead. Besides, there were a couple of hang-ups in the months after she disappeared. And one on Christmas Eve. I know that was Theresa trying to reach out, but whoever took her must have caught her, must have stopped her. That's why I'm doing this show. I think whoever has her will see all the publicity, and they'll let her go."

"I hope so," I said quietly.

Linda sat back, triumphant. We continued the interview for another twenty minutes, but I had the sound bites I wanted. The ex-boyfriend was obsessed, Theresa had possibly lied about her plans on the day she disappeared, and her mother had a salacious theory as to her whereabouts. It would all play beautifully.

Sixteen

W hen I got home I had to step over a dead bird that some neighborhood cat must have left outside my front door. It was beautiful and peaceful looking, except for the way its neck flopped to the side. I got the broom and swept it into the grass.

Once in the house, I made myself a cup of tea. I pushed aside the chamomile and mint teas Frank was, for a brief time, passionate about and took a tea bag from a brand I bought at an Irish import store. I preferred black tea with a touch of milk. It was the right beverage for the mood I was in. Coffee implies a sense of purpose, alcohol means either celebration or defeat, and colas are for hot days and greasy meals. Tea is comforting, traditional, and healthy without being pretentious. I sat on the leather chair in the living room, turned the TV to a decorating show, and sipped my tea.

But it was no use. My body wanted to relax, but my mind kept going back over the interview. Linda was delusional. The idea that her daughter was a kidnap victim, alive and being held, was possible, of course, but it was unlikely. But the other choices, that Theresa was dead or that she had intentionally inflicted this hell on her mother by running away, were unacceptable. Of all the terrible things that could have happened to her daughter, for Linda Moretti, a crazed kidnapper was the most reassuring.

It made me wonder if I'd been a little delusional myself. Six months ago I would have said I knew everything there was to know about Frank, but I obviously didn't. A week after his death I was still uncovering secrets. So why was I sure it was a heart attack? Detectives had come to my door and called my colleagues, which should have been evidence that he'd died of something other than natural causes, but I'd dismissed the possibility without a second thought.

I guess it's one thing to be an observer of the effects of violent crime; it's another to have it touch my life. I didn't want to imagine myself on the other side of the camera, weeping about the years we would never have. I wanted Frank's death to be the one thing about our relationship that was neat and simple. Like Linda, I was looking not for the good outcome but for the one that would hurt the least.

But seeing Linda ignore the facts to find her own truth, I was suddenly uncomfortable. I didn't want to be that kind of person either. If Frank hadn't died of a heart attack, then what had happened? If I didn't owe it to him to find out, surely I owed it to myself.

I put my tea on the end table, put my shoes back on, and walked out to the car. Without even knowing what I was going to do once I got there, I drove back to St. Anthony's Hospital. There were other places to start, of course, but I thought like a producer. If this was an episode of one of the true-crime shows I'd worked on, it would begin with the narrator saying something like this:

> Thirty-seven-year-old Frank Conway had everything to live for. Though his fifteen-year marriage had recently collapsed, Frank was already starting a new life. He'd fallen in love, rediscovered painting, and was looking forward to a reunion of his high school basketball team. But Frank never made the reunion.
>
> One hot night in mid-July, he collapsed and was rushed to the hospital. While his estranged wife and his new girlfriend met uncomfortably in the waiting room, doctors worked to save him. They couldn't. His family and friends comforted themselves with the diagnosis of a fatal heart attack and tried to get on with their lives.
>
> It was only because of the suspicions of an emergency room doctor, and the persistence of a weary detective, that the truth—and a killer—was finally revealed.

While the narrator spoke, there would be video of an ambulance racing to the hospital and doctors working on the reenactment version of Frank. In true crime, we always start with the crime. Then we tell the backstory, introduce the suspects, show the evidence, and, finally, reveal the killer.

Dumb as it was, if I was going to figure out what had happened, the only place I could think to start was at the beginning of the show.

"I'm looking for Dr. Milton," I told the nurse at the desk.

"He's with a patient. You'll have to wait." She seemed not to notice my urgency or care when I expressed it. When I didn't move from her desk, she said it again.

It was the same waiting room, the same knot in my stomach. I sat and watched the families come and go. They all looked worried then relieved, or worried and then sad. Life was beginning and ending, and they were all waiting to find out which end of the spectrum they were on.

After about an hour, Dr. Milton came down the hall. He looked about to pass me, so I stood in front of him.

"I'm not sure you remember me," I said.

"I remember you. What can I do for you?"

"I'd like to talk to you."

He seemed uncomfortable at the idea. "I only have a few minutes. It's a busy night."

"I wanted to ask why you called the police."

That made him even more uncomfortable. I changed tactics.

"Can we sit down?" I asked, a calm, reassuring, and completely fake tone in my voice.

He gestured toward two seats as far away from other people as was possible. "Mrs. Conway," he started.

I could hear dismissal in his voice, so I interrupted him. "Dr. Milton, if you remember me then you remember that I wasn't alone in this waiting room. I was with my husband's new girlfriend."

"Vera."

"You know her first name?"

"She brought me carrot cake the day after. She wanted to thank me for doing my best."

I laughed. "I'm sorry. I don't know her well. It's just—odd, I guess. I'm sure the whole situation looked odd to you. It might even have looked suspicious."

"Look, Mrs. Conway. I didn't get in touch with the police because your husband's girlfriend was with you in the waiting room. I don't care about his personal life."

"Then why did you? I know how this looks, my coming here to find out what you know, but I just need to understand. You must encounter a lot of people faced with the same news I got, and we're all looking to the only person we can think of who might have some answers." I could see him nodding in agreement, so I asked what I'd wondered about since the night Frank died. "Did he tell you something?"

"No. He never regained consciousness."

"Then what made his death suspicious?"

"He had the symptoms of a heart attack, but I didn't think he had one. It didn't feel right. And the autopsy confirmed it. His heart was fine."

"Then what did he die of?"

He shook his head. "As far as I know, the medical examiner has listed the cause of death as undetermined. They're testing tissue samples they took from his body, but it could be weeks before there are any results."

"Do you think he was murdered?"

"I don't draw conclusions like that. That's for the medical examiner and the police. That's why they were asked to get involved." He stood up. "I'm sorry, Mrs. Conway. I have to get back to work."

For the second time in a week, Dr. Milton had delivered life-changing news and then walked away. At least this time I didn't have my husband's mistress clutching my hand. But that was small comfort. If Frank's death were a story I was producing, Vera would be the person I spoke to next.

It only occurred to me as I was driving away from the hospital that I didn't know where Vera lived or how to get in touch with her. I called Frank's cell phone, since it was still in her possession, and was startled by the sound of his voice telling me he wasn't available but would get back to me soon.

"Fat chance," I said, but I had to pull the car over to the side of the road. Hearing him again left me shaking.

I wondered for a moment why his phone was still working. Then I remembered we still shared a plan, so I was the one who would have to cancel it. Vera had the last "I love you" and I had the phone company.

"This sucks," I yelled. "This fucking sucks." I slammed my fists on the steering wheel, accidentally hitting the horn and beeping at a woman walking her dog.

"I'm sorry," I said to her. She smiled a little but turned her dog around and started walking in the opposite direction.

"Why did you leave me, Frank?" I asked the dark sky. Even as I posed the question I wasn't sure which time I was talking about.

Seventeen

"I'm here to see Detective Rosenthal," I said.

It was eight fifteen a.m. and already almost eighty degrees. Chicago weather is like that, so cold in the winter that tears freeze on your face, so hot in the summer that everything, including your brain, turns into a puddle. Andres and Victor had picked me up at my house. Driving together would make things easier since we were hitting more than one location in the day. I'd left them to haul lights and other equipment out of the van, while I went from the heat into the overly air-conditioned Ninth Police District. I spent the next several minutes trying to get the attention of a receptionist at the missing persons division.

"Excuse me," I said louder. "I'm here to see Detective Rosenthal."

"I'll call her," the receptionist said, making it clear she was doing me the biggest favor of my life.

Finally a tall, thin, thirtysomething woman came toward me from another room. "I'm Yvette Rosenthal," she said. "You must be Kate."

When Andres and Victor arrived with the equipment, Rosenthal showed us options for the interview and Andres and I picked the conference room. Technically on a shoot, I'm the boss, but if the camera person is really good, like Andres, it's a shared responsibility, more like sixty-forty, with the producer in the lead. I get the extra points because, among other things, I decide when to break for lunch.

"It's going to take us about an hour," Andres said to me, which was code for "Kate, get her out of here so we don't have to chitchat while we work."

I touched Rosenthal's arm. "I'd like to grab a cup of coffee and go over some of the details of the interview while we wait."

"Perfect." She led me toward a small eating area the detectives shared. "The coffee is strong, if you like it that way."

"Fine with me."

Even when the interview subject isn't the family member of a victim, the bonding experience is a little awkward. It's the "I'm a person, you're a person" part, where they see I'm not intimidating and begin to feel, without my actually saying it, that I will make them look good. I don't actually say it because I don't always make them look good.

Detective Rosenthal would have nothing to worry about, though. True-crime shows are usually tipped in favor of law enforcement. If she was also a mom or had devoted some of her off-hours to the case, it would only sweeten the image I was trying to create.

We sat at a small orange table with an open package of doughnuts on it. I avoided mentioning the cliché and just sipped my coffee.

"You must do this all the time," she said.

"I work on a lot of different kinds of shows," I told her. "I've done a lot of true crime, but it's mostly homicides. This is my first missing person."

"They're tough. I came here from homicide two years ago, and I never get used to it."

"Theresa's mom thinks her daughter is being held captive."

She nodded. "I think the only way she's holding it together is because she believes she'll see Theresa alive again."

"She won't, will she?"

Rosenthal took a deep breath, slowly letting the air leave her lungs. "I doubt it," she finally said. "It's been too long. We don't often have good outcomes this long after a person has gone missing."

"Linda said she's gotten hang-ups. She thinks that it's proof Theresa's alive."

"I hope she's right." Rosenthal shifted in her chair. "But think about it. You've picked up the phone and no one is there. So have I. We probably get as many hang-ups in the course of a year as Linda does. We just don't read anything into it."

"That poor woman," I said, more to myself than to her.

"Can I ask you something?" Rosenthal sat up straight. "Why Theresa? She's just an ordinary person. Nothing special about her life or, sadly, her disappearance. Happens every day."

"That's exactly why. We want people watching the show to think, 'That could be me or my sister or my wife.' That way they're invested in the outcome."

"And they stay through the commercial breaks."

I nodded.

"So no dead hookers or drug addicts?" she asked.

"Only if it's a housewife or college student leading a double life," I said. "Any chance of that with Theresa?"

"If you find that out, I hope you'll tell me."

"Well, I did notice the police report had a few things blacked out."

"Nothing that would affect your show."

"For instance?"

Rosenthal just smiled. Not that I was expecting she would tell me, but she seemed a little too pleased with herself that she was keeping a secret.

"Police work has got to be frustrating sometimes." I took my own deep breath and turned the conversation in a different direction. "I did a story once where a man died of an apparent heart attack, but the autopsy revealed his heart was fine. It didn't look like much, but there was a cop who just kept asking questions until he found out the truth. That must happen a lot—homicides that look like natural causes."

"Sometimes. Most killers are more straightforward. They shoot or stab or choke. To stage a murder as a heart attack would take some medical knowledge. Is that what happened in that case?"

"Yeah."

"Was it on *Caught!*? I think I might have seen that episode."

I nodded.

"So who did it?"

I started to blush. "The girlfriend."

"It usually is. The wife or the girlfriend. The husband or the boyfriend. People are so scared of a stranger murdering them in their homes. Don't get me wrong, it happens. But if you really want to know the person most likely to kill you, look at who's in bed with you. That's who you have to worry about."

"I guess I'm lucky I'm sleeping alone."

When Andres and Victor were ready for us, Detective Rosenthal and I sat opposite each other, just as I had with Linda. Rosenthal had been interviewed many times before, so softball questions weren't necessary. Besides, this wasn't personal for her. She was just here to give the facts and one "I won't rest until we find her" sound bite, and I would have what I needed.

"How did you get involved in the case?" I asked.

"I got called in when Theresa had been missing for about a day. I spoke with her mother, Linda Moretti, who had reported Theresa missing. I interviewed several of her friends, people at the hospital where she volunteered, as well as her current and former boyfriends. Unfortunately I wasn't able to develop any leads as to her whereabouts."

"How long does someone have to wait before filing a missing persons report?"

"That's an urban myth—the waiting period. I can't speak for other states, but in Illinois there is no waiting period. If someone is missing, you can file a report right away."

"But in the case of an adult, if it's only been a day or two, will the police take it seriously?"

"Absolutely. First of all, if the person was known to disappear for days at a time, it's unlikely their family would bother to report them missing. So if a wife or a mother or a son comes in and says, 'My loved one has disappeared,' that's an indication that this is out of character for the person. Secondly, we look at the person's activities right before they disappeared. If they withdrew large sums of money from their accounts, if they were in some kind of trouble at home or at work, or had legal trouble, these would be indications of a voluntary disappearance." She took a breath and I nodded for her to continue. "If someone disappears who has no history of walking away, and no reason to, we start looking right away for other possibilities."

"What was your instinct with Theresa?"

"She didn't walk away. That would be my assessment. She seemed happy in her relationship with her boyfriend, Wyatt. She was close to her family. She had friends. Add to that, the money in her account has not been withdrawn since she disappeared. To me, this wasn't voluntary."

"How much money did she have in her account?"

Rosenthal hesitated. "Nothing unusual." There was a catch in her throat.

I thought for a moment about pursuing it, but I knew I'd get stone-walled and I had too many questions to ask to make an enemy of Rosenthal now. Instead I went for safer territory. "Where was Theresa going that day?"

"We don't know. She told her mother she was meeting a friend for coffee. Her friend, Julia Kenny, later told me they didn't have plans, so we really have no idea where she was going."

"Was she lying to her mother?"

"That's one scenario. Perhaps the women got their plans mixed up."

"Or Julia is lying."

"We checked Julia, of course. We didn't see any reason she would have to hurt Theresa. I think it's more likely there was a misunderstanding."

"Did Theresa even get to the coffee shop?"

"We have no evidence she was there. We also don't know that she wasn't. It was a pretty busy place and not a place she frequented often. No one recognized her photo, but that doesn't mean she wasn't there."

"Her mother indicated that her ex-boyfriend Jason Ryder had been obsessed with her."

"Mr. Ryder is a person of interest in this case. He made some harass-ing phone calls to her home and had a confrontation with her brother. But we have no evidence that he saw Theresa the day she disappeared or even in the week prior."

"No phone calls between them?"

"None that I'm aware of."

"And her current boyfriend?"

"We have nothing that would indicate he has special knowledge in this case."

"Meaning you don't suspect Wyatt Brooks?"

"It's an open investigation, so we suspect everyone and no one. But as far as we know, there wasn't a motive for Mr. Brooks to have harmed Theresa, nor is there evidence he was in her neighborhood on the day she disappeared."

"What do you think happened to her?"

"I think Theresa left her house and encountered someone who kept her from continuing with her day, and that person is the reason she hasn't been seen since."

"Do you think she's dead?"

"I wouldn't speculate on that."

Off camera, of course, Rosenthal had done exactly that, but I wasn't expecting her to repeat it on the record. That wouldn't be the sort of sound bite that Theresa's family would want from the lead detective on their daughter's case. And it wouldn't make her look like the hero cop I had in mind. I had to follow up, though, so she wouldn't think I was letting her off too easy.

"But it's been more than a year," I pressed. "What are the odds she's alive?"

"I'm not much of a gambler. I would say that unless I find evidence to the contrary, I am working this case under the assumption that Theresa is alive."

"When will you give up on this case?"

She shifted uncomfortably. This was the money quote and I could see her struggling. "There are new people missing every day. We don't give up on any of them, but I admit a fresh case will get more attention, because, well . . ."

I stopped her. "What I need you to say is, you will never give up."

This is another dirty secret of TV producers. We often tell our interview subjects what we want them to say. I prefer it if they come to it on their own, but I have to get what I have to get.

Rosenthal seemed relieved at the interruption. "You're not going to use the other stuff, about the new cases?"

"No. I think someone watching this show doesn't want to hear that old cases will inevitably be at the bottom of the pile. I think they want to hear that if they were in Linda's shoes, their loved one will be as much a priority to the police as they are to the family."

She nodded. "Can you ask me the question again?"

"When will you give up on this case?"

"I will never give up on Theresa. Ever. Each case, each person, is as much a priority to the members of this department as it is to the

families of the missing. I'm going to work this case until I bring Theresa home."

I smiled. "We've got it. Thanks, Detective."

"You made that easy," a more relaxed Detective Rosenthal said as
Victor removed her microphone.

"It's easy when you speak the truth," I told her, without a hint of
irony in my voice.

Eighteen

"Tell me we can take lunch," Andres said as he packed the last of the equipment back into the van.

"I don't want hot dogs. I don't want pizza," I said. "I want healthy food. I'm sick of gaining weight every time I do a shoot. We're going someplace that has salad."

Victor walked up behind me. "Screw that. Let's get Ukrainian. There's a great place down the block."

"Healthy Ukrainian," I said, wondering if there was any such thing.

Twenty minutes later, we shared varenyky topped with bacon and sour cream, stuffed cabbage rolls, and plates full of sausage. And we did what we always did—Andres and I discussed the case, while Victor listened to music and drummed annoyingly on the table.

"I'd put my money on the ex-boyfriend," Andres said as he shoved another potato-filled varenyky in his mouth. "Getting into a shouting match with the brother seems kind of sketchy to me."

"We talk to him tomorrow, but I don't know," I said. "Theresa may not have been the good girl everyone thought."

"Based on?"

"She's just too perfect. No one is that squeaky-clean. Plus, her mother was a little too clingy. The whole 'Theresa wouldn't buy shoes without me' thing. I just don't buy it."

"You think her mother killed her and buried her underneath the bakery?" Andres was laughing at me.

"I'm just saying, if I were Theresa I would have rebelled against all that family togetherness. And the whole 'I'm her mother, so I knew everything about her' thing. No parent knows everything about their child. Especially their twenty-two-year-old child."

"I don't know anything about my kids, and the oldest is eleven." He pushed his plate away. "What's on the schedule for this afternoon?"

"B-roll."

Interviews are considered A-roll, and the visuals that supplement the story are referred to as B-roll. I'd shot B-roll footage of Detective Rosenthal going through Theresa's case files (or really just pretending to go through them; we used someone else's file that happened to be on her desk). I'd also shot Linda looking wistfully at photos of her daughter. These shots are used in nearly every true-crime show I've done. They can be a little boring—who hasn't seen the "guy walks purposefully down the hall" shot—but they're necessary to cover edits and make the story more than just a bunch of talking heads.

The B-roll material I liked shooting was the atmosphere stuff. In this case, shots of the places where Theresa spent time, and the last place she was seen alive. It gave me a much better sense of the person than just talking to her friends and relatives.

We drove through the streets of Bridgeport, getting general neighborhood shots, then spent time getting footage outside the school where she'd just finished her studies, the hospital where she volunteered, and finally, exterior shots of Hank's Restaurant, the coffee shop where she was supposed to meet Julia.

It was a large place, old and run-down. Even through the window I could see that the vast majority of the clientele would go straight from the coffee shop to the local bar.

We set up the camera across the street, with Andres nearly hidden from view by the van on one side, and Victor and I on the other. We didn't have a permit to shoot in the street, but we never do. Cops weren't our concern. It was the owner of the coffee shop. While he couldn't stop us from shooting his business, since we were on public property, he could stand in front of the camera and yell at us. It had happened on many shoots. Some people enjoy a little free publicity, even when it will associate their business with a crime. But the ones who don't can get very vocal about it. And looking at the place, with its faded signs, graffiti on the door, and cigarette butts littering the entryway, I sensed the owner wouldn't be welcoming.

"This doesn't look like the kind of place two women would come to talk wedding plans, does it?" I asked.

Victor took a puff of his cigarette and shrugged. "Looks okay to me."

Andres looked up from his camera. "There's a place on the next block with big couches and nice artwork. A place where you can get a decent cappuccino. That's where they would have talked wedding plans. Not here."

"Told ya." I nudged Victor. "Andres knows women."

"I've known more women than Andres ever will."

"You can't count the ones you've paid for," Andres told him.

Victor grunted a few times in a show of exaggerated offense.

"Who said Theresa was meeting her friend here?" Andres asked me.

"Her mom, I guess. It was in the police report."

He slowly panned the camera from left to right, getting a full view of the shop. "She must have gotten the wrong place."

We were only a half mile from Linda's bakery and had more than two hours before the crew went into overtime, so I decided to swing by and see if we could get some shots of her at work. Theresa had spent a lot of her free time at her mother's bakery, and even worked there while in high school, so it made sense for the backstory. Plus I knew they would have lots of wedding cakes in the window, and if luck was with me Linda would be working on one. What better shot could there be than a mother decorating someone else's wedding cake, knowing she might never have the chance to do the same for her missing daughter?

We hadn't discussed my stopping in, but I knew Linda would go along with anything that she thought would help, so I didn't even bother to call. Though maybe I should have. As we parked across the street, I could see two people—Linda and a young man—screaming at each other in front of the bakery.

"Who the hell is that with Linda?" Andres asked.

"Her son. I recognize him from the photos at the house."

"So much for a close-knit family."

We watched Linda throw up her hands and walk into the bakery, still crying and yelling while her son stood on the sidewalk staring at the ground. Eventually, he too went back into the bakery. I noticed that no one in the dry cleaner's next door bothered to come outside and see if there was trouble. Obviously it wasn't the first family argument to spill out onto the street.

"What do we do?" Andres asked.

"I have no idea," I said. "I guess we wait."

We sat in the car for about five minutes, waiting for things to cool down, before I left the guys and went in to talk to Linda.

"Hi," I said, sounding a little too fake and cheery.

"Oh, my heavens, Kate!" Linda's excitement was even more phony than mine.

"We were just driving down the block and I saw your bakery. I thought maybe we could get some footage of you working?"

She froze. "We're just closing up. We're putting everything away."

It was only four in the afternoon and the sign on their door said they were open until five, but I nodded. "I figured," I said. "Is it too late to grab something for the boys?"

"Not at all. I'll make you a box. And some coffee. You must want coffee."

Before I had a chance to answer she had disappeared into the back room. I was left standing alone in the bakery, which had a homey, old-fashioned feel to it. There was a long counter with cookies, small cakes, and fruit tarts sitting on doilies. Two Styrofoam wedding cakes decorated as samples sat in the window.

On the far wall, there was a bulletin board with a poster of Theresa and dozens of photos of her. They were all pretty similar to the ones I'd seen at the house, happy family shots reminding everyone of better days. But there was also a photo of Theresa with a young, dark-haired woman. It was unremarkable, except that a pushpin had been used to gouge out the woman's eyes. Another photo, with the same woman, had an ink mustache drawn onto it.

As I stared at the images, Linda reemerged holding a large pink pastry box neatly tied with ribbon.

"I didn't mean to put you to any trouble," I said. "I'm sure it's been a busy day." Why I would be sure of that, I have no idea.

"Not at all. Slow day. My son, Tom, and I were just sitting here doing nothing."

She smiled. It was wide and sincere. Exactly the kind of smile I give to interview subjects when I'm lying to them.

"What do I owe you?"

"Absolutely nothing. My way of saying thank-you."

"It's not necessary. I don't even pay for it," I explained. "The production company reimburses me for the crew's lunch or any expenses I have." I took money out of my purse.

She pushed the money away. "I don't want it. I'm just so happy this is finally getting some attention." She grabbed a full coffeepot, poured three cups of coffee into large paper cups, and placed them in a take-away tray. "Can you handle this by yourself?"

"I think so. I'm just disappointed I didn't get to shoot you at work. Any chance for later in the week?"

"Of course. Anytime."

"Who is the girl in the photo?" I pointed to the damaged images on the wall.

Without looking, Linda answered, "Julia."

"Theresa's friend? Someone must not be very fond of her."

"Julia did that herself. She thinks she looks bad in photos." She moved toward the exit. "I'm so grateful you're doing this story. My whole family is. Whatever we can do to help, I hope you know that."

Just as she almost had me out the door, Tom emerged from the back room. With his head down, he walked quickly past his mother and me.

"You must be the son," I said.

"I must be," he answered without looking up. He walked out of the bakery without another word to us.

"He's in a hurry. He's got tickets to a Sox game," Linda said.

"Lucky him."

I didn't bother to mention that as we stood there, the White Sox were playing the Yankees in New York.

Nineteen

"She's a pretty good liar," I told Andres and Victor once I was back in the car.

I explained what had happened in the bakery, but the guys were mainly interested in the coffee and desserts.

"What was she supposed to say?" Andres pointed out. "My family is fighting. Get your camera out and film this."

"I'm just saying she didn't seem flustered, which means she has some practice with telling lies. And it's just weird about the photos."

Victor inched up from the backseat and popped his head between Andres and myself. "I'm with Kate on this one. I can see drawing a mustache on a photo of yourself, but gouging your own eyes out? That's screwed up."

Andres gulped the last of his coffee, crushed the cup, and threw it in the backseat, missing Victor by an inch. "What do we do now, boss?" he asked me.

"We have more than an hour in the day."

"So, a bar?" Victor suggested. "A drink to wind down the day."

"Nice try," I told him. "Head toward my house and I'll figure something out."

As we drove from the South Side to the North Side, crossing an invisible border that separates what has been traditionally blue-collar Chicago from the more hip, more moneyed side, I knew where I wanted to go next.

I keep a bright orange binder next to my laptop in a tote bag I carry with me on all shoots. In the binder I have everything I need, from interview questions to a list of needed B-roll images. I may not always enjoy my profession, but the necessity of being organized at least plays to my strengths. I went through my production binder and found

Julia's number. When I called, I explained to her that Friday, when we were scheduled to interview her, would be a very packed day, and I was hoping to get some B-roll footage of her now. I made up a bunch of stuff about getting tapes to New York, as if there was some kind of rush to get footage of her. Julia acted as if she understood what I was talking about and agreed to meet us at Angel Food Bakery, a coffee shop near her Ravenswood apartment. I guess the reason I knew Linda was such an experienced liar was because I recognized a fellow practitioner when I saw one.

"Why can't this wait until Friday?" Victor asked as we pulled up in front.

"I don't know," I admitted. "But Friday is the last day of the shoot, and I just think there might be something she tells me that I need to know before I talk to the ex-boyfriend, and before I see Linda again."

It was a gut feeling, based on a disfigured photograph and Linda's insistence that Julia had been wrong about meeting Theresa. I knew there wasn't time for the interview; that would have to wait until Friday, but there was a chance I could get something to help me better understand what was really going on. Or maybe I just didn't want to go home.

Angel Food Bakery was miles away, literally and figuratively, from Linda's bakery in Bridgeport. A bright place, with a cheery retro feel and offerings like homemade Twinkies that reimagined childhood comforts, it fit its trendy neighborhood in the same way that Linda's bakery fit its more traditional Bridgeport patrons.

"Julia?" I asked the pretty, dark-haired woman munching on a cupcake at one of the tables.

"Kate?" She hugged me. Why do people insist on hugging strangers? She was with a man about her age with a slight build and eyeglasses. "This is my husband, David."

"I hope you don't mind my tagging along. I've never been around a camera crew before," he said.

"Actually this works out great. We can shoot the two of you here, eating, and maybe outside walking down the street," I told him.

After checking with the artsy owner of the place, I had the

permission I needed, and Andres began taping the couple sitting at one of the tables, talking and enjoying their cupcakes. It was exactly what they'd been doing before we arrived, but now that it was being taped, they were self-conscious. Julia giggled and David kept glancing toward the camera. In frustration Andres looked toward me, eyebrows raised. I nodded. After working together for so long, even a small facial gesture is code for something. He put the camera on its tripod, aimed it at them, and walked a few steps away.

"Andres and I need to figure something out," I told the couple. "You guys just hang out and we'll start taping again in a minute."

Andres and I stood in the corner, pretending to chat. The camera was, of course, still running, but since they didn't know it, Julia and David relaxed, and we were able to get the footage I needed.

They were obviously very much in love. It wasn't just in the way he ran his fingers across her wedding ring, or in the way she smiled at him. It was something else—the way they were both excited just to be with the other person. For so many years Frank and I held hands across the dinner table and curled into each other when we sat on a couch. We had looked like that. Did that mean someday they would look like we ended up?

"Okay," I said after a few minutes, "I think we're going to go outside and get some stuff of you walking down the street."

Julia and David jumped up. "This is fun," Julia said. "I feel like a movie star."

"I'm glad you feel that way," I said. "It can be difficult to participate in a story like this, to relive all those old memories."

Her smile faded. "I miss her. It's been this total nightmare."

"Is that why you moved from Bridgeport all the way up here?"

"Sort of. I guess. We got married. We wanted a fresh start."

"And better bars," David said.

"Can't argue with that." I turned back to Julia. "Do you talk to her family much?"

David slid his arm around Julia, an unmistakable sign of support. Which meant she needed support.

"Not often," she admitted. "I think they kind of blame me."

"Because you were supposed to meet Theresa."

"I wasn't. We didn't make plans." Her frustration was obvious. She had clearly made the same statement many, many times.

"Theresa had a lot of stuff going on in her life that her mother didn't know about, didn't want to know about," David offered. "I think Theresa said she was meeting Julia so she wouldn't have to get into it."

"Her mother does seem overprotective."

David glanced at Julia, seemed to get approval to speak, and turned to me. "She was crazy. She wanted Theresa to be nine years old forever. No wonder she did the things she did."

"David," Julia interrupted. "Theresa was a great person. She wanted her mother to be happy but she also wanted to be her own person."

"And that led her to do what?" I asked.

Julia shrugged. "She maybe got around. It was a long time ago. I don't know that it really matters."

"She was dating someone else other than Wyatt?"

"I think so," Julia said. "She never said she was but something was going on."

"Maybe she was getting back with Jason?"

"Not a chance."

Still by Julia's side, David seemed to tense up at the mention of Jason's name.

"You didn't like him," I said.

"No. And I don't think Theresa was that stupid."

Julia wavered. "I don't know. There was something going on," she said. "Maybe someone new."

I wasn't sure if any of this would get into the show. If we were painting Theresa as ripe for sainthood, we wouldn't want to offer anything that would deter from that. On the other hand, if the network wanted to hint that Theresa somehow brought this on herself with late-night hookups and dark, dirty secrets, I could be on to something.

But for the moment, I was thinking about the photo. "I saw a couple of pictures of you in Moretti's Bakery," I started, looking for any indication Julia knew what the photos looked like. There wasn't any. "They'd been defaced."

"Asshole," Dave whispered.

"Who?" I asked.

Julia looked at David, shaking her head, but he didn't seem to care. "Tom. Theresa's brother. The guy has issues."

I was dying to ask the next logical question—could he have hurt Theresa?—but now I was sure I wanted this on camera. I'd have to wait until Friday for my answer if I wanted it to feel fresh and unrehearsed.

"We're going to go into overtime if we hang around too much longer," I said as my excuse to end the conversation. "Let's just get a couple of quick shots of you walking down the street. And listen, don't smile, don't look too happy. We have stuff of you happy, which I will need when I talk about how you were getting married when Theresa disappeared, but I also need sad stuff. I don't want it looking like you've completely forgotten Theresa."

This time they played along, walking down the street looking as though their world had collapsed. It was exactly what I needed, but there was something artificial about it. And not just because it *was* fake. There was nothing in Julia that actually seemed sad about the disappearance of her friend. It had been a year—but is that enough time to get over the sudden and inexplicable loss of your best friend since childhood? Maybe Theresa's brother had a good reason for mutilating Julia's photos.

Twenty

It's not just thumbs that separate us from the rest of the animal kingdom, it's the ability to compartmentalize. All day I had thought mostly of the shoot, of Theresa Moretti and the people who knew her.

Once I was home it rushed back over me and I couldn't push it away. Frank was dead. And I still hadn't figured out what I felt about him. My feelings, my lack of feelings, my confused and contradictory feelings—it was the sort of thing I would have indulged in when I was in my twenties. I would have called girlfriends and talked for hours. But excessively analyzing romantic relationships is like wearing a crop top. At some point, you realize you don't have the stomach for it anymore.

Not that it mattered. When I walked into the kitchen, I knew my feelings weren't my biggest priority. Something in the room seemed out of place. The photo albums of Frank and me that I'd left on the floor were stacked more neatly than I'd left them, and the pictures of Theresa on the table looked to be in a different order. It was just weird enough that I walked around each room holding a frying pan, a useless weapon if there really was someone in the house. Of course there wasn't. People don't break into other people's houses to see what kind of photos they have.

"This is stupid," I said. "I must have done this myself." I was half convinced I had done it and forgotten, but just in case, I left the frying pan on the kitchen table, next to my laptop.

In a nod to Frank, and because I was out of my own stuff, I made a cup of one of the green teas he had left at the house. It was good. Maybe I'd mocked him for nothing. I sat at the table and began hunting for the answers in my own personal true-crime show.

Dr. Milton had said Frank's death had been listed as undetermined. I looked online for what that meant and got nothing helpful. I did know a few people in the coroner's office from past episodes of *Caught!* but none of them well enough to get a peek into Frank's file. There was only one person who could give me more information than I already had.

Now that Detective Podeski had supplied her last name, it was surprisingly easy to find Vera's phone number and address. She lived in the Gold Coast neighborhood, the wealthiest in the city. It seemed an odd address for someone who had dressed as simply as Vera had the night we met. I guess she could be one of those people who lived in an expensive shoe box so she could impress others with her address. Though when I thought about it, Frank would never have gone for someone like that. His mother was someone like that, and Frank despised his mother's shallowness.

Voice mail picked up with a cheery greeting from Vera to leave a message, which I did. Nothing special. I just told her it was Frank's wife, Kate, and I wanted to ask her some questions. What questions they would be I hadn't yet figured out.

An hour later, the doorbell rang. I answered, assuming it was someone wanting to pray for me, sell me something, or mug me. Instead it was Vera.

"What are you doing here?"

She was holding a large box and seemed about to drop it. Out of instinct, I reached out for it, and we carried it into the living room.

"You called me," she said.

"I didn't ask you to stop by. How do you know where I live anyway?"

"I came here with Frank once."

"You did?"

"I stayed in the car while he picked up some clothes." She smiled a friendly, neighborly smile. "You have a great place. You have really nice taste. I love your couch."

"Okay." I stood for a moment waiting for some explanation as to why she was in my house. None came. Finally I asked, "What's in the box?"

"Frank's things. I thought you might want them. I thought we could go through them and maybe each pick out some mementos."

She knelt beside the box and pulled out his Bears cap. "I didn't bring his clothes, but I figured we could decide what to do with those another day."

"Are you drunk?"

She sat on the couch, making herself a little too comfortable for my taste. "Of course not."

"Then you must be crazy."

She got up and walked over to me. I was afraid she might hug me again, but thankfully she refrained. "You said you wanted to talk to me."

"I did."

"About Frank?"

"Yes."

"So talk to me."

I was chickening out. I'd asked people if they'd killed someone many times, but only in interviews. The interview subjects were usually expecting me to ask it, and there was a crew a few feet away, ensuring that the whole reaction would be on camera. Lacking the context of a television interview, the question seemed, for lack of a better word, impolite. So I stood there silently.

Vera seemed not to notice my awkwardness. "Do you have any wine?"

"Excuse me?"

"You're hurting and I'm hurting, and I think we could just hurt separately or we could help each other get past this. And either way, I think we both need a drink."

That was the first time she had said anything I could agree with, at least the part about needing a drink. I poured two glasses of pinot grigio and sat on my leather chair. Vera sat again on the couch she had admired, and we both drank.

"The coroner listed his cause of death as undetermined," I said.

"Which means it could be natural causes."

"Or someone could have killed him."

She watched me for a moment, then turned her eyes to her wine. "Someone like me?" she asked quietly.

"Or me."

"Well, you know *you* didn't and I know *I* didn't, so there must be another explanation."

"Like?"

"I don't know."

"Has Detective Podeski called you?" I asked.

"He's a very unpleasant man."

I smiled. "He is. I feel like a criminal just being in the same room with him."

"Then you should avoid that." She smiled. "It's not like either of us has done anything wrong."

It was all I could do not to point out that she wasn't being entirely accurate. One of us had done something wrong. Vera obviously reached the same conclusion. She brought her glass to her lips quickly and took a fast sip while I enjoyed watching her squirm.

Twenty-one

"I didn't set out to have an affair with a married man, Kate. I'm really not that kind of person."

"Except you must be, or else you wouldn't have."

"I just wanted to be with him so much."

"I assume you don't walk into someone else's house and take a painting off a wall, no matter how much you might want it. So why is it okay to take someone else's husband?"

Vera's expression turned earnest and thoughtful. "A piece of art doesn't consent, but a husband does," she said as if we were debating ideas in ethics class. "Not only does he consent, he often instigates. If a painting flung itself out a window and into my arms, am I really stealing it?"

Touché.

Vera stared at the rug. "I was married a long time ago but it didn't last long. I met a few men along the way. Nothing ever stuck. And then I was alone for so long, I didn't even know how lonely I was until I met Frank." She glanced my way, looking for my approval the way my interview subjects always do. Only this time I sat in expressionless silence. "I just fell for him so quickly that before I knew it, well, we had crossed a line. I feel so bad about it."

"Okay, stop right there," I said. "If you're hoping to be forgiven and turn this into some kumbaya moment, then you might as well leave now. In fact, you probably should leave now."

Vera didn't move. "I'm not asking for forgiveness, Kate. I'm just explaining. I'm not the sort of person who sets out to hurt other people, but I did hurt you. The worst part is that for those months that Frank was still living here, I didn't even feel bad about what I might be doing to you. I didn't think about you as a real person until the night Frank died. Until I heard your voice on the phone." She looked around the living room, as if she were studying it. "He had this whole life I never knew anything about. Those people at his funeral, who knew him and loved him. I didn't know who any of them were."

"Did you expect to?"

She shrugged. "I don't know."

"You knew Neal. He was Frank's best friend. I know you met."

"Only a couple of times. He seemed embarrassed around me."

"Did you double-date with Neal and his wife?"

I don't know why I was torturing myself, but I just had to know.

"No, nothing like that." She paused. "I met him a few times. And not that long ago we ran into him at a restaurant. He and Frank stepped outside, and they must have exchanged some words because Frank was in a foul mood the rest of the night."

"When was that?"

"Two or three weeks ago. Why?"

"No reason, I've just never known them to argue."

She put her wineglass on the coffee table. "Do you want to go through the stuff? I know that it's probably, legally, yours, but I was hoping you might let me keep a few things."

"You brought it over here, hoping I'd give it back to you? If you wanted some of this stuff, why didn't you just keep it?"

"That wouldn't be right."

"Now you want to do the right thing?"

"Look, Kate. We can yell at each other. We can focus on the negative. Or we can just try to be the decent people I know we both are." Vera's voice was shaky, so I knew she was nervous, but her gaze was steady and determined. "Frank took a lot of his stuff, maybe things that meant something to you too. You'll want those back. I was just hoping what you don't want, I can keep." She reached into the box and pulled out a decorated tin. "I almost forgot. I brought you a present."

I was half expecting it to be one of those old-fashioned joke tins, where a fabric snake pops out, but when I opened the tin it was full of candies wrapped in gold cellophane. "It's butterscotch," I said. "I love butterscotch."

She looked pleased. "I know. These are imported from Scotland. They're heavenly."

She turned back to the box, started removing items and spreading them on the floor, like some preauction display. She hummed as she did it. She was an odd duck. So nonantagonistic, so not sarcastic, so unnegative. So unlike me. She reminded me of someone. When I realized who, I laughed. She reminded me of Frank.

She saw me laugh. "I know how nuts this looks, my coming here. I know it *is* nuts, but I can't help myself. I miss him. I miss the way he used to draw little pictures on everything, and the way he would shout at the TV during a Bulls game. I miss the way he laughed and the way he smiled and his voice. I even miss the way he tied his shoes."

"Bunny ears," I said.

She smiled. "And no one understands. But you."

"Vera, I was with him for twenty-one years. We dated for almost six and were married for more than fifteen. You were with him for, what, three months before he left and four months after."

"Seven months before he left," she corrected me.

Frank had told me three. Another lie. I should be used to it by now.

"Whatever," I said. "We're not in comparable situations."

"I know that," she said. "And I know you think I have no right to any claim on him."

"I didn't say that." I thought it, but I didn't say it. "That's why you went to the wake." It had suddenly dawned on me. "If you didn't go, it would be like saying you were his mistress, some secret, unimportant tryst. But if you went, if you stood with his friends and family and publicly mourned him, then you weren't his mistress, you were his girlfriend."

She nodded. "Frank said you could read people well and were impossible to fool."

"Not always, obviously."

As I spoke, something on the floor caught my eye. It was a book with a familiar cover, but the title was covered by a Cubs banner.

"What's that?" I pointed toward it.

Vera grabbed the book, and I saw that it was a copy of *Travels with Charley*.

"That must have gotten in there by mistake," I said.

"No. It was Frank's. He was reading it. He said someone he knew really loved it and he wanted to understand why. He was only about halfway through, but I think he was really enjoying it." She handed me the book. "You keep it."

I held the book in my hands and stared at it. My hands were shaking, and I felt flushed and woozy. It was the same way I'd felt when Frank kissed me for the first time.

Twenty-two

After Vera left, I went to bed with Frank's copy of *Travels with Charley* and, without really meaning to, I ended up sleeping with it wrapped in my arms. And even though, as I've said before, I don't think there are ghosts, I kept picturing Frank hovering above me, a huge smile on his face. Frank was always so pleased with himself whenever he did anything I liked, and I knew he would love the image of me clinging to a reminder of him. Which, of course, I wouldn't want him to see.

Thinking that made me feel slightly ashamed of myself. What was wrong, exactly, with Frank doing something that made me happy? When we were first married everything he did made me feel good; even taking out the garbage was, to me, a sign of his love. Toward the end it was rare for Frank to do anything to please me. Was it because he stopped trying or because at some point I just refused to find happiness in him?

I was glad the next morning to be back to the relative safety of a television show and the case of a missing twenty-two-year-old woman. We had two interviews, which would make it a very busy day, and one where I could put my personal life completely out of my mind. The first interview was with Grayson Meyer, an ex–assistant state's attorney and friend of the family. The second was with Jason, Theresa's ex-boyfriend. I didn't care about Meyer's interview, since it would be more of the same "Theresa was a saint" stuff. It was Jason's interview that would really make or break the story.

"Have you met this guy before?" Andres asked as we pulled into a parking spot of the building where Meyer had his office. It was a beautiful high-rise on Wacker Drive, a place for some of the wealthiest and most politically connected Chicagoans to do business.

"Never met him," I told Andres, as he loaded the equipment cart.

"I just know he used to be a prosecutor. Now he's doing some pro bono defense work and using an office in a fancy law firm to do it."

"He's dreamy," Victor said, offering up an theatrical swoon.

Victor had the sort of skinny, nonmuscular body that often begged the question, does he do coke? He heightened the effect with black jeans, black T-shirts, a spiked, sometimes dyed haircut, a nose ring, and several very colorful tattoos. He despised any male who might be considered more traditionally attractive.

"I don't care what he looks like," I told him. "I just want to get in, get a few sound bites, and get out. We're just using him to give us some family information, plus a little legal info on missing persons."

Andres grabbed his camera. "I shot an interview with the guy about six months ago. It was for some congressman's campaign. And Victor's right, he is kind of dreamy. We'll understand if you want to extend the interview and just enjoy the view for a while."

"Are you going over to the other side, Andres?" I teased.

"See how they are?" he said to Victor. "I can't notice another man is attractive without her turning it into some sexual thing."

"Women. It's all about sex with them," Victor agreed.

I laughed. "I love my boys," I said and slapped them both on their butts.

There are two parts of field producing I love: learning about things I would never have otherwise learned and hanging out with the crew. Though spending the morning in a beautiful building interviewing a "dreamy" man didn't exactly suck either. It was exactly what I needed to put Vera completely out of my mind.

On the twenty-eighth floor of the building, in the offices of one of Chicago's most prestigious law firms, we were led to the law library and offered coffee, which we accepted. The guys started to set up and I watched the clock. Twenty minutes went by, and then forty. Andres was almost ready, and we still hadn't met the man we were here to interview.

"This asshole is going to put us behind schedule," I said, just as the door was opening.

"I'm so sorry I'm late. I got a phone call. I'm Gray Meyer."

He was, as promised, dreamy. Early forties, about six foot one, dark brown hair and green eyes, with the slim but muscular build I would associate with a tennis player, not an attorney. Though judging by the Italian shoes, I'd guess he was a very successful attorney.

"No problem," I said. "We're just finishing with the lights."

He introduced himself to me, then Victor, and he remembered Andres from the previous shoot. He even asked how Andres's mom was. Apparently she had been in the hospital when they'd met six months before.

"You're going into politics," I said once we sat opposite each other. Andres and Victor were making final adjustments, so I would have little time to bond with Meyer, but he didn't seem to need it.

He smiled. Perfect white teeth. "Why would you ask that?"

"You have a politician's memory for people."

He laughed. "You have a journalist's knack for finding the story."

"You are going into politics?"

"I already am, in a way. I helped get Bobby Rosenello elected to Congress. You know Bobby."

"No. Should I?"

"He's your congressman, isn't he? Don't you live in Bucktown?"

I blushed. First there was the embarrassment that I didn't know my own congressman, and then the shock that he knew where I lived. My interview subjects never know anything about me. "How would you know that?"

He shrugged. "I guess I like to know who I'm talking to. Bucktown's a great neighborhood. Great restaurants. Very artsy. Are you an artist in your spare time?"

"My husband was an artist." I glanced down at my wedding ring, which had not left my finger since the day of the funeral.

He leaned a little toward me. "I'm sorry about your husband. I heard he just passed away."

Who the hell was this guy?

"Where do you live?" I asked, just trying to think of something to get him off the topic.

"Lincoln Park. My wife is a lifelong resident."

"That's a nice neighborhood too."

Lincoln Park is about a mile away from Bucktown, but in a whole different tax bracket. Higher. Much higher.

"We're ready," Andres said, and I practically jumped up and thanked him. Restraining myself, I took a moment to study my notes and then told Grayson Meyer to keep his eyes on me the whole time and answer as completely as he could. No yes or no answers, since they wouldn't play well on camera. He nodded.

Now the conversation would be back on my terms.

Twenty-three

"Grayson," I started. "Can I call you that?"

He made a face. "No, I hate that name. It's a horribly pretentious name. Call me Gray, which is better, if only slightly."

I took a breath and relaxed a little. "Gray, let's start with how you knew Theresa."

He nodded, straightened himself in the chair, and looked at me. "I know Theresa through the Kenny family. Her closest friend, Julia, is the daughter of a friend of mine. I've met Theresa a number of times through the years. She's a lovely young woman, very close to her family, very proud of being from Chicago. And if I remember correctly she had just finished her nursing studies. I think that shows she's a giving person."

"How much time did you spend with her?"

"Not much. We were only linked through the Kennys, but she did come to a Halloween party my wife and I threw a few years ago. We got into a conversation about politics. She thought there ought to be a law making community service mandatory. Something like the draft, but for helping people, not for war." He smiled warmly, and a little sadly. "She's probably right, though I doubt we could get it through Springfield, let alone Washington."

"She seemed very keen on the idea of helping in the community. She even won an award . . ."

"Yes, I know about that. Theresa is the sort of person who gives you hope for the next generation. She really wanted to make a difference and she was willing to do more than sign up for a cause on Facebook; she was willing to actually go out there and create a better world. I really admire that kind of passion."

"So you spoke about that with her?"

"Not in depth. As I said, I knew her mainly through the Kenny family."

"If you didn't know her that well, why am I talking to you?" I said it in a casual way, but I meant it.

"I think because I organized the search party and helped with the media. Julia's dad called me the day after Theresa went missing. It was one of those things where everybody wants to help, so they reach out to people who might be able to do something. I did what I could."

"Which was what?"

"I called the people I know at the *Tribune* and *Sun-Times*, the local news stations. I kept in touch with Detective Rosenthal, so I could help her and the family with the distribution of flyers. I just helped get the word out."

"There was a large color poster of Theresa on the Morettis' door. Are you talking about things like that?"

"We put them everywhere. We hired a private detective, searched the neighborhoods, tracked down leads that went as far as Los Angeles. Unfortunately, we haven't had the outcome we've wanted so far."

"That's great that you were willing to give so much, but it sounds expensive and the Moretti family doesn't really have that kind of money, do they?"

"I helped a little. And so did the community. There were a lot of fund-raisers, especially in those first few months. You never want to find out the way Linda has, but a community will come together to help. And they, we, came together to help the Morettis."

"Were there leads?"

"That's something Yvette Rosenthal could help you with. As far as I know, there haven't been."

"Did you know her boyfriend or her ex?"

He nodded. "I met them. Wyatt was the boyfriend's name. He seemed nice, maybe a little overwhelmed. I don't think they'd been together very long. But he hung in there. The ex, Jason, he took it harder. I know there was some trouble with him before she disappeared, but nothing serious. He showed up once to help, but Theresa's brother didn't want him there."

"That's Tom, right? What did he do?"

He paused. "He just didn't want him there."

There was finality in the statement that made me want to ask more, but Gray Meyer looked like the kind of guy who wouldn't be pressed. And frankly, what did I care? I wasn't here to solve the disappearance, just get a story that would fit into the template of true-crime shows.

"What about Julia?"

He sighed. "Poor thing. She was in the midst of planning her wedding to David. In the morning she would go to a dress fitting; in the afternoon she'd pass out flyers all over Bridgeport. She was destroyed. She wanted to cancel the wedding, but David wouldn't let her. And the Morettis—not only did they come to her wedding, which had to be hard, but Tom Moretti made Julia's wedding cake. He said Theresa would have wanted him to."

"I got the impression they, maybe, blamed Julia."

"You got the wrong impression."

"Do you think Theresa could have just walked away and started a new life?"

"No. There's no way. She wouldn't have done that to her family."

"You don't think she had a secret life? Maybe a lover somewhere?"

He shifted a little. "I didn't know Theresa well enough to know what social activities she engaged in, but I think that sort of speculation is without merit." His voice was even but firm. "I think to even suggest it damages a good person who can't defend herself."

I was kind of amused by how politely he was telling me off.

"What do you think happened?" I asked.

"I don't know." His voice softened, almost to a whisper. "I hope she's alive. I hope she comes home soon. She had her whole life ahead of her. I just hope she gets the chance to live it."

As the words came out of his mouth, I knew his last two sentences would be the sound bite that ended the episode, a photo of Theresa with Wyatt or her family on screen as he spoke.

"That's it," I said. "I have what I need." Behind me, I heard Andres shut off the camera.

Gray sat back. "I forgot I was on camera. You have such a conversational interview style. I did some interviews, when I was in the state's attorney's office, where producers practically told me what to say. Can you imagine that?"

"No," I said with a straight face.

He stared at me for a long moment then snapped out of it. "Let me show you something in my office." He put his hand on my arm, leaving me with the feeling I wasn't being asked. I was being told.

Twenty-four

His office was large with expensive midcentury-looking furniture and a window that faced the Chicago River. There was modern art on the walls and a photo of a Grace Kelly–type blonde on his desk.

"Your wife is beautiful," I said.

He nodded. "No idea what she saw in me." False modesty. Smoothly delivered.

On his desk I noticed a copy of the *Tribune*, opened to the society page. Gray and his wife were photographed at some party. Underneath it the caption read, "Elizabeth Meyer, Chairwoman of the Help for the Homeless Dinner Dance, pictured with her devoted husband, Gray Meyer."

"Nice photo."

He rolled his eyes. "One of the other lawyers brought it in to give me crap about it."

"I'm glad somebody did." I waited as we just stood and stared at each other. Eventually I said, "I need to get back to my crew."

"Right. Won't take a minute." He rummaged around in a file cabinet before coming up with a business card. "This is the bar where Wyatt and Theresa met. Did you know about this place?"

"No. They met several months before she disappeared, so I'm not sure that's something that will get into the story."

"It's an interesting place. Theresa spent a lot of time there with Wyatt."

"We only have twenty-two minutes to tell the story," I explained. "We focus on the disappearance mostly."

He handed me the card. "Well, in case you want to stop by there."

"Okay. Thanks." I could tell there was something else he wanted to say, but I had to get to Jason's interview, so I walked to his office door.

"Kate," Gray said, with a touch too much familiarity, "I feel bad I said anything about your husband. I could tell you weren't expecting it."

"I wasn't," I admitted. "The people I interview don't usually check into my background."

"I understand. I guess I'm just used to being careful."

"Well, there's no need to be. You've done enough media to know that the hour we spent interviewing you . . ."

"Will end up being about thirty seconds of screen time," he said, finishing my thought.

"Exactly. This story isn't about you. It's about Theresa."

"Which is why I wanted to help."

"You like to help, don't you?"

"I do. When I feel that something isn't right, I want to do something that may help make it right."

"Superman complex?"

He smiled. "Maybe. I think everyone in law enforcement, in the law, and in politics all starts out with a bit of a need to be a superhero."

"It seems to me a lot of people lose that need along the way."

"I suppose. Hopefully I'm not there yet. Which is why I wanted to say that if you need anyone with you when you talk to Detective Podeski next time, I'm available. Or I can recommend someone."

It took me off guard but I tried not to show it. "A lawyer, you mean."

"Yeah. Just if you felt you needed someone."

"Why would I need someone?"

"If you were questioned."

I closed his office door and walked toward him. "Why would I be questioned?"

He moved back a few steps, as if he were slightly intimidated. I took this as a small victory. "I was in the state's attorney's office for fourteen years," he said. "I know a lot of people in the police department."

"You obviously know Podeski. And you know he's investigating my husband's death."

He nodded. "He thinks your husband was murdered."

"By whom?"

"You."

I leaned against his desk. I looked down at my slightly scuffed tan shoes against the deep-red Persian rug. A rug the color of blood.

"Can I get you a glass of water?" Gray asked.

I shook my head. "Why does he think Frank was murdered?"

"They found digitalis in his system. That's heart medicine. It can bring on the symptoms of a heart attack in someone who doesn't have a heart condition. He didn't have a heart condition, did he?"

I shook my head again. It took me a minute to let it sink in, then I looked at Gray. "Why are you telling me this?"

"I've looked into the faces of thousands of criminals over the years. There's something they all have in common. It's in their eyes. I can't tell you what it is. I just know it when I see it. It's not in your eyes."

"And so you're sharing inside information on an ongoing police investigation because I don't have a killer's eyes?"

He flashed a small smile.

I looked up at him, studied his perfect features and bright green eyes. All I saw was the sincere, kind expression of a man who was truly interested in helping me. The same expression every politician has when they want something.

Twenty-five

"His charm made her catatonic." Victor poked me in the side as we drove west on Chicago Avenue toward Jason's apartment.

"What was that for?" I snapped.

"Touchy, touchy." Victor leaned back in his seat and looked hurt. "Guys like him have that effect on women."

I could have told Victor and Andres about the conversation; they would have understood. But I didn't want to say out loud that the police—that anyone—thought I had killed Frank. Instead, I checked my cell phone for messages. There were two. One was from Alex, asking me to call him when I got the chance. The other was from Jason. He was running late, he said. He'd call me when he was at his apartment. That could only mean cold feet. I dialed his cell and got voice mail.

"Jason, it's Kate. My crew and I are headed over to your place. I can delay by an hour or so, but I've got to do this interview today if we're going to include it in the show. I've talked with Theresa's mom so I know what they've said about you, and I really think you should give your side. I'll be at your place at two thirty, ready to set up. I hope you'll be there."

"So what do we do now?" Andres asked once I'd hung up.

"Lunch," Victor suggested.

I thought about my conversation with Gray. I was being played, and by someone who had a lot more information than I did. I didn't have his connections or his clout, but I knew how to lie. I was hoping that would be enough to get something that might level the playing field.

"I want to make a stop first," I said.

Andres and Victor waited in the car, blasting the radio and arguing about what music to play. I walked into the police station.

"Hi, remember me?"

The receptionist looked up, stared at me blankly.

"I was here yesterday interviewing Detective Rosenthal."

More blank stares.

"For the television show."

"Oh, yeah. She's not here. Do you want me to call her cell?"

"No, that's okay. It's just that she promised me a copy of the police report on the Theresa Moretti case and I was wondering if you could give it to me."

She sighed, got up from her chair, and after ten agonizing minutes in which I wondered if it was a felony to lie to a police receptionist, she returned with a manila file folder.

"I made you copies." She dropped into her chair. The effort had apparently exhausted her.

"Thanks. Really appreciate it."

She was back to a blank stare.

I was barely in the car before Victor grabbed the back of my seat and shook it. "Lunch?"

"Yeah, lunch. Let's go someplace near Wrigley Field. You guys really like that barbecue place on Clark, don't you?"

"What's the occasion?" Victor asked.

Andres knew. "She wants us to shoot something in that neighborhood."

There was a Cubs game going on, so we overpaid to park and walked to a bar on Sheffield. It was midday, and the Cubs were in the fourth inning, so it would be a while before the place filled up. I asked the guys to get some exterior shots, just in case we would need them. I went inside to see if there was anyone to talk to.

The way I saw it, Gray had either given me that card as an excuse to talk about Frank or he'd talked about Frank as an excuse to give me the card. If I could figure out which, maybe I'd know how seriously to take his revelation about the investigation into Frank's death.

"Hi," I said to a large man in his forties. He was standing behind the bar, looking bored.

"What can I get you?"

"I'm working on a television show." I pointed to the crew outside. "We're shooting an episode of a new show called *Missing Persons*. It's an offshoot of the show *Caught!*"

"I love that show," he said.

I smiled. That just made things a lot easier. "Yeah, it's a great show," I agreed. "The episode we're doing is about a girl named Theresa Moretti . . ."

"Theresa? I knew Theresa. She dated Wyatt. Are you talking to him?"

"Yes, tomorrow. You know Wyatt?"

"He used to work here. That's how they met. She came in and they got talking. Wyatt is a bit of a ladies' man."

"Were you here the night they met?"

"Yeah. It was a busy night and I couldn't get Wyatt to wait on anyone other than a group of women sitting in that corner." He pointed to the end of the bar. "After that, Theresa was in here all the time."

"Did they make a nice couple?"

"Yeah. Okay. Not toward the end, though."

"The end being a breakup, or her disappearance?"

"She went missing before they could break up, as far as I know, but I could tell that's where it was going."

"Were they fighting?"

"Just the one that I saw, but it was huge. Theresa was sitting over there." He pointed to a stool at the end of the bar. "It was maybe three days before she went missing. It was a slow night and they were just hanging out in the corner talking. Then all of a sudden, she started telling Wyatt off. Yelling at him about something. He said later she was just drunk. But she stormed off, and then he left."

"Did she drink a lot?"

"She could hold her own."

"Which is a yes."

He raised an eyebrow and considered the question. "Yeah, I'd say she drank a lot. But with Wyatt bartending, a lot of her drinks were free, so maybe that had something to do with it."

"What was he like after she disappeared?"

"He went through the wringer. I don't think he slept for the first week or so. He looked like hell when he'd come in. Then he just quit one day. Maybe two or three weeks later. I think he made finding her his full-time job, poor guy."

"Do the police know about the fight?"

"Not from me. I don't gossip." Then he blushed, realizing what he was doing. "This is different. This is for a TV show. If you want I can say all of this again, on camera."

Which, of course, I wanted.

Twenty-six

We put the bartender outside in front of the bar, since the dark bar would have taken too long to light properly. He repeated most of what he'd said off camera. At first it was all compliments. Theresa was nice, friendly, polite, seemed close to her family and friends. Then he talked about the drinking and fighting, which were new parts to the picture, at least on camera. Theresa was still a wonderful person, but the halo was beginning to tilt a little.

When we were done with the interview, Andres got a couple of interior shots of the bar as quickly as he could, but we were behind schedule. Barbecue was out. We grabbed hot dogs from a stand and raced over to Jason's apartment. We pulled up at two forty p.m., and I jumped out, hoping that Jason was curious enough about what the others had said to show up for the interview.

He was. He opened the door in a blue oxford shirt, khaki pants, and what appeared to be a new haircut. He looked like his mother had dressed him.

"I'm Kate," I said casually. "This is going to be much easier than you think."

"I hope so, 'cause I really don't want to do this."

As Andres and Victor set up, Jason and I went into the kitchen. I noticed one of those photo booth pictures. Four snapshots of Theresa and Jason smiling and making goofy faces. They must be required in the first few months of a relationship because everyone seems to have them, including Frank and me. Only this photo booth picture was beautifully framed and hanging in a prominent spot in Jason's kitchen.

"You miss her," I said.

He blushed a little. "We were really in love."

I studied the photos. "I can tell. This is a nice place. Have you lived here long?"

"About a year."

"Did you move after Theresa disappeared? I know her friend Julia wanted to leave the old neighborhood. Too many memories. Must be the same for you."

He seemed nervous, but then a TV crew was setting up in his living room. Being nervous made sense. "I actually moved just before she went missing."

"Was it her idea to hang the photo of the two of you in the kitchen?"

"No. She was never here. We were broken up by the time I moved."

I nodded and smiled and tried to relax him. He had a small silver medallion I recognized as a saint's medal, and he was twirling it in his fingers.

"Which patron saint is that?" I asked.

"Saint Catherine. Patron saint of nurses."

"Nurse? Like Theresa?"

"And my mom. She's a nurse too. She gave this to me to keep me healthy. I kind of consider it my good luck charm."

We chatted about the hot weather and Jason's new job in a candy factory. He worked in the room where flavoring and color are added to a sugar mixture to make hard candies. It was something he found fascinating. I'd done a couple of shows in candy factories and it gave us a starting point for the conversation. He relaxed as he told me about his job and the people at work. They all seemed to get along, and he felt it was the sort of place where he had a future. He loved to cook, he told me, and even though he only needed to know a small part of the process, he planned to take some classes in candy making, just so he would better understand the science behind the sweets.

I asked him a lot of questions about candy but let my questions about Theresa wait. Jason struck me as a sweet guy, young for twenty-five, and very sensitive. If the kitchen was his favorite place, and that was where he chose to keep Theresa's picture, then he was still trying to include her in his day-to-day life. That meant there was a lot of emotion just underneath the surface. I didn't want to unleash it before we got on camera.

But an hour later, when we sat across from each other, Jason seemed determined to remain positive, helpful, and composed. Every question, from how they met to why they broke up, elicited the dullest of answers. We'd been rolling tape for thirty minutes when I thought to ask about the day he and Theresa took the photos he had framed in the kitchen.

"We were at Navy Pier, just hanging out," he said, smiling at the memory. "Theresa liked doing date stuff, so we did it."

"Date stuff?"

"Like going dancing or to the zoo. She didn't just want to sit in a bar and watch a game. She wanted to do stuff that we would remember."

"I was like that too," I admitted. "And I do remember those days. They were really happy ones, so Theresa was right." I could feel tightness in my throat as I remembered Frank and me during our zoo and dancing days. But I was getting off track. I pushed away the memory and returned to the photo. "That day at Navy Pier must have been special, Jason."

He shrugged.

"Well, you chose those photos to frame and hang in the kitchen, so there must have been a reason. I'm assuming you have other photos of Theresa."

"We talked about our future a lot that day. We were going to get married, have a couple of kids. We talked about, maybe, someday, building a vacation house in Wisconsin. Just ordinary stuff, that's what we wanted."

"But Theresa's mother said you broke up because she wanted a commitment and you didn't."

A flash of anger. Then, a deep breath. "Not true. I wanted the same things Theresa did."

"But Linda Moretti said Theresa told her that." I was lying, but I was close to the truth.

"I don't care what Mrs. Moretti said; that's not why we broke up."

"Let's get back to that. The breakup."

"I already answered that question. We were just going through a downtime. We needed space. We would have gotten back together."

"But she was dating Wyatt."

"It wasn't going to last."

"Isn't that just wishful thinking on your part?"

He looked about to punch me. "The hell with this," he said and started to get up.

"Stop, please," I said. "I know this is difficult, and I hate asking, but I do understand what you went through. My husband left me for another woman. I thought he would come back too."

I could see Jason soften. He sat back in his chair. "When did he leave?"

"Four months ago."

"Maybe he will come back."

"He won't." I said it out loud for the first time. Just hearing the words left me with tears in the back of my eyes. This is what I wanted Jason to feel, not me. "I just want to know why you were sure."

"I'm sorry about your husband." His voice was warmer. "I guess it's hard to know. It's hard to give up on someone you love. I guess maybe I didn't know if she would come back. But we'd been talking. Things seemed good."

"When was the last time you talked?"

"The day before she disappeared."

I hadn't heard that before or seen it in the police statements or the pre-interview packet I'd received from Ripper Productions. And it didn't seem to be something Detective Rosenthal knew when I interviewed her.

"Did you call her?" I asked.

"She called me."

"What did she say?"

"Nothing. She just wanted to talk. I kept feeling like she was going to tell me something, but all she said was that she was just glad I was in her life. She said she always knew who I was. I never surprised her."

"What do you think she meant?"

"I don't know. I figured that guy she was with had done something and she was finally seeing I was the better man."

"Did you see her after that?"

"No. I was going to call her the next day, but I didn't want to be pushy. I thought it would be better if I played it a little cool, you know." His voice was shaking, and he seemed on the verge of breaking down.

I almost reached out to comfort him but stopped myself. I didn't want my hand in the shot.

"Do the police know about the call?" I asked.

He rolled his eyes. "They haven't done anything to find Theresa. They just filed reports and listened to her mother."

"Jason, where do you think Theresa is?"

"I don't know."

"Do you think she's dead?"

Tears filled his eyes. "I don't . . ." He stopped. "I'm done," he said to Andres. "I don't want to talk anymore." He pulled the mic off and walked into the kitchen, where we could all hear him burst into tears.

Twenty-seven

"That guy knows," Victor said as Andres drove away from Jason's apartment, with me in the passenger seat and Victor in back.

"Knows what?" I asked.

"Come on, he did it," Victor insisted. "He knocked that chick into eternity. She's probably in six pieces under the floorboards in his bedroom."

"That's disgusting." I turned away from him and focused on Andres. "He didn't seem like a killer to you, did he?"

"I don't know, Kate. He seemed a little too into her. She was his ex-girlfriend. If my woman had left me for another man, I don't think I'd be crying about her a year later."

"But he loved her and she's missing. You don't think he would still be sad even if it was a year later?"

"Unless he's the reason she's missing," Victor said.

"I've got to go along with Victor on this," Andres said. "He's the only one so far who seems to think that they were getting back together. Her mother sure as hell didn't think so and neither did Julia, did she?"

"No," I admitted. "But you never really know what goes on in someone else's relationship. And if he had done something to her, wouldn't he be saying he was over her, instead of making himself look like some wishful sap? His version of the story makes him look too guilty to be a lie."

"Kate, he doesn't have a better story because he's stupid." Victor inched himself up so he was practically sitting between Andres and me. "It's simple. She leaves him for someone hotter, and he kills her. We must do twenty episodes a year where that happens."

"People get dumped without resorting to murder," I pointed out.

"He's a loser."

"Based on what?"

"Based on his being dumped. Losers get dumped. And he's a big-ass loser because a year later he's still got her picture on his wall."

Andres beeped at the car in front of us for not moving on green fast enough.

"Come on, Kate, you have to agree with me," Victor said excitedly. "It's not natural to be so weepy about some chick who leaves you. If someone kicks you to the curb, you don't sit around remembering the good times. You get revenge."

Andres made a sharp right turn and went just a little faster than the posted speed limit.

"I'm not saying," Victor continued, "that you wouldn't miss her. Theresa was hot, in a buttoned-up kind of way. I'd have done her."

"I'm sure she'd be thrilled to hear that," I said.

Victor was ignoring my sarcasm. He was intent on making a point. "And, you know, that Jason kid is okay looking, but he was out of his league with her. He's not getting laid by her kind again."

I turned toward him and said my words slowly. "So you would kill someone who left you for someone else?"

Andres braked suddenly, and Victor flew forward. "What the hell?" Victor yelled.

"Sorry, you should buckle up back there," Andres said.

Victor flipped him off. "Kate and I are trying to have a conversation."

"Sorry." Andres smiled. "Hate to get in the middle of a good conversation."

A few minutes later, Andres pulled up in front of my house. He jumped out of the driver's seat just as I was getting out of the car.

"I'll walk you to the door, Kate."

"It's not necessary."

Andres followed me up the stairs. "He's an ass."

"I know that."

"It will be ten o'clock tonight before he realizes what he said."

"It's fine."

"And besides, it isn't the same thing. What happened in your marriage is totally different from what happened with Jason and Theresa."

"I know."

Andres gave me a hug. "I'll pick you up tomorrow morning at eight sharp. What do we have?"

"The two final interviews, the boyfriend and Julia. And B-roll at the mother's bakery."

He smiled. "We'll be busy all day, so that should keep Victor's mouth shut. And we'll go out for a drink afterwards, just the two of us. We'll hang out."

"You don't have to take care of me," I said.

"Yes, I do. Most of the producers I shoot with are idiots. I have to keep the good ones in working order."

Victor stuck his head out the car window. "Jeez, Kate, I just realized what I said. I wasn't talking about you. You're hot, so you don't need to feel bad you got dumped," he shouted, sharing his insights with the whole neighborhood. "Besides, it's not like your old man was murdered."

Andres walked back to the car shaking his head, as Victor sat back, feeling as though he had sidestepped a land mine. I went inside the house wanting a stiff drink and a cyanide capsule.

Twenty-eight

Neither was waiting for me. Instead there was another message from Alex, sounding more urgent than the first. I called him on his cell.

"Sorry, it's been a busy day," I said, leading off the conversation.

"I know, kiddo. You're back doing another one of those TV shows. I just thought we could talk."

The last thing I wanted was to talk. "Sure. What's up?"

"Let's do it in person. Margie's Candies okay?"

"I guess. Alex, is everything okay?"

"A half an hour?"

I'd barely said yes when he hung up.

Margie's Candies is a Chicago institution. They've served their hot fudge sundaes and banana splits to nearly everyone who has spent some time in Chicago, including Al Capone, the Beatles, and me. I knew Alex had chosen it because it was close to my house, but I didn't want to go there. For years, Frank and I had spent summer nights sitting in one of their booths. I hadn't been there since he left, and as good as their ice cream was, I hadn't intended to go back.

But a half hour after his call, I was walking through the door of Margie's Candies looking for Alex. He was there ahead of me, sitting nervously at Al Capone's booth, sipping a cup of coffee.

"Hey, there." He jumped up and kissed me on the cheek. "You look tired."

"I just got back from work." I sat down and looked at the menu, but I knew what I wanted. "I'll have a half caramel, half hot fudge sundae," I told the waiter, a sixtysomething man who had waited on me at least two dozen times.

"You also want some English toffee to go?" he asked.

"It's nice to know there's a man who knows me so well," I said, smiling. I turned back to Alex. "What's wrong?"

"Nothing."

"Yes, there is. I could hear it in your voice."

He smiled. "I guess it's nice to have a woman who knows me so well." The smile faded. "It's the insurance, kiddo. There's a delay."

"The cause of death."

His eyes widened. "You know about that?"

"Did you talk with the police?"

He shook his head. "The insurance company is talking with them."

"A detective came to see me," I said. "And then someone I interviewed mentioned it. A guy named Gray Meyer. Have you ever heard of him?"

Alex's company had done a lot of work for both the city and the state. I hoped their paths had crossed.

"Yes, Gray Meyer. He's a smooth one. He's a good guy as far as I can tell. I've only met him at fund raisers and things. He does a lot of work for inner-city kids."

"Noblesse oblige?"

"I don't know what motivates him. I heard he was going to run for the state senate about a year ago, but then he decided not to announce."

"Do you know why?"

"I heard there was some infidelity."

The waiter brought my sundae and refilled Alex's coffee. I dug in before the hot sauce melted the ice cream. Alex sat back and watched me, as if he was my father and I was his little girl. It was a nice feeling to be part of Frank's family again, if only for the few minutes of silence we shared before Alex brought up the reason we were meeting.

"I don't think there's anything to this delay," Alex finally said.

"I don't either."

"Frank's mother has gotten wind of the insurance and I'm nervous she'll figure out the beneficiary before it's all completed. She's already so upset."

"If I were her, I would be too. If there's any possibility Frank was murdered . . ."

"Which he wasn't."

"Of course not. But if there was, why wouldn't Lynette be upset? I'm upset. We all are."

Alex reached across the table and squeezed my hand. "She wants me to get Frank's things back from that woman. Some of them are family heirlooms. There was a watch I got on my twenty-first birthday that I gave him for his twenty-first birthday. And my father's tie clips, the diamond cuff links we gave him on your wedding day, my dog tags from the army . . ." He sighed. "I don't know how to reach that woman. I thought maybe you would."

"Is that why you called me?"

"And I wanted to see how you were doing." He paused. "It's just a mess, the way he left things. After all you've been through, I couldn't just ask you over the phone. I shouldn't come to you for this, but, well, you know Frank's mother. She won't rest."

"I know."

I thought about all the phone calls over the years. If Frank and I planned to skip Easter dinner or her birthday or any holiday, real or imagined, she would bawl into the phone until we relented. One year we were forced to return from our vacation a day early so we could be on hand for her bunion surgery. Frank would have cut her out of his life, but I couldn't. I pushed him into going along with all of her requests. She was his mother. I wanted him to respect that. And, more than that, I wanted her to like me. A colossal waste of time, as it turned out.

"If you know anything about this woman of Frank's. Even her last name," Alex said.

"I know her," I told him. "She came to my house last night and brought some of his stuff." When we had divided the contents of the box, I was left with his Bears hat, wedding ring, a few CDs, the photos of him as a kid, and *Travels with Charley*, which was still in my bed. "She still has his clothes and his paintings and other things. I'm sure she'd give you what you asked for."

"What's she like?"

"All right, I guess, as far as home wreckers go."

He looked embarrassed. "Kate, you know that when Frank left, his mother and I were so angry at him. I thought he was going to throw away his life on that woman. But I don't think . . ."

I stopped him. I didn't want to hear that even though he'd chosen someone else, Frank would always love me. Being first runner-up in a love triangle isn't much of a consolation.

"Her name is Vera Bingham," I said. "I have her number. I can call her and tell her you would like Frank's things."

"You should have some of them too. We can divide up the family heirlooms. You are still family."

"That's okay. I don't need more reminders," I said.

After we'd paid the bill, and I'd gotten my English toffee, I walked Alex to his car.

"You sure I can't drive you home?" he asked again.

"It's five blocks. And I need the exercise after that sundae." I smiled, but there was something else I needed to say. "Alex, I think the police consider me a suspect."

He stared at me, as if taking in my words. "Not possible."

"I'm going to find out what happened."

He hugged me. "That Detective Podeski is a fool. You loved Frank. And he loved you. I know that with everything in me."

He kissed me on the cheek one more time, told me to take care of myself one more time, and drove away. As I watched his car drive north, I realized he knew Podeski's name. It wasn't just a call from an insurance agent that had prompted this visit. It was a call from Podeski. That meant there was Andres, Gray, Vera, me, and now Alex. How many more people had heard Podeski's theories on Frank's death?

Twenty-nine

"Can I see Detective Podeski?" I asked the desk sergeant.

"I'll call him. What's your name?"

"Kate Conway."

After I'd left Alex, I'd walked home. I had the uneasy feeling that someone was following me, but I was walking on a crowded street in a major city, so I tried not to get too paranoid about it. I had something more important on my mind.

Once I'd reached my house, rather than going inside, I'd gotten in my car and driven to the police station. I'd answered his questions; now I wanted him to answer mine. It had seemed like a good idea on the drive over, but waiting in the reception area, I was losing my courage.

After ten minutes of standing there, I was about to leave. But before I could, Podeski, in the same bad suit I'd seen him in before, walked into the room. "Can I help you, Mrs. Conway?"

"I don't know, but I think we need to talk."

He led me to a small room with a table and four chairs, brought me coffee, and sat down opposite me. I still had the English toffee with me and, out of politeness or nervousness, I offered him one. Much to my surprise, he accepted.

"You've been asking around about Frank's death," I said. "I'm hoping you'll tell me what you've found."

"Why?"

"What do you mean, why? He was my husband. If someone killed him I'd like to know who."

Podeski leaned back and bit into his toffee.

"Detective," I continued, "I'm asking if you've found evidence that my husband died of something other than a heart attack."

"You and I are both used to asking questions, not answering them," he said.

"What does that mean?"

"Just an observation."

I ignored him. "I understand you found digitalis in Frank's system. Is that a preliminary finding or the results of a complete tox screen?"

"Where did you hear that?"

"I've worked on a lot of true crime. I understand how cause of death is determined."

"I'm talking about the digitalis."

I paused. I was about to say something about not revealing my sources, but I'm not really a journalist. Instead I said, "I have friends."

He smiled. "You're probably a well-connected lady."

"You think I killed Frank."

"I don't know that anyone killed Frank. But you're right about the digitalis. That's probably what killed him. How it got in his system is the next question. When I answer that, I'll know if there's a need for further investigation."

"If you want to know anything, then ask. Ask me everything you want. Search my house. Search my car. Call all of my friends. Just leave his parents out of it. They've been through enough."

"I've already talked to his parents. His mother is a big fan of yours."

He sounded sincere but I assumed sarcasm. "We've always had different ideas about what was best for Frank," I said.

"She told me you were the best thing that ever happened to her son. She seems to think his girlfriend is who I should be looking at."

"She said I was the best thing that happened to Frank?" I needed to hear it again. My world really was going upside down if Lynette actually defended me. "Did you tell her who gets the insurance?"

He didn't answer. Instead he finished his toffee, then looked at me for a long time before speaking. "Mrs. Conway, I want you to understand something. I'm not considering this a murder investigation. I'm considering it an investigation. A healthy man dies suddenly. A drug that would be toxic if taken in large amounts is found in his system. There is an insurance policy of two hundred and fifty thousand dollars and the beneficiary is the man's soon-to-be ex-wife. Isn't this the sort of thing that would appear on one of those true-crime shows you work on?"

I sighed. "We always make some poor idiot look guilty for the first three acts of the show before revealing the real killer. And I can see how you would want to cast me as that idiot. But I didn't know about the insurance policy, so that removes motive. I hadn't seen Frank in weeks, so that removes opportunity. And I don't have access to digitalis, so that removes means. Even on a TV show I wouldn't look like a good suspect."

He leaned forward and folded his large hands together, resting them on the table in front of me. "All I have is your word on that. Frank had the policy for the entire time you were married, so it's possible he mentioned it at some point. He was in your house the day he died so it's possible that you did have contact with him. Maybe he waited back. Maybe you told him you wanted to talk after work," he said. "And you've interviewed a lot of people, learned a lot about how to commit a murder from your work. It's possible you know how to acquire the drug and what it does. You could have gotten digitalis from nearly anywhere, including your mother-in-law, who's taking it for her heart." He paused. "And even if you really didn't know about the insurance, there's always the fact that you were a woman scorned. You wouldn't be the first."

"And I'm the only person you're considering?"

He shook his head. "There's Vera Bingham. I bet you'd like it to be her."

"I'd like it to be no one. Believe it or not, Detective, I'd like to be arguing with Frank right now over which one of us gets to keep the toilet scrubber. What I don't want to be doing is burying my husband of fifteen years, splitting up his belongings with his mistress, or sitting in a police station with you."

He just sat emotionless and waited for me to finish talking. "What do you know about Ms. Bingham?"

"More than I'd like to know."

"She was with your husband for almost a year, but you were only separated for the last four months, is that true?"

"That's what I understand." I sat back, suddenly exhausted and desperate to go home. I can see why people confess to crimes they didn't commit. Police interrogation rooms are stuffy, soulless places. "I'm tired, Detective."

"You don't want to hear my concerns about Ms. Bingham?"

I didn't, but then again, I did. "What are they?"

He nodded. He was testing me. Hoping to wear me out, catch me saying something I hadn't intended. I'd played this game many times, though I'd always been on the other side of it.

"Ms. Bingham is the granddaughter of Walter Knutson. Of Knutson Foods." He waited for a reaction, which I wouldn't give him. "Do you ever shop at one of their grocery stores, Mrs. Conway?"

"Everyone has shopped there. Even you, I'll bet, have shopped there."

"They have a pharmacy in every branch of their stores."

"That's stretching it, don't you think? Just because her family owns the place doesn't mean she knows anything about it." Why I was defending her, I don't know, but Podeski was annoying. I didn't want him to be right about anything, on principle.

"She would if she were a pharmacist."

"She's not," I said, though honestly I had no idea if she was. She just didn't seem the type.

"She owned a pharmacy for a time. She's owned plant shops, a dance studio, a make-your-own-pottery place. She's had eleven different businesses in the last twenty years."

"All failures?"

"No. Most were successful. She owned them with friends. She put up the capital, and when the business was strong enough, each friend bought her out. She hasn't made much money off each deal, as far as I can tell, but for the most part she's recouped her investment."

"Good for her."

"Her love life wasn't as successful until your husband came along. Did you know they were talking about opening an art studio together?"

"No."

"And they were engaged?"

"Since he wasn't even divorced, I think that might be wishful thinking on her part."

"Not according to Frank's friend Neal."

"Neal said they were engaged?"

"Neal has been very helpful."

"Meaning?"

Podeski smiled and popped the last of his toffee in his mouth.

Thirty

After throwing Neal's name at me, Detective Podeski was suddenly anxious to go on his dinner break. I left the station with the feeling that he was trying to get me to do something, but I couldn't figure out what it was.

My offer to let him search the house had gone unnoticed. I did it mainly because several cops had told me it was something innocent people usually said, and I was hoping it would make Podeski realize I had nothing to hide. Instead, as I walked out of the police station I wondered if I did have something to hide. Was there something else I didn't know about my marriage?

If it were an episode of one of my true-crime shows, I'd have a pretty slim list of suspects. Me, because of all the reasons Podeski outlined, and Vera, who had money and potential access to the right drug. But did she have motive? If they were opening an art studio and planning a wedding, what reason would she have to kill Frank? Assuming he had been murdered, and I wasn't conceding that he had. I just couldn't figure out how he could have gotten digitalis in his system, especially since Podeski had said something about large amounts.

Ever since Podeski had first shown up at my door I'd had a knot in my stomach. Every unpaid parking ticket, every questionable tax deduction became another reason I might look like a killer. I'd told myself it was irrational, but it kept getting stronger. And now, with Podeski more or less calling me a suspect, the knot was beginning to take over my whole body. Knowing I hadn't killed Frank provided me little comfort. I just kept imagining Podeski flashing an arrest warrant and handcuffs.

I wanted to go home, crawl into bed, and hide from the world, but Podeski's final taunt sent me in a different direction. I drove by Neal's house, not knowing what I was going to say but hoping to catch him alone. Instead Neal was on the lawn with his twins and a few neighbors. I was about to drive past when I saw him looking at me. I pulled over.

"Kate, is everything okay?" Neal was at my car window before I'd even turned off the engine.

"I don't know. I guess I'm not having the best night."

As soon as I got out of the car, he threw his arm around my shoulder. "Let's grab a beer. Come into the garage." He turned to the twins, now nearly six. "Kids, go inside and tell Mom Aunt Kate is here."

As the kids went inside, we went to the garage. Neal had fixed it up to be a sort of den. He had two overstuffed reclining chairs, a television, and a minifridge on one side, leaving just enough room for one car on the other. Or there would have been, except for a dozen or so boxes and a tarp-covered pile of more stuff they obviously didn't want but couldn't seem to get rid of.

He grabbed a bottle of beer from the minifridge and handed it to me. "You want a glass?"

"In these elegant surroundings"—I smiled—"I think I'll manage without it."

"Beats drinking a beer surrounded by stuffed bears and princess costumes," he said, laughing. "You don't know how lucky you are." Then he blushed.

Frank and I had tried for three years to have kids, with no luck. It wasn't exactly regret, especially when I saw how overwhelmed and broke our friends were, but it wasn't exactly a choice either.

"You looked like you were having fun with the kids," I said.

"It's bedtime anyway. What's going on?"

"I just wanted to see how you were doing."

"Okay, I guess. I keep grabbing the phone to call him, and then I remember, you know."

I nodded.

Neal smiled. "You miss him too, don't you?"

"I've missed him for a long time. Months. Years."

"It wasn't such a bad marriage. You guys had some great times together. Like the night he proposed, and you were so drunk, instead of saying yes, you just kept hiccuping."

"I knew he was going to propose, and I was nervous. I was just drinking to calm my nerves." I laughed. "Poor Frank couldn't tell I was saying yes through all those hiccups."

"And remember when you guys first bought the house? He spent every waking moment fixing it up."

"He did," I admitted. "I forgot about that. He stripped all the woodwork, and he refinished the floors. He was very good with his hands."

"And he planted the garden."

I nodded. "Every summer he'd cut a big bunch of roses for me on my birthday. And paint me a card. He said it was a better expression of his love than buying some lame present."

"And cheaper." Neal laughed.

I lightly slapped his hand. "It was damn romantic. And I loved it." I looked down at the bottle of beer in my hands. "I haven't thought about that stuff in a long time."

"I know he wasn't the perfect husband, Kate, but every marriage has its bad times."

I shook my head. "That's kind of an understatement, Neal. Besides, I really didn't come over for a trip down memory lane. I talked with a detective. His name is Podeski. Do you know him?"

He nodded. "He talked to me too. I wouldn't worry about it, Kate. He's just filling out paperwork."

"So you don't think he has any reason to be suspicious?"

"Of who?"

"Of me."

He directed me to sit in one of the chairs, then he pulled up a cooler and sat on it, facing me. Our knees were inches apart, just like I conducted interviews. "Why would you have killed Frank?"

"Aside from the obvious reason?"

"But that's crazy."

"What did you say to Podeski?"

He turned white. "Nothing." He took a long chug of his beer, while I waited.

"Neal, you said something. If it's about the engagement . . ."

"You knew about that?"

"Only after he died."

"That was something he never wanted you to find out."

"I would have found out when they got married."

"No." Neal got up and started pacing. "You don't get it. He wasn't going to marry her. He got a little carried away. It was a mistake."

"He told you that?"

"He wanted to come back to you."

I could feel the blood drain from my face and my heart begin to move upward into my throat. I was going to pass out.

"Is that what you said to Detective Podeski? Because he told me you confirmed Frank's engagement to Vera."

He hesitated. "I didn't say anything about what Frank told me. I didn't know if you would want to know, and I figured, what difference did it make? But Kate, I promise you, Frank really did love you. He was even interviewing for a job teaching art at a community center. The one near you on Augusta."

I got up and handed Neal my beer.

"You're lying," I said. "You think you're helping me. You think it's what I want to hear, but you're lying."

I walked out of the garage and toward my car.

"Kate, don't go," I heard Neal call after me. Out of the corner of my eye I saw his wife, Beth, walk out from the house.

"Kate," I heard Beth say.

I didn't respond. I got in my car and pulled away.

I knew I was overreacting but I couldn't stop myself. I used to get so mad at Frank that I would storm out of the house and stay away for hours. When I'd get home, he'd be sitting on the couch, watching TV. He'd smile as if nothing had happened. I'd get angry about his indifference and we'd start the cycle all over again. I knew even as I was doing it that I was just trying to get a reaction, any reaction, trying to get him to *do* something, to fight—not just with me, but for me. It didn't work. The angrier I got, the more he withdrew.

It made us both miserable, but at least while it was happening, I could hate him and feel certain of it. Now nothing made sense.

Thirty-one

"Kate, are you okay? I've been in a panic about you."

It was Ellen. And she didn't sound panicked. She sounded completely in control.

"Why were you in a panic?" I asked.

"I got a visit today from a police detective."

I could feel myself turning red. It wasn't just frightening anymore. It was embarrassing. "It's fine," I said. "He's just asking questions."

"Well, don't worry. I took care of it."

That worried me. "What did you say, Ellen?"

"I told him that you didn't love Frank a bit and you didn't care what happened to him. You thought of Frank as a liability, so his leaving you was a good thing," she said. "I also told that detective that since you didn't want him back, you didn't have a motive to kill Frank. It's not like you were going to inherit anything."

"There was a two-hundred-and-fifty-thousand-dollar life insurance policy. His dad took it out."

Silence. "Well, the point is I said you didn't kill Frank. I think he'll just forget about you."

"Sure, I mean, with character references like yours, why would Podeski think I'd kill Frank?"

"Kate, honestly, it's fine. I was very clear in saying you aren't the killing type. And I teach seventh grade, remember. I know sociopaths when I see them. Don't worry about it anymore and just get some sleep."

I did not sleep. I lay in bed for about two hours, then I got up and paced. I thought I might get sick, but after ten minutes of hanging my head over a toilet, I went away a failure.

I wanted to kill Frank. An irony not lost on me since at least one person thought I had. If it was true that he was hoping to come back, why hadn't he said anything to me? Was he afraid of what I might say? I guess that made sense, since I had no idea what I would have said. Half of me hated him and only remembered the bad times. The other half loved and missed him. I don't have any idea which half would have won.

And it didn't matter. Frank was gone.

It's an odd thing about losing someone. It doesn't hit you all at once. Obviously Frank was gone. He'd left the house four months ago, and died over a week ago, but every time I said the words, it surprised me.

"Frank is gone," I said out loud. "He's never coming back."

It still felt like a punch in the gut, and I waited for the umpteenth time for tears to flow, but none came. What was wrong with me that I couldn't let myself cry for him?

I thought about my conversations from earlier: Gray's insider information that Frank had died from digitalis poisoning; Podeski's insistence that I had means, motive, and opportunity to kill Frank; and Neal's revelation about the engagement. Why did so many people know what was happening in my life and I knew so little?

I turned on my computer hoping somehow technology had the answers that I did not. I started with Vera. I searched for information on the Knutson family and its many heirs. There were the usual scandals of the very rich: a cousin of Vera's had died of alcohol poisoning in the mid-nineties, several other members of the family had been through messy divorces and custody fights, and an uncle had been accused and then cleared of insider trading. But there was nothing as interesting about Vera. She attended an occasional charity event for animal welfare and was photographed at several of those dull-looking luncheons that end up being written about on the society page. She'd written a letter to the editor of the *Chicago Tribune* about education reform and had recently attended a fund-raiser for the governor. That was getting me nowhere.

I got even less information searching on Podeski's name. Aside from a line in one article saying he was the lead detective in a homicide from 2007, there was nothing on him. Clearly he wasn't the flashy type looking to make a name for himself. Though one line in the article caught my eye. Podeski was quoted as saying, "I'm only interested in finding the killer. And I'll keep looking until I do." Somehow the fact that I wasn't a killer didn't put my mind at ease.

Finally, I did a search on digitalis. I found out it came from foxglove, a plant with a pretty purple flower and toxic leaves. It was from those leaves that digitalis was made. According to several websites, though it was an effective and lifesaving heart medicine, a large overdose can be fatal. Even a small one can cause nausea and a jaundiced effect in the eyes. That explained Frank thinking the white sheets were yellow on the night he died. What it didn't tell me was how Frank got it in his system or who put it there.

Whatever answers I was looking for weren't in a search engine. I turned off the computer. But just as I was about to go back to bed, my home phone rang. No one called me at home. Anyone who knew me used my cell number because it was so much easier to reach me that way. The only calls I got on the landline were people looking to sell newspaper subscriptions or refinance my mortgage. And, as annoying as they were, telemarketers wouldn't call at two a.m. I raced to pick it up.

"Hello?"

Breathing. Not the cliché heavy breathing of obscene phone calls. Just breathing.

"Who is this?"

Click.

The caller ID said "private number." For my own peace of mind, I decided that meant wrong number. But the phone rang twice more, and twice more there was a breather.

I wasn't generally one to overreact to strange phone calls, but things were starting to build up. The weird feeling I was being followed, the dead bird on the porch, and most of all, the rearranged photos. If someone was trying to unnerve me, they were doing a good job.

I called information and told the very nice operator about the calls, hoping she could get someone to trace them for me. She couldn't. Instead she suggested I call back after nine a.m., speak with a supervisor about setting a trap on my phone for any future calls, and file a police report.

Maybe I would do that, I told myself, but probably I wouldn't. By morning, I was sure I would feel slightly foolish about the whole thing and try to pretend it hadn't happened. But in the meantime, sleep was out of the question.

I remembered the copy of the police report I'd gotten from the world's worst receptionist. I'd been too busy to look at it before, but now I had nothing but time. Just as I was hoping, this copy didn't have any black marker covering valuable information. I laid it out on the floor in the living room next to the copy with the black marker and checked for the missing information. On the first few pages, Rosenthal had blacked out an entry that said Theresa had been at the Kitty Cage two days before her disappearance. The Kitty Cage was a strip club just north of Chicago that had been in the news recently when it was raided for selling drugs as a secondary business. And on the complete copy, she had handwritten Gray's name with a question mark next to it, blacked out on the version I'd been sent.

Then there was Theresa's bank account. According to the complete police report, deposits had remained a fairly steady two or three hundred dollars, until six months ago when four deposits had been made, each over two thousand dollars, for a total nearing ten thousand. Then, two weeks after her disappearance all of the money had been withdrawn.

Rosenthal had specifically said that Theresa's account hadn't been touched since she went missing. Obviously that wasn't the case. And there was a bigger question: where does a twenty-two-year-old unemployed nursing student get ten grand in six months? And why would she go to a strip club? Maybe, despite what Rosenthal had told me, Theresa really was living a double life.

It made the show more interesting, but I was a little disappointed. I had, in my own disinterested, exploitive sort of way, come to like Theresa. I didn't want to have to expose her as a stripper or drug mule. I wanted her—I wanted somebody—to be exactly who they seemed to be.

Whatever the truth was, I wasn't going to get an answer and my mind was beginning to get a little wobbly. I wanted to sleep, but the odd phone calls and the unanswered questions wouldn't let me, so I turned on the TV.

I changed the channel about fifty times. Nothing was on. When I was a kid, before cable television, there was always something to watch. And now, with a hundred and fifty channels, pay-per-view, Internet downloads, and DVDs, I can never seem to find anything worth my time. Including—no, make that especially—the shows I work on.

Finally, I came across an episode of *Matlock*. Andy Griffith as a cranky Southern defense lawyer. It was one of Frank's favorite ways to waste time. He was always telling me about how one station played marathons of it, and he would get sucked in.

"You have to watch a bunch in a row to get the essence of the show," he would say, as if he had figured out the Tao of Matlock. "If you ever stopped analyzing everything, and just relaxed, you would love it."

So, too late for Frank to know, I put the remote down, curled up on the couch, and watched Andy Griffith use country good sense to solve crimes.

Thirty-two

Six hours later, my doorbell rang.

It was Andres. "Hey." He sounded cheery until he noticed I was wearing sweats and a camisole. "Did you forget about the shoot?"

"No, sorry. I fell asleep watching a *Matlock* marathon."

He smiled. "Seriously?"

"It's a really good show."

"I've heard that."

"Well, sometimes you just have to let yourself relax and stop analyzing everything." I could see I was amusing Andres. "I'll get dressed," I told him. "Give me five minutes."

I tried to compensate for my lack of sleep with two large cups of coffee and three doughnuts—two glazed and one chocolate—but sugar and caffeine weren't doing it for me. I tried to think of the questions I'd planned to ask but nothing came to me. I was starting to feel like I was ready to finish with Theresa Moretti's life and get back to my own. Not entirely accurate. I wanted someone else's life—someone with no problems, no hang-up calls, no dead husband's girlfriends, and preferably beachfront property.

On the way to the shoot, I told the guys what I'd learned about Theresa.

"So she was a hooker." Victor sat back, satisfied that people were as sleazy as he wanted to believe they were.

"We don't know that," I pointed out.

"But that's how you're going to play it in the show, right?" Andres looked worried.

"I don't know. If it didn't have anything to do with her disappearance," I said, "why should we drag her name through the mud? So Crime TV can get ratings?"

"Isn't the point of doing this show . . . so that Crime TV can get ratings?" Victor asked.

"Yeah, it's just . . ." I stumbled. "I feel bad."

"Okay, but before you grow a career-ending conscience, consider this. We don't know it had nothing to do with her disappearance," Andres said. "Maybe that's exactly why the police crossed it out. Maybe they want us out here chasing our tails."

I considered it. "Maybe they are. What do we care? We're not looking for the truth. We're looking for a good story."

"Which is why we usually play up the 'secret life' shit. Whether it's true or not."

I looked at Andres. I could see that he didn't feel any better about it than I did. We both just stared ahead of us for the rest of the trip.

"We're here." Andres pulled up in front of Wyatt's elegant apartment building and pointed toward the doorman standing at the entrance. "What does this guy do for a living?"

"He's an aspiring actor."

"Must have a side gig."

I approached the doorman, who called upstairs to Wyatt, and after waiting for several minutes, we were directed to the fifteenth floor. Wyatt was waiting for us at the door to his apartment, looking as if we'd just woken him. He was a good-looking guy: tousled dark blond hair, muscles pressing against his T-shirt, an all-American grin. He looked casual and relaxed, but in his eyes I could see the "tell" of every actor: the need to be liked.

We brought the equipment into the apartment, which was as beautiful as the building. It was perfectly furnished with oil paintings on the walls, sculptures decorating the tables, and cashmere throws tossed over the couch.

"This is your place?" Victor asked.

"My girlfriend's." Wyatt smiled. "She's a doctor."

"How long have you been together?" I asked.

"About a year now, I guess." He set out some mugs and a pot of coffee. "Make yourself at home, guys. There's milk and sugar, and some bagels, I think. I need to change into something a little better than this." He pointed to his T-shirt and sweats.

"Take your time. We'll be setting up for an hour or so," I told him.

Once he'd left the room, Andres whispered to me, "Didn't the mom say Wyatt had a photo of Theresa next to his bed?"

"I guess he's moved on."

"How long has Theresa been gone?"

"Just over thirteen months."

"So he waited a whole, what, six weeks before hopping into bed with someone else?" Andres shook his head. "I change my vote from the ex-boyfriend to this bozo."

"Come on," Victor said. "Look at this place. What intelligent man would turn down a chance at this view—or that one?" He pointed to a photo of Wyatt with a very pretty woman who seemed about ten years his senior.

I shrugged. "Maybe Victor's right. Maybe he wasn't getting any support from anyone, and he needed someone. A friend, maybe. Someone who believed in his dreams, who would watch TV with him. And then the friendship turned into something else. It doesn't make him a bad guy."

Andres gave me a look. "Yes, it does, Kate. He stepped out on his wife. That's not what good guys do."

"They weren't married," Victor said, unaware of what had been so obvious to Andres. "Besides, look at this place. She's hot, she has a great apartment, probably buys him clothes and vacations. It's a sweet gig. Any guy would go for this. It's not like Theresa was around to shine his pipes."

"Jesus, Victor," Andres said. "Just a little class, sometimes, would be nice."

"What?"

"Play nice," I said.

"I didn't do anything wrong." Victor was the most thin-skinned insensitive person I knew.

"Doesn't matter," I told him. "I'm interested in what you were saying. Your theory on this case."

"Thank you, Kate," Victor said, his hurt feelings put away for the moment. "I'm saying that it doesn't mean anything that Wyatt didn't stick around waiting to find out if Theresa resurfaced. He needed some comfort. And what's more comfortable than a place like this?" He did a *Price Is Right* Showcase Showdown hand gesture of the living room.

If Victor was right, maybe more than just Wyatt had gotten sucked into a nicer lifestyle with a new woman. Maybe Frank had gotten caught up in all Vera could offer: an art studio, a nice apartment, new clothes, a forty-two-inch flat-screen television. And maybe just before he died, he'd realized it was meaningless because he was in love with me.

"You're saying that a man can have his head turned by a woman with a lot of money, even if he's in love with someone else?"

Victor scrunched his face in disbelief. "No. Jeez, Kate. Never took you for a cynic. If a guy is in love, really in love, nothing and no one can take him away."

Ouch. Back to square one.

Thirty-three

"Tell me about Theresa."

Wyatt had reemerged in a light-green shirt and dark jeans. He said he was anxious to get to the interview, but once we started, he wouldn't stop shifting in his chair. For an actor, he seemed remarkably uncomfortable in front of a camera.

"She was nice," he said. "You know, pretty, smart, easy to be with. We had fun together."

For ten minutes I threw him softballs and in return got well-prepared answers about Theresa, the saint. Finally, after he started to relax, I got to the questions that interested me.

"I was under the impression she was looking for work and had been volunteering. Did she have a job I don't know about?"

"No."

"What about an income, maybe gifts from Linda or even something on the side that maybe she didn't tell her mother?"

He smiled. "Theresa was broke all the time. Her mom gave her some money for gas and stuff, maybe a couple hundred a month, and she had a credit card she maxed out."

"So no way to get something like ten thousand dollars?"

"That would have been sweet. We could have done stuff with that. We talked about going to New Orleans a couple of times but neither of us had the juice for it. If Theresa had ten g's we would have gone. And we should have. My girlfriend now, she and I went down there a few months ago. Cool place."

"It is," I said. "Did Theresa ever talk about the Kitty Cage?"

"The strip club?"

"Yes?"

"Why would she talk about a place like that?"

"Just curious," I said. I should have pushed harder, but his blank expression made it clear he didn't know anything. I changed to a different line of questioning. "How long had you and Theresa dated?"

"Four or five months, nothing serious. She mostly came to the bar where I used to work and she'd hang out."

"Did you go on dates?"

"What do you mean?"

"Like go dancing or to the zoo—something like that?"

"No, not really. She seemed pretty happy at the bar, so we never bothered." He took a deep breath, trying to rid himself of his nervousness.

"Didn't she want to do things like that?" I asked.

He shrugged. "If she did, she never mentioned it. She liked hanging out where I worked."

"And after work, what would you do?"

He turned slightly red. "You know, we'd go back to my place."

"So your relationship was hanging out at the bar where you worked or at your apartment?" I didn't know why, but I was annoyed at Wyatt and I was letting it show.

Wyatt picked up on it. "She came to see me in a couple of plays," he offered.

"That's right; you're an actor."

"Yeah. I'm doing something right now. It's sort of experimental and we're doing it at this really small theater next to a Laundromat, or really in a Laundromat, but it's great. I have head shots if you need them."

"I might." I never turned down photos of possible suspects, no matter how self-serving they might be. "Let's get back to Theresa. Were you in love?"

That took him by surprise. "It was too soon to tell."

"Four or five months? That seems about right to know if you're serious about someone."

"I guess. Maybe we weren't."

"You had a big fight at the bar a few nights before she disappeared. What was it about?"

"How do you know about that?"

"Did you have a fight?"

"Yeah, it was nothing. Theresa was pissed at me about not being more attentive. She wanted me to notice what she was wearing and crap like that."

"She screamed at you. That sounds like more than just about being attentive."

He chewed on his lip for a moment, then looked at me. "She was drunk. I didn't really pay attention to what she was saying. My feeling was if she wanted to be with me that was cool, but if she didn't, then that was cool too."

"She was dating someone named Jason when you met, wasn't she?"

"Yeah, he was just some guy who lived in her neighborhood."

"And she broke up with him for you."

"I guess. I think she was breaking up with him anyway. When something's not working, it's not working, you know what I mean?"

"I suppose. Did she ever talk about him?"

He thought about it for a minute. "Yeah. She said he called her a lot. He showed up a couple of times where she was volunteering."

"Did it bother her?"

"It was a little pathetic."

"But she wasn't worried he would do something?"

"I don't think so. He seemed like a nice guy."

"You met him?"

"After Theresa went missing."

"Tell me about meeting Jason."

"It was a couple of days after. Her family set up a call center and I went down to help. He was there for a while."

"He was helping?"

"No. Her family didn't really want him around. I didn't get it. He was a nice enough guy. He wanted to help find Theresa and they needed help, but . . ." He shrugged. "Her family didn't like him."

"What about her brother, Tom? What was his relationship with Theresa?"

"Tom's okay. He's had some trouble but he's okay."

"Trouble?"

"You know, problems with the law. Theresa said he was going to go to New York for bakery school when he got enough money together. I thought that was crazy because the guy already knows how to bake, so I figured maybe he had other reasons."

"Like?"

"I don't know. You'd have to ask him."

"I'll do that," I said. "Let's talk a little about what happened after Theresa disappeared. What were those first few weeks like?"

"I was torn up. Everyone was. A lot of people came to help."

"Like Gray Meyer?"

"He's a great guy, isn't he?"

"Why do you think he got so involved? My impression is he didn't know Theresa very well."

"Gray is just one of those guys who likes to help, I think. He even introduced me to an agent who is thinking about taking me on."

"You were in the middle of searching for your missing girlfriend and he mentions an agent that might represent you?"

Wyatt squirmed. "No. Not like that. I'd been spending a lot of time with the police, at the call center, you know, helping out. I was neglecting my career. Gray thought it would be good for me to get back into it. That's why he set up a meeting."

"Okay." It left me with more questions for Gray. Questions I would never have a chance to get answered, since *Missing Persons* didn't have the budget for follow-up interviews. "What did you think happened to Theresa?"

"At first I figured she just took off, but then when she didn't call her mom and days were passing, I knew something had happened."

"She was close to her mom."

"Crazy close."

"What do you mean by that?"

He shifted in his chair again. "I just mean her mom's opinion meant a lot to her. I like my parents too, but Theresa . . . it was like she was a kid, trying to please her mom."

"But her mom said that you and Theresa were serious. If they were close wouldn't she know that wasn't true?"

"Theresa probably just said that to get her mom to calm down. Mrs. Moretti was really angry when Julia got engaged before Theresa."

Now I was the one taken off guard. "She was angry? Why?"

"Julia and the guy she married were together, like, six months before he proposed. Theresa's mom would go on and on about how Julia didn't know the guy. Shit like that. Sorry, I'm not supposed to swear on camera." He looked toward Andres.

"It's fine. Just tell me again. Did Linda not trust Julia's husband?"

"I don't think she even knew the guy. I met him once, at their engagement party. He seemed okay. A little dull, but a good guy. But Mrs. Moretti didn't like him. It was like he was stealing away Theresa's chance to be the first of the kids to get married. I don't get it, but Theresa used to say that her mom liked the limelight, and now Julia had it and that pissed her off."

"She doesn't strike me as someone who craves the spotlight," I told him.

"You should have seen her after Theresa disappeared. She couldn't do enough interviews."

"Her daughter was missing. She was desperate."

He shrugged. "I guess."

"I was under the impression that you spoke with Linda every week."

"She calls me. What am I supposed to do? If I don't pick up, she calls again and again. My girlfriend said I should just change my number, but I'd feel like a heel. I get that she's lost her daughter, and I get that she thinks she and I share that. But how long am I supposed to stop my life?"

"It doesn't seem like you stopped it for very long. You were dating someone else pretty quickly."

"I was in bad shape. I needed someone to be there for me." He was getting defensive. "I met Karen when she came to a play I was doing. We just hit it off right away."

"What play?"

"It was a production of *Peter Cottontail*, an adaptation of the TV special."

"A children's play?"

"Yeah. Karen came with her niece."

"But *Peter Cottontail* is an Easter story, isn't it?"

"Yep. We had a really cool production. Great costumes and stuff. I have a flyer around here somewhere, if you need it."

"You never know."

"And listen, I know you guys put reenactments in these kinds of shows, so if you can pass my résumé to your casting guy I'd appreciate it."

Thirty-four

"If I were Theresa I'd have run from these people," Victor said, as he, Andres, and I ate lunch at an Indian restaurant. "They all seem like freaks."

"And the way he handed Kate four different head shots," Andres added. "What was that about?"

"He's doing this for some TV time," I said. "Not the first."

"But it was like Theresa was some booty call," Andres said. "You would think he would be smart enough to at least look like he cared about her."

I finished my samosa. "Last year Easter was early April?"

"Yeah. So?"

"And Theresa went missing in late May," I pointed out. "More than a month after he met his new girlfriend."

"Is that a motive? Why not just break up with Theresa if he's into somebody else?"

"I don't know, but it might be an interesting angle for the show. Maybe we imply that he tried," I said. "Maybe she was persistent, like her mother. Maybe she called and called."

"Why would she?" Andres asked. "She had the ex-boyfriend in her back pocket."

"Unless she didn't want the ex. If Theresa was lonely, if she decided Wyatt was the one for her, maybe she wouldn't let go. Maybe, even if it wasn't the greatest relationship in the world, we could get some sound that suggests she would have done anything to keep it."

I didn't know Theresa, but it didn't seem far-fetched. If she did want to get married, she could have married Jason. But that was not what her mother wanted. Her mother wanted Wyatt. And Theresa wanted to please her mother. Besides, if she loved Wyatt, she might do anything.

"So she won't let go, and Wyatt can't take it?" Andres was seeing where I was headed. "Or maybe she was dumping him for the other guy Julia mentioned, and his ego couldn't take it. Or maybe he found out about the money, or the strip club."

"And, maybe by accident, he kills her," I said. "Pushes her, head hits the coffee table, that sort of thing. It would look great in a reenactment."

"And then what?" Andres asked. "He buries her somewhere?"

"Maybe. Or he dumps her in the river or in the middle of Lake Michigan. Who knows?" I sat back.

"Or she said to hell with this, and she's sitting on some tropical island somewhere."

"Or the guy who gave her the ten grand killed her and took back the money," I said. But as the words were coming out of my mouth I changed my mind. "There's records of those things, right? If Theresa had taken the money, or someone else had, the police would be able to trace it. So why hasn't it led them anywhere? And why did Rosenthal want to hide it from me?"

"It's got nothing to do with money." Victor finally chimed in with an opinion. "It's Wyatt."

Andres shrugged. "I don't know. I can see how he might have killed her but it's been more than a year. The longer he talked, the more it seemed like he'd be too stupid to get away with murder."

"Didn't care for the guy the moment I met him," Victor said. "Did not care for him."

"You didn't like him because he's good-looking," I said.

"I didn't like him because he's not telling the truth about something. You have to remember, the two of you are staring at the guy. He can charm you with his pretty-boy looks. But all I'm doing is listening. And I heard something."

"What?" Andres asked.

"A lying douche bag." Victor sat back, put his headphones on. "Mark my words. He knows where Theresa is."

"Yesterday you were sure it was the ex-boyfriend," I pointed out.

"I didn't have all the evidence. Now I do. When Theresa's body shows up, that Wyatt guy will be her killer." Victor clicked on his iPod and sat back, content to end his part of the conversation with a prediction.

"It doesn't really matter, does it," Andres said. "Without a body, we can make all the guesses we want, but there's no evidence that a crime was even committed."

"Like the cause of death being listed as undetermined," I said, more to myself than to Andres.

"What do you . . ." He suddenly understood. "Is that what it's listed as . . . Frank, I mean?"

"I think I'm officially a suspect," I whispered.

"That's ridiculous."

"That's what I tried to tell Detective Podeski, but Gray Meyer said Podeski thinks I killed Frank."

"What does Gray Meyer have to do with it?"

"No idea," I said. "But it doesn't matter. Without a cause of death, there is no crime, so I don't need to get freaked out that the police are going to show up at my door."

"You didn't do anything, Kate."

"Remember that story we did about the guy who spent ten years in prison for killing his neighbor?"

"The one for Science Television? That was all about DNA. What's that got to do with Frank?"

"An innocent person got sent to prison. That's what it has to do with Frank. It happens, Andres. Innocent people get convicted. But if the cause of death remains undetermined, they can make all the guesses they want and I don't have to worry."

Andres moved his fork back and forth across his curry. "Except, Kate," he said quietly, "if someone did kill Frank, don't you want to know? Do you really want to spend the rest of your life like Theresa's family, wondering what happened?"

Thirty-five

That question was still on my mind as we set up the interview with Julia at her Ravenswood apartment. Her husband, David, arrived early from work to offer his support, and the two held hands and spoke softly in a corner while Andres and Victor set the lights.

Julia seemed to have moved on quite easily with no answers about Theresa. So had Wyatt. But Linda and Jason were stuck reliving, and rewriting, the past. Did I need answers? What would it change if I knew why Frank had died? If Vera had killed him—and who else could it be?—would seeing her in prison make me feel vindicated?

I know the answer to that is supposed to be a resounding yes. But I wasn't sure that knowing Frank was the victim of a homicide would make his loss easier than thinking of it as just an untimely end. I'd been around enough families of murder victims to recognize the hollow misery they shared. They can't let go, can't stop wondering "What if," can't stop imagining the last moments of their loved one's life.

I didn't want that for myself. I wanted to be Julia and Wyatt. But even as I thought it, I knew I couldn't be. If there was a chance that someone, and by "someone" I meant Vera, had killed Frank, I had to know.

"Hey, Kate, we're ready." Andres tapped me on the shoulder. "You've been off in your own world."

"I was just looking at Julia and David."

They were still in the corner, hands touching, whispering, smiling and gazing at each other. I'm not sure they remembered the rest of us were even in the room.

"Newlyweds," Andres said. "There ought to be a law where they're banned from public view."

"I think it's called a honeymoon."

"Two weeks is not long enough to stop the newly in love from being annoying," he said. "It's just hard to believe my wife and I were ever like that."

"I know the feeling."

Once Julia was in the chair facing me, I maneuvered things so that David sat in the corner of the room, out of camera range and with Julia's back to him. If he was within her line of sight, I knew she would spend the entire interview looking at him for approval, instead of me. But I could see David, sitting on the edge of the couch, hanging on her every word.

The first few questions were the softballs. Julia and Theresa had met in grade school. They had known each other for all of life's turning points from the first kiss to the first heartbreak. Theresa was supposed to be Julia's maid of honor at her September wedding.

"At first I was going to cancel the wedding. I figured David and I could wait until Theresa was found, but no one thought that was a good idea," she said.

Out of the corner of my eye, I could see David frown.

"Even Theresa's family?" I asked.

Julia looked about to cry. "I think they did. They insisted on making my cake and the whole family came to the wedding. But I did hear Theresa's mom had told someone that she thought it would have been more appropriate if David and I had gotten married more quietly, you know, instead of having a big party and a band."

"But Theresa had been gone for nearly four months by then."

"Exactly! Life has to go on. I can't sit and wait for Theresa to come back. She might never come back."

"But you can understand that her mother doesn't share that view. For her, life can't go on without Theresa."

"But for the rest of us, it has to."

I could tell she was getting frustrated, and we were getting off track. "Tell me about the day Theresa disappeared," I said.

"I got a call from Mrs. Moretti at about midnight. She said she hadn't seen Theresa since the afternoon. She thought Theresa and

I were supposed to meet up at some coffee shop. I told her we didn't have plans to do anything and that I'd been shopping all day."

"Alone?"

"Yes. I was buying gifts for the bridesmaids, so obviously I wouldn't want Theresa with me."

"Was Theresa close to her family?"

I could see panic in Julia's eyes. She looked around for David.

"Julia," I said, "there's no right or wrong answer. Just tell the truth."

She nodded and took a breath. "She was close to her family." There was hesitation in her voice. "I think, though, that she was growing up and it was hard for her mom to see that."

"I've been told that her mom wasn't pleased that you were getting married before Theresa."

Another deep breath. "I think Mrs. Moretti had been planning Theresa's wedding since she was a little girl. When I picked robin's egg blue for the bridesmaids' dresses Mrs. Moretti tried to get me to change it. She said robin's egg blue was Theresa's favorite color, but if I used it, Theresa would look like she was copying me when she got married."

"Was Theresa close to getting married?"

"I don't think so. She was dating Wyatt but it wasn't going anywhere."

"Mrs. Moretti seemed to think they were serious."

"That's what she wanted to think."

"Was Theresa in love with Wyatt?"

Julia sat quietly and we all waited in silence for her answer. "I think so," she said. "Or at least I think she wanted to be. Theresa wasn't a rebel. She may have done some drinking and some . . . some other stuff her family wouldn't have approved of, but she did want to please her mom. I think she did want to get married, and I think maybe at least for a while, she convinced herself she was in love with him."

"But he wasn't in love with her."

"It didn't seem that way. I only met him a few times, but I didn't get the impression he put much effort into Theresa. I think he was just going to have fun until she became a nuisance and then he was planning on dumping her." She paused. "He said something like that to David at our engagement party."

I looked to David, who nodded.

"I have to say it's never made any sense to me why Linda Moretti would prefer Wyatt, a struggling actor, over Jason, who has a good job, ambition, and genuinely seemed to love Theresa. What did she have against him?"

"Jason is a good guy but he loved Theresa a little too much, if you know what I mean. When they were dating he would call her ten times a day, show up at her school—things like that. Even after they broke up, he still called."

"He was stalking her."

"I don't know if I'd call it stalking. He was just around a lot."

"Was she afraid of him?"

"You know, in a weird kind of way, I think she liked it. I think she encouraged it. I told her one time that she should make it clear to him that she wasn't interested, but I think she wanted him hanging around. Just in case."

"In case of what?"

"I don't know. In case she didn't find anyone better."

"That doesn't make Theresa seem like a very nice person."

She nodded. "She was. But she wasn't perfect. She wasn't the saint her mother wants to remember her as. She did some things that she probably shouldn't have. She took advantage of Jason, because he let her, and Wyatt took advantage of her because she let him. It's screwed up, but that's love, isn't it."

"In my experience, yes." I shifted gears. "Would it surprise you that Theresa had nearly ten thousand dollars in her bank account deposited over the six months before she went missing?"

Julia's face told me that it did surprise her. "That can't be right," she finally mumbled.

"Any idea where she got that money?"

"No."

"Not her mother?"

"She would never give her that kind of money. She didn't have that lying around. She's just getting by like everyone else."

"Not a wedding fund, maybe?"

"If her mother had money put away for her wedding, she would never give it to Theresa. Her mother is too controlling for that."

"Or maybe some job, something she didn't talk about? Maybe something illegal or something no one would approve of?"

"Like what? Like a drug dealer? Theresa wouldn't be that stupid. She wanted to be a nurse, and a mom. I don't know where the money came from but Theresa didn't do anything illegal to get it." Her defense was the first spark of friendship I'd seen from her.

"What about a strip club called the Kitty Cage?"

Julia turned bright red. "She'd booked it for my bachelorette party. They have a smaller club that's for, you know, ladies. It's next door to the original."

I almost laughed at my stupidity. I'd been producing salacious television shows for so long that something as innocent as a bachelorette party had never occurred to me. Still, it didn't explain the money.

"Tell me about her brother, Tom," I said.

She turned and looked to David and met his eyes. Whatever they had almost told me the other day, it was pretty clear they'd decided against saying it now. When Julia turned back to me, she said, "He's a great baker. Have you eaten at his mom's bakery?"

"I have."

"Well, then you know."

"I heard he had some issues with the police. What did he do?"

"I think you would have to ask him."

"Before Theresa disappeared he was planning to go to New York," I said. "He seems to have abandoned that dream to be with his family."

"I didn't know he was planning to do that."

"Theresa didn't talk about him?"

"They weren't close."

"Because of his temper?" It was a guess, but I'd seen a glimpse of anger at the bakery.

One look in Julia's eyes confirmed I was right. "I think all siblings have differences" was all she would say.

I took a breath. Maybe off camera she would tell me something, though if she did, I wouldn't have the quote on tape. Still, I was curious. "What do you think happened to Theresa?"

"I don't know." Her eyes got watery. "I just don't think she walked away, though I hope she did. I hope she's somewhere having a blast. But I can't picture her doing that. I just think . . . I don't know. I just think something bad happened."

"You think she's dead?"

Tears came. "I ask myself that every day. Is she dead? Is she okay? Where is she? Even when I'm happy. Especially when I'm happy. It's always there. It's hell."

"I think she needs a break." David jumped up from the couch and came over to his wife, wrapping his arms around Julia.

"Of course," I said. This was why I hated having friends and relatives hanging out at interviews. The interview subject can't see my manipulations, but the bystanders often can.

"It's great you were able to get off work," I said to David, while Julia went to touch up her makeup.

"It's not a big deal."

"What do you do?"

"I work at the DMV."

"That must be an interesting place to work. Lots of crazy people coming in every day."

"I don't work with the public," he said, a touch of disdain in his voice at the thought. "I work in an office downtown."

"And how did you meet Julia?"

"At a party to raise money for some state candidates. We just clicked right away."

"Was Theresa at the party?"

"I don't remember."

"Did Gray Meyer throw the party?"

"What difference does that make?"

Julia reemerged. "I'm ready for the rest of the interview."

She returned to her chair, and I asked her several more questions, but I could feel David looking at me, and I knew that I'd gotten everything from Julia I was going to get.

"You said Theresa did some things she shouldn't have," I said. "Like what?"

Julia thought for a moment. "Like dating the wrong man. Not everyone is as lucky as I am."

I could see by the smile on David's face that Julia had given the right answer. Or at least the answer he wanted her to give.

Thirty-six

I wasn't sure what to expect at the Morettis' bakery, but when we arrived it was clear that Linda had planned each moment. The pastry case had been scrubbed and stocked with perfect-looking desserts. The windows had been cleaned, letting in more light. The café tables had cherry-themed tablecloths on them. Even the photo wall had been reworked. The defaced photos of Julia were gone, replaced by a half dozen new photos of the Moretti family in happier times.

Linda greeted us in a pair of tan pants, a white shirt, and a pink check apron. She was so neat and put together that she looked more like Hollywood's version of a baker than anyone I'd seen in the real world.

"Before you start," she said, "you have to have something to eat. Tom just made cream puffs."

That was all it took. Andres and Victor sat at one of the tables, a plate piled with cream puffs in front of them. I admit to taking one or two for myself, but mostly I was interested in the photo wall.

"This looks different," I pointed out.

"We wanted to spruce the place up," she said. "We don't want Theresa thinking the place has gone to pot in her absence."

"You think she'll watch the show?"

"If she can. Wouldn't it be great? She'd see that we were still looking for her. That would boost her spirits."

"You don't, even for a second . . ." I couldn't bring myself to ask her the question again.

She shook her head. "My baby is alive. I know it."

Tom had opened the kitchen door slightly, and I could see him listening and rolling his eyes. And there was something else too. Anger, maybe. Resentment. Hatred. I couldn't be sure.

"We'll want to get footage of you at work, Tom," I said.

"I don't like to be on TV."

Linda opened the kitchen door fully to reveal Tom, with flour and dabs of frosting all over his apron. He looked like a real baker.

"You have to be on the show. Theresa needs to see her brother."

"Theresa is dead, Ma."

"You have to be on the show." Linda's voice was stern, uncompromising. I could see Tom relent.

"We won't get in your way too much," I said.

"I'm finishing the Murphys' wedding cake." He turned and went back into the kitchen.

"Never mind him," Linda said. "He's just shy."

Twenty minutes later we were setting up in the kitchen. Tom was ignoring us, focused on the wedding cake he was decorating. It was a masterpiece of five layers of square cake, each layer resting slightly askew on the layer below. It looked, quite purposefully, like it might fall over, but it was clear from the way Tom moved it as he worked that he had no concerns. Each layer had tiny pearl-like dots of icing at the base and white and cream flowers climbing the sides. It was the kind of cake featured in magazines and cake contests, far more upscale than one would expect in a local bakery.

"Fondant?" I asked just to make conversation.

"Buttercream."

"Wow. You get it so smooth."

"I guess."

"I've been eating your pastries, and they really are spectacular."

"Thanks."

"Are you trained? I mean, not just at your mom's bakery?"

He looked up momentarily from the cake. "I mostly picked it up from working here. I took some bread-making classes but I haven't gone to culinary school."

"Was that what you were planning to do in New York?"

"Who said I was going to New York?"

"It was something I heard."

"You heard that, did you?"

"I also heard you might have had some trouble with the police."

Tom ignored me. I was getting nowhere. I stepped back and let Andres get several good shots of Tom working on the cake, then some wide shots of the kitchen.

"Get the rest of the pastries in the case and shots of Linda waiting on a customer," I told him. He and Victor left me alone with Tom in the kitchen.

"Did you and Theresa get along?" I asked.

"She was my sister."

"Yeah, I know. I have a sister. We get along okay but we also get on each other's nerves."

He looked at me. "What are you wanting to ask me?"

"Some people think you and Theresa didn't get along, and maybe you have some issues." It occurred to me that I had no reason to ask these questions. I wasn't interviewing Tom. I wasn't using any of this in the piece. I just wanted to know.

"Everyone has issues, Mrs. Conway."

"It's Kate."

"Maybe in Bucktown people like to stick their noses in other people's business, Kate, but we like to be respectful in this neighborhood. We like to mind our own business."

"How do you know I live in Bucktown?"

"It was just something I heard."

His stare was icy and he held the decorating bag of buttercream icing like it was a weapon. When Andres called to me from the other room, I was glad of the excuse to walk away.

"I need you to be a customer," Andres said when I joined him in the front of the bakery. "Go outside, count to ten, and come in."

I nodded and went outside. Whether it was the July heat or Tom's coldness, I couldn't be sure, but suddenly I felt shaky. I forgot to start counting and then just guessed and walked in the store.

"You looked at the camera," Andres said.

"Sorry."

I walked outside again and this time forced myself to count to ten.

If anyone had been a huge fan of my work, and no one was, they would have seen me in a dozen or so television shows. I've been a diner at restaurants, a dead body in reenactments, a lady trying on shoes, and a housewife taking cookies out of the oven. Whenever we've needed someone for a B-roll shot, and no civilian was handy, I'd fill in. Unless we needed a guy; then it was Victor's moment of glory.

I walked up to the counter and chatted fake chat with Linda, who played along beautifully. After Andres got the wide shots, I ordered two dozen cookies. While she packed them, Andres got close-ups of her hand putting them into a pink box. She had to do it several times so he could be sure he had exactly the right shot. When Andres was satisfied, Linda tied the box, handed it to me, fake chatted some more, and I left the store. When I got the nod from Andres, I came back in and returned the box to Linda.

"Thanks so much. I think we have everything we need," I said.

"Keep the cookies. In fact, I'll send you each home with a box. Just my way of saying thank you."

"That's very nice. And completely unnecessary."

She waved off my protest and started packing two more boxes. "What happens next?"

"I look at all the tapes, write the script, and it goes to New York for editing. It will probably be three or four months before it hits the air, but someone from Ripper Productions will be in touch with a specific date before then."

"I'm amazed at how fast you do this," she said.

"Four ten-hour days for twenty-two minutes of show," Andres said.

Linda nodded. "You all worked so hard. Someday I hope you'll cover the story when Theresa comes home."

I smiled as warmly as I could. "Absolutely."

Out of the corner of my eye, I saw Tom watching from the kitchen.

Thirty-seven

I overnighted the last of the shot tapes to Mike in New York, and then Andres, Victor, and I went out for a few drinks to celebrate our final night of the shoot. It felt good to relax and talk about something other than dead husbands and missing women, two subjects we had banned for the evening. While I had a few too many beers, Victor told us about his new band, which played some combination of punk and rap, and Andres talked about his golf lessons.

It was nearly midnight when Andres dropped me off. I hadn't left the porch light on, so I nearly tripped over the package that sat at my front door. It didn't have stamps or some marking of a delivery service, but it did have my name and address carefully printed on it, so I brought it inside and left it on the kitchen table next to the pink box of Linda's cookies. I intended to dive into the cookies but first I needed actual food, so I made myself a sandwich.

I can cook, I just don't bother. It was fun to cook when there were two of us, and when Frank was around to finish the leftovers. And there was a time when Frank was very into cooking. He took some classes and talked about going to culinary school but never did. I used to bring him cookbooks from any food shows I worked on, and he'd make all the recipes. He even grew herbs and a few fruits and vegetables in the garden, carefully finding ways to outwit the rabbits who liked to eat his strawberries. I used to love coming home to his meals. Everything from the bread to the lemonade was homemade and often homegrown. But then he lost interest. All the recipe books collected dust. I took over the cooking for a while, but without his talent or enthusiasm. And once it was just me, I resorted to takeout and whatever sandwiches I could put together quickly.

I sat at the kitchen table with my plate, a glass of water, and two aspirin for the almost certain hangover I would have. I stared at my name and address written in block letters on the plain brown wrapping paper covering the shoe box–size package.

"It looks like I ordered porn." I laughed. "I wonder if the neighbors saw it and think that I'm burying my grief in sex tapes."

I ripped open the brown paper, and sure enough, it was a shoe box. Women's shoes.

"Someone sent me shoes," I said to myself.

I opened the box and it was not shoes.

I threw the box on the table and jumped back. It was the dead bird from the other day, decidedly worse for the time that had elapsed.

"Your statement is that you came home, discovered the package, opened it, and found the same bird that had been left on your porch several days ago. Is that correct?" Detective Podeski sat on my couch in a dark, worn suit, while his partner stood nearby taking notes. I sat on the leather chair, my hands still shaking.

"Yes. That's what I just told you."

I hadn't called Podeski. I'd called 911 to report a bird. In a shoe box. Maybe in some places that would have constituted a criminal act, but this was Chicago. I hadn't expected anything. But I got quite a lot. First, a patrol car showed up, and then Detective Podeski, who had heard about my call on his police radio.

"Has anyone made threats against you?" he asked.

"No. Why would anyone make threats against me?"

"That's what I'm trying to find out." He was a little grumpy. I guess getting a threatening package didn't fit into his idea of me as cold-blooded killer. "You mentioned the other day about letting us search your house. Does the offer still stand?"

"Of course. If you want to."

"It will take us about a half hour."

"I'll make coffee, if you like."

It occurred to me as I set out coffee mugs and Linda's cookies that I had some very private things in drawers in my house. The electric bill with a Second Notice stamp on it, the nude sketch Frank had made of me years ago that I kept in the closet in case my mother dropped by, and most embarrassingly, the vibrator my sister, Ellen, had gotten me as a predivorce gift. I knew finding a vibrator wouldn't faze the cop who was probably looking through my underwear drawer right now, but it bothered me. I felt even more violated than the bird on the porch had left me.

Podeski drank coffee, ate more than his fair share of the cookies, and watched, with clear delight, how nervous I was becoming. But he said nothing. One of the officers who had arrived in the patrol car walked into the living room and motioned for Podeski. The men walked into the hallway that led to the kitchen. I could see them chatting for a few minutes and then Podeski came back, holding a pair of black leather pumps.

"Are these yours, Mrs. Conway?"

"Yes. I bought them for my husband's funeral."

"Did you throw the box out?"

"No. I had my shoes in them. That's how I store my nicer shoes."

"Where were they?" he asked.

"In my closet," I said, then it dawned on me. "That isn't . . ."

"These match the box. Whoever left that bird on your front porch used a box from your closet."

I stood up. "The other night I thought someone had been in the house, but I wasn't sure."

"Was something taken?"

"No." I felt a little stupid even saying it. "I had photos and photo albums in the kitchen. They looked"—I hesitated—"neater. Like someone had arranged them."

"But you didn't call the police."

"And say what? Someone broke into my house and straightened up?"

He nodded. "It's possible that someone is trying to frighten you or warn you. And it's possible you put a bird in a box and called the police so we would think someone was trying to frighten you."

"And I used my own shoe box? Wouldn't it have been smarter to buy a pair of men's shoes, dump the shoes, and use the box?"

The corners of his mouth turned up into a slight smile. "You are a clever woman, Mrs. Conway."

I let that pass without comment. "There might be fingerprints," I pointed out.

"We'll check the paper and the box. You call a friend or go somewhere to spend the night. Maybe Ms. Bingham would come over."

"Vera? Why would she come over?"

"Why did she come over the other day?"

"To bring some of Frank's things back. Are you watching the house?"

"No, ma'am." He nodded toward the other officers and they left the house, taking the box and its contents with them. "Lock the doors behind us, Mrs. Conway."

I did. And then I checked that the locks were secure, the windows were latched, and even the flue to the fireplace was closed.

I thought about calling someone, but by the time the police left, it was nearly three in the morning. I couldn't imagine getting my sister or one of my friends out of bed because of a dead bird. But for the second night in a row, I wasn't going to sleep either.

I grabbed a quilt my grandmother had made and wrapped it around me. I lay on the couch, turned on the TV, and watched an infomercial about a new brand of makeup. According to their spokeswoman, a once-famous sitcom star, their product didn't just make you look better; it brought with it romance, success, and glamour. All of that would be nice another time. Right now all I wanted was daylight.

Thirty-eight

I left the house early and went for a walk. I saw a few neighbors out with their dogs and stopped each of them. No one had seen anyone at my front door the day before.

I went to a diner for breakfast but just pushed around the eggs and hash browns. I had a raging headache, not all of which could be blamed on alcohol. I'd slept maybe two hours, and even then I'd had terrible dreams.

It had to be true. Someone had killed Frank and was now trying to scare me. I had asked questions. I'd gone to the doctor, then Podeski, Vera, and Neal. Was Frank's killer really afraid I'd find the truth? Because if that was the case, the killer had greater faith in my investigative skills than I did.

Or maybe it was someone connected to Theresa's disappearance. Maybe I'd asked a question that made it look like I knew something I didn't. But that was even more absurd. A few days from now, I could be working on a three-part documentary about the origins of man or an hour-long salute to cheese, and Theresa would just be one more entry on my IMDb Web page.

Besides, we were done shooting the episode. If I had spent any part of the last week with her killer, then so be it. The good news for that person, and me, was we would never have to see each other again.

I left my plate barely touched, paid my check, and walked a few blocks. I didn't feel like going home. It wasn't that I felt too afraid to enter my own house, though that was certainly part of it. I just felt restless. I'd been putting off a phone call. I was even more reluctant to make it now, but I was running out of excuses. Besides, if I were making a list of people who might want to keep me from uncovering a killer, one name seemed obvious.

"Vera? You mentioned something about going through the rest of Frank's stuff. Is today okay?"

I heard dogs barking in the background. "Sure," she said. "Come over now if you like. I'm home all day. Do you like dogs?"

"Love them."

I don't really. They drool, and they sniff inappropriate places. They assume you want to spend time with them, even when you don't, so they push their way in and demand your attention. I suppose they're nice enough, but whatever you give them they want more. They remind me of producers, so maybe that's the problem.

Vera lived in a gray stone building a few blocks from Lake Michigan. A lot of these wonderful old houses have been converted to condos, but it was clear from the single name on the mailbox that this one wasn't. And why should it be? She was a Knutson Foods heiress.

I was greeted at her door by two enormous but harmless-looking greyhounds. They must have found me equally inoffensive because neither went for my throat.

"This is Daisy and this is Jay." Vera petted the heads of each dog as she spoke.

"Like characters from *The Great Gatsby*?"

She smiled. "Do you know most people don't get that reference? I loved that book and I figured it would be sweet if the two lovebirds got together in the end."

"But they don't. Daisy stays with her husband, and Jay Gatsby ends up dead in his swimming pool."

Vera shrugged. "Well, my Jay and Daisy are having a happy ending." She led me from the entryway through a hall that led to a large kitchen with modern appliances surrounded by solid, expensive woodwork.

"This is a beautiful place," I said, which hardly did it justice. It was filled with the details of hundred-year-old houses: carved wood moldings, stained glass, and inlaid tile. Outside was a decent-size backyard for a city lot. Except for the neglected garden it would be a nice place to spend a summer evening. "How long have you lived here?"

"Almost twenty years. My father gave it to me as a wedding present, but smart man that he is, he stipulated that it would go to me alone in the event of a divorce."

"Why did you get divorced?"

She blushed. "He cheated on me."

I raised an eyebrow.

"I know. It's ironic. Except my husband didn't just cheat on me, he turned it into something of a mission to bed every woman in the Chicago phone book."

"Where is he now?"

"Probably on the *M*s."

I laughed. I was, unfortunately, beginning to see what Frank saw in Vera.

"You have more of Frank's stuff to sort through," I said.

"Yes, upstairs. But there's no hurry. Have some coffee first. Tell me about your week."

She got us both coffee and then directed me to a small table near the back window. I sipped my third coffee of the morning and just enjoyed the view for a while before speaking.

"Nothing to tell," I said eventually. "I've been working on a show called *Missing Persons*. We're doing an episode on a twenty-two-year-old woman from Bridgeport."

"What happened to her?"

"I don't know. She walked out of her mother's house a year ago and hasn't been seen since."

Vera rested her hand on the head of one of the greyhounds, who was in turn resting its head on Vera's lap. "That sounds like such exciting work."

"It can be," I said.

"I envy you having a career like that. I find the days just run together because I don't really have anywhere to go."

"I thought you started businesses with friends."

She shrugged. "I help people who need start-up capital. I'm not sure they're friends. I'm not very good at making friends." She laughed, a self-conscious, embarrassed laugh.

"You have that woman who came to the wake with you."

"Susan."

"That can't have been a fun evening for her, but she went because she's your friend."

Vera stared at me a moment, as if considering what to say next. "I guess so," she said. "How are you doing? Are you sleeping? I'm not sleeping through the night yet."

"Slept like a baby last night," I lied.

I looked for signs of surprise but couldn't find any. If Vera was a nut job who broke into my house and left dead birds on my porch, she was hiding it well.

Sitting with her it was hard to imagine her that way. She didn't seem like a nut job. Or a home wrecker, for that matter. Maybe I was just looking to blame her for everything. Maybe she was just a nice woman who turned out to be the final straw in a marriage already about to collapse. Besides, the dogs liked her. I may not be a dog lover myself, but I do think they're a pretty good judge of character.

"Are you okay?" Vera asked. "You look a little sick."

"I'm fine. I was looking at the dog. Greyhounds are an unusual choice."

"They're rescue dogs. From the racetrack. When they retire from that, there are organizations that find them homes where they'll be loved and allowed to enjoy the rest of their lives."

"You take in retired race dogs and help your friends start businesses. You need to be needed," I said.

"Don't you?"

"No. I actually don't like being needed," I admitted. "Was Frank a project? Someone who needed you?"

She smiled. She should have been insulted and maybe she was, but her smile was warm and open. "I hope he needed me. I needed him. I think that's what brought us together."

Even though I'd asked the question, that was as much insight into their relationship as I wanted for one day.

"We should go through Frank's stuff," I said.

We went upstairs to her bedroom, a smallish room by modern standards, but beautifully decorated, with a Matisse hanging over the bed. Must be nice.

We sorted his jeans, T-shirts, dress shirts, belts, and shoes in less than an hour. Vera held on to a couple of shirts they must have bought together. I took two T-shirts, one from a Bruce Springsteen concert we'd attended, the other from a long-ago trip to Bermuda. The rest we boxed up for a Goodwill store in my neighborhood and I promised to drop them there during the week.

Vera gave me Frank's watch, the tie clips, and his father's dog tags, as well as his wallet and a box of souvenirs from his high school basketball days.

"I'll give all of this stuff to his parents," I told her.

"I also have some of his sketches they might like. I think they're downstairs."

She left me in the room alone, and as I'm inclined to do, I snooped. Nothing too intense, I just peeked into her closet and the top drawer of her dresser. There was nothing special until I looked at the nightstand. In a simple silver frame was a photo of Frank and Vera, holding each other and smiling.

When Vera came back into the room, she caught me staring at it.

"He looks so happy," I said. "He looks like he's in love with you." I could feel my face flush from the realization that it was the same beaming expression I'd seen in the photos of our wedding reception.

"I think he was in love with you too," she said quietly.

I took a breath. "Maybe."

I had a feeling Vera was on the verge of crying, but thankfully my cell phone rang and interrupted the moment. I didn't recognize the number but I picked up anyway.

"Kate? This is Yvette Rosenthal," the woman said. "Is this a good time?"

"Of course, Detective, but we're done shooting the episode so—"

"You might want to change your mind. We found a lead on Theresa. Her purse was discovered in a forest preserve near Brookfield. We're setting up a grid search now."

"I'll see if I can get the crew together," I said, "if it's okay to shoot it."

"Are you kidding me? I think you must be my lucky charm. I had pretty much given up on this case until you came along, and now"— she paused—"we may actually be close to finding her."

Thirty-nine

As soon as I hung up with Detective Rosenthal, I called Mike.
"You're never going to believe this," I said. "They found Theresa's purse in a forest preserve just west of Chicago."

"Who's Theresa?"

"Missing Persons, episode one."

"Shit!" Mike yelled. "They found something. That's amazing. Call Andres. Get him to meet you there. Get lots of stuff of dogs sniffing things, cops looking concerned. You know the drill. Is the family going?"

"I don't know."

"Call them. Call everyone. Get statements. They're hopeful, they're excited. Man, we can end the show with stuff about how the family is so close to knowing the truth. All we need now is the public's help. Great work, Kate."

"I didn't actually find the purse."

"Yeah, but the detective liked you enough to call. That's great work."

I'd never heard Mike so excited. And I was a little excited too. It was rare for us actually to be there while a story was unfolding. It made me feel a little like I was working in news again.

"Listen, Kate." Mike's voice sounded more serious. "One full day, no overtime. Okay?"

I called Andres, who promised to call Victor and meet me at the scene. I tried Linda Moretti but didn't get an answer. Same for Julia and Wyatt. All that was left was the half-hour drive to Brookfield, but when I stood up, I felt a little dizzy.

"Are you okay?" Vera asked. "You've seemed out of it all day."

"I haven't eaten anything yet," I said. "And maybe I didn't get as much sleep as I needed."

"I'll drive. I'm not doing anything and it sounds kind of fun."

Before I had a chance to protest, she had me downstairs and into the passenger seat of her hybrid Mercedes, three boxes of Frank's things in the backseat. I grabbed a burger at a fast-food place hoping some food would make me feel better, but it only made me feel worse.

By the time we got to Brookfield, a nice little town most famous for its world-class zoo, I was feeling the effects of heat, bad food, and no sleep. The thing I'd done right—put the image of the dead bird out of my mind—came back when we passed a dead deer lying on the side of the road.

"Rest in peace, little deer," Vera called to it.

"You're a big animal lover, aren't you?" I asked.

She smiled. "Yes, I guess."

Nut job or nice person. I stared at the unassuming woman who had given up her afternoon to drive her lover's widow to work. The evidence might be tipping in her favor, but as far as I was concerned the jury was still out.

Though it was a large wooded area, it was hard to miss the right spot for the search. There were several Brookfield police cars, two patrol cars with the Illinois State Police logo, and half a dozen other vehicles all parked haphazardly. The parking area looked down on a clearing where the cops and several others had gathered.

Andres and Victor were standing by the van, waiting.

"What do we do?" Andres asked.

"Start by following Rosenthal, wherever she is," I said. "We'll get statements later."

Detective Rosenthal, as it turned out, was consulting with the Moretti family. Linda, Tom, and a dozen others were huddled together about a hundred feet from the cars.

"There's your boyfriend," Victor said as we approached the Morettis.

I looked where he was pointing and saw Gray Meyer approaching the group. In jeans and a light-blue T-shirt, he looked even more handsome than he had in his suit. But he also looked serious and slightly angry.

"You know Gray?" Vera asked.

"*You* know Gray?" I asked back.

"We went to school together."

Once Gray saw us, and particularly Vera, the serious expression transformed to a bright, friendly smile. He and Vera hugged and chatted. I left them to their reunion and approached Detective Rosenthal, who was walking away from Theresa's family.

"Can you show us the purse?" I asked.

"It's being taken into evidence."

"If it's bagged already we'll shoot it through the bag."

She nodded. Within minutes, Andres was getting close-up shots of Theresa's driver's license, her debit card, a lipstick, and a torn piece of paper with the numbers *4*, *3*, and *7* written on it in ink. All the items were remarkably well preserved, having been inside Theresa's purse the whole time. And now these small items from her everyday life were sealed in plastic bags with bright red evidence tape across them.

The purse itself was not in good shape. It was dirty and wet and the handles were torn. Her mother had said that Theresa's purse was tan, but this purse looked more gray than tan. Still, Linda had identified it as belonging to Theresa. The ravages of Chicago weather were likely the cause of the color change, Rosenthal explained. It made me wonder what Chicago weather had done to Theresa's body, assuming she was somewhere in these woods. One look at Rosenthal, and I knew she was thinking the same thing.

Forty

"The state police received a call this morning from a man who was out taking photographs. He found the purse," Detective Rosenthal said. "They checked their database, found that there was a missing persons report on Theresa Moretti, and called me."

We were standing away from the others, with the police cars and activity in the background. There wasn't time, or the need, for a proper interview. We just set up the camera while Victor held a boom mic and I started asking questions.

"Why did it take so long for her purse to be found?"

"It might have been buried, probably under less than a foot of dirt. During the winter the ice and snow would have displaced some of the soil. And, of course, animals would have too. A deer or even a raccoon could have dragged it a dozen yards or more from its original spot, which is why we have to create a wide search area."

"How important is this?"

"It's the first piece of evidence we've had that even suggested Theresa's whereabouts. We know her purse was here, and judging by the condition, it looks like it's been here awhile."

"That would suggest Theresa might be here too," I said. "Her body might be in these woods. The weather and animals might have displaced some of the soil over her body."

"We're setting up a grid search right now. We'll go through the area searching for evidence, see what we can find. If Theresa is here, we're going to do everything we can to find her."

With that Rosenthal headed back to the rest of the growing police presence. Crime scene tape had been put up around the trees on the perimeter, leaving us with little to do but sweat. The temperature closed in on ninety degrees, making my headache worse. I leaned against Andres's van and tried to close my eyes, but there was too much activity and I didn't want to miss a good shot.

Julia and David arrived about twenty minutes after I did, and they were sitting on the grass with the Moretti family, waiting for news. Whatever their differences, the possibility of finding Theresa had left them seeking comfort from each other. Sort of like Vera and me the night in the hospital. A few minutes later Wyatt came, waved hello to me, and sat next to Linda, who rested her head on his shoulder.

"I don't want to interrupt," I said to the group.

"Then don't," Tom replied.

"Tom," Linda said. "I'm sorry, Kate. As you can imagine . . ."

"That's the thing, I can't imagine. I can't even begin to know what you're going through. I don't think anyone who hasn't been in your situation can." I reached out for her hand, which she took and held tight. "I'm just wondering if any of you would like something to drink. I can get water or some food."

"Maybe some water," Linda said. "If it's not too much trouble."

"Not at all."

I went back to the car and sent Victor to the nearest convenience store to buy three cases of water, whatever snacks he could get for no more than fifty bucks, and some aspirin for me. When he returned, we distributed the water and food to the police and growing number of friends and family members that had begun to arrive. Everyone was, naturally, grateful for the act of agenda-free generosity. Victor and I accepted the thanks, while Andres hung back, shaking his head.

After a few minutes, I returned to the group. "I hate to do this." I crouched down between Linda and Wyatt. "My boss just called and he insists on getting a statement from the family. I told him I didn't want to disturb you, but, well, you know bosses. I think Wyatt will do if you aren't up for it, Linda. I feel so bad . . ."

"Not at all." Linda got up from the grass. "Anything I can do, after all you've done for us."

We set Linda up so her friends and family were in the background, several yards behind her. She looked as though she'd aged twenty years since the day before.

"What information do you have about what's going on today?" I asked.

"Very little. Detective Rosenthal called this morning and told us that Theresa's purse had been found. Naturally we drove here right away, and we're just waiting now."

"Waiting for what?"

"Information. More evidence. Something that will tell us where to find Theresa."

"Do you think Theresa is here?" It was a tough question, but it had to be asked.

Linda shook her head, unwilling to let go of her theory on the disappearance. "No. I think her kidnapper dropped her things here. But maybe we can find something that will give us a lead."

"Like fingerprints?"

"Exactly." Her face lit up. "His fingerprints could be on her things. The things found in the purse. Then we could find her."

"Who called Wyatt and Julia?" I had, of course, but I hadn't reached them. I didn't leave messages, so they hadn't shown up because of me.

"I did," Linda said. "I thought if there was a search, the police might need volunteers, so we called everyone we could think of to come help."

I looked behind her and saw a team of cadaver dogs and their trainers. It wasn't the search team Linda was hoping for. I also saw Gray introducing Detective Rosenthal to Vera.

"Thanks, Linda," I said. "I think we have what we need."

I saw Andres shooting Vera and Gray with Rosenthal. I almost placed my hand in front of his lens, but I knew he was just getting the necessary B-roll we'd need of all our interview subjects at the scene. It was weird, though. Vera had been inching her way into my life since the day Frank died. Now she was becoming part of my work as well.

"Who is that woman?" Andres asked. "The one standing next to Gray. That's not his wife, is it?"

"It's Vera."

I could see Andres's camera dip. "Not your Vera."

I watched her smile and touch Gray's arm. "Apparently she's everybody's Vera."

Forty-one

"Hi," I said to Gray. "I'm sorry I haven't come over sooner."

"I see you guys are shooting this. That's great." He flashed the same perfect smile from the day of the interview. "And listen, thanks for all the water. I know the family really appreciates what you've done."

"I'm glad to help. I see you know Vera."

Vera, who had been standing next to Gray but watching the crowd, suddenly turned to me. "What are the odds?"

"Two wealthy Chicagoans who live in adjacent neighborhoods, both of whom get their pictures on the society pages? I'd say the odds were very good you'd know each other."

Gray blushed. "Hopefully the society pages aren't all we have in common."

"Is Vera your source of information about my husband?"

Vera seemed confused. "What are you talking about?"

Gray didn't answer. He just stood there, studying me. The thing about people born to a certain amount of money and influence is that they're used to dividing the world into "us" and "not us." I was definitely in the latter category for Gray Meyer, and therefore, I suppose, not expected to challenge him. As much as I didn't want to be at odds with a man I might have to interview for another story, I was also tired of being mouse to Gray's cat.

I was about to say something to that effect, but before I had a chance to, the search dogs started barking furiously.

"I'll be back," Gray said and ran toward the noise.

Tom got up to join him, but he was turned away by the police. We all stood, waiting for what seemed like forever. I caught Andres's eye and motioned for him to shoot the family. He nodded.

Within minutes, a young officer came out of the woods and shouted, "False alarm."

Instead of relief, the announcement just added to the tension.

"How do you take all of this pain?" Vera asked.

"It's not my pain."

"But it's all around you. I saw that woman, the missing girl's mother. She was grabbing on to you."

"She needs support."

"It has to be so draining. I think it's so admirable that you care about these people so much."

As she was talking about my compassion, I watched Andres push in on Linda's face. That's the great thing about cameras. He had never moved from the same spot he'd been in the entire time, which was at least fifty feet from Linda, yet I could tell just from the way Andres positioned his foot that he was getting a close-up of Linda's fear and worry.

I turned back to Vera. "It can be hard sometimes."

"I don't think Frank understood what you have to deal with every day," she said. "He should have been more supportive."

I smiled a little. "He didn't really know what I did. I tried to explain it, but I could see his eyes glazing over and I just gave up."

"He never came to a shoot?"

"No, but then I never asked him to."

"Maybe you should have."

"Too late now, Vera." I motioned toward her car, parked only a few yards away. "I appreciate the ride but I can get Andres to take me home."

She considered my suggestion but stood her ground. "I kind of want to see what happens, if that's okay."

"The more the merrier, I guess."

While the police organized a volunteer search party, Andres, Victor, Vera, and I sat in the car, blasted the air-conditioning, and waited. Since I had a full day to shoot, I figured we might as well stick around, just in case. Vera and Victor sat in the backseat and talked about music while Andres and I took turns complaining about Mike, Ripper Productions, and TV in general.

After about a half hour had passed, Andres tapped on the driver's-side window and pointed. "I wonder who called him."

"I did," I confessed. "I thought it might be interesting to see what happened if he showed up."

Jason stood by his car, watching the police and Theresa's family huddled together. He seemed unable to move toward them but also didn't seem to be in a hurry to leave.

Andres grabbed his camera. "You coldhearted bitch." He laughed. "This is the reason Mike loves you."

Vera leaned forward. "Who is that?"

"The ex-boyfriend," Victor told her. "And the guy Gray is setting up to take the fall."

I turned to him. "When did you come up with that theory?"

"When that Gray guy showed up this morning all muscles and pretty-boy smiles. He's always around. Always wanting to help. Did you notice that? I think it's weird. I think he's using poor old Jason as a patsy."

Andres frowned. "Why?"

"I think he was having an affair with Tom. Tom looks like a guy with a secret. I'll bet that's it. Theresa found out, threatened to tell his wife. Maybe she even blackmailed him. That's where she got the dough. But she wanted more money, so he killed her."

"Why Tom? If he's having an affair, why not Theresa?" Andres asked.

"Look at that Gray guy. There's no way he's straight. He's too well-groomed."

I laughed. "It's really hard to keep up with you, Victor. You change suspects every five minutes. Next you'll say Vera did it." I looked to Vera. "You ever murder anyone, Vera?"

It just sort of popped out of my mouth, the question I'd been wanting to ask since we'd met.

She just laughed. "Not that I know of."

"You'll let us know if you do, though, won't you?" Victor asked.

"You mean you won't figure it out for yourself, Sherlock?" I said.

"Laugh at me if you want to, Kate, but I'd bet serious cash that someone in this crowd is a killer."

"Maybe more than one." I smiled at Vera, then got out of the car to talk to Jason.

Forty-two

"The police are organizing a search party," I told Jason.

"I'd like to help," he said.

"Is that why you came?"

"You called me."

"I know. But why did you come?"

Andres held the camera five feet away, but I could tell Jason was feeling penned in.

"I don't know," Jason said. "I just thought, maybe I should come."

As I was about to ask another question, Andres turned the camera. I immediately saw why. Tom had realized that Jason was there and was coming toward him at full speed.

Andres and I stepped back.

"What the hell are you doing here?" Tom screamed, but without giving him a chance to answer, he tackled Jason and began punching his face. As much as I wanted a bit of drama, this wasn't what I had in mind. Tom was turning Jason into hamburger.

Andres looked over at me. "You do realize that one of us has to shoot this, and one of us has to break it up."

"Sorry, Andres, but you probably take a punch better than I do."

He handed the camera over to me. "Don't drop my camera."

"Don't block my shot."

As Andres went to break up the fight, Gray, Wyatt, and Dave ran up the hill to help. Within seconds Gray had pulled Tom off Jason and Dave and Andres had pushed Jason away from Tom. After a little more shouting, Jason walked away, and Wyatt took Tom back to his family. As I was turning off the camera, Gray walked over to me, yanking my arm so hard that the camera nearly fell out of my hands.

"What the fuck are you doing?" I yelled.

He pulled me away from the others. "Did you get all that?" He wasn't shouting but he wasn't hiding his anger.

"I was invited here by Detective Rosenthal to shoot what was going on."

"You don't have to get the bad stuff."

"Is it just occurring to you now that I work on a television show that exploits people's pain for ratings?" I said the words slowly. "I'm not quite sure what your agenda is, Gray, but that's mine."

His eyes flickered. There was something—anger, disappointment, I couldn't tell. "It's just—isn't it kind of sleazy to be doing this now?" he said. "This is a family in crisis."

I said nothing. Just clenched my jaw. He was right. It was sleazy, but I wasn't about to take ethics lessons from a politician. I turned my back on him and went to see the playback of the video we just got.

Three more hours passed. For the first hour we shot the searchers as they walked the forest preserve. People lined up, arm's length apart, and walked an area, carefully looking at just the space around them. Once they were done, they reassembled to walk another area, in a grid pattern. We got about twenty minutes of footage, then retreated to the car. There was only so much tape of searching we were going to need. And now that David had convinced Jason to leave, there was only so much excitement I could create.

"How much longer?" Andres said.

"We have three more hours until overtime," I pointed out.

"I'm hungry," Victor announced from the backseat.

"I still have some chips," Vera told him.

Vera was with us, still waiting to see what happened. Maybe it was a bit masochistic of me to let her stay, but I was curious. I wanted to know who it was that Frank had left me for, and if she was the reason he was dead. It was easier to tolerate her with the guys around. She and I didn't have to chat too much, but I could still observe her. And a little part of me, maybe a large part, wanted to reassure myself that of the two of us, I was the better woman.

Unfortunately it wasn't working out that way. Vera was unfailingly cheerful, friendly, and helpful. It turned out to be handy to have an unpaid production assistant on the team. She got us food when we were hungry, and she watched the equipment when we went into the woods with the searchers. She kept Victor amused, which was no small feat, and she gave me the rundown on Gray Meyer.

"He was pretty shy in school," she told me. "He had one girlfriend for a long time but they broke up in college. He was athletic, smart, the kind of guy who should have been popular but he sort of kept himself apart. He's gotten more assertive as he's gotten older."

I chuckled. "Clearly."

"You don't like him, do you?"

"There's just something about him," I admitted. My arm didn't hurt from where he'd grabbed it, but my ego was a little bruised.

"I don't think he makes a great first impression. I think he's very sincere, and people sometimes misread that as politicking."

"Given his professional interests, I think that's a smart way to see him."

Vera tilted her head. "He had an older brother who died. It was after Gray went to college. We were out of touch for a while, so I don't know the circumstances, but I think it was sudden. I'm sure it's affected him."

"Or he paints himself as a tragic hero to win sympathy."

She laughed. "Frank said you were hard on people. Boy, was he right."

I didn't want to get into Frank's opinions in front of the crew, so I let it go. Vera, however, seemed to realize what she said.

"I just meant you're tough. That's a good thing."

We both seemed content to drop the matter and sit in silence, but it was too late. A lightbulb was illuminating over Victor's head.

"You're *that* Vera?" Victor said. "The one who was doing Kate's husband?"

"We were friends," she said gently, trying to deflect the situation.

"Jesus, Kate," Victor continued. "You're hanging out with Frank's bit on the side. That is so cool. I'll bet he's spinning in his grave 'cause he never managed to get you guys in a threesome."

I was spared from more of Victor's excitement when a group of people came running out of the woods. "Let's get out of the car," I said.

Vera and I jumped out while Andres grabbed his camera and Victor took his boom mic. Andres's camera was off, and lowered to his side, but we stood on the hill, away from the gathering crowd, just in case.

"Should we go down there?" Vera asked.

"No," I said. "If we need to shoot, we'll want to be at a distance so no one notices us."

She nodded and stood waiting with the rest of us.

Linda and Tom walked out of the woods and toward their friends, but judging by their faces, they didn't seem any more informed than we were. Julia and David joined them, and Wyatt stood back, talking on his cell phone.

"Do you think they're done for the day?" Andres asked.

I shook my head. "Who knows?"

A few minutes passed. Gray came out of the woods, followed by Detective Rosenthal. The two spoke quietly for a moment before Rosenthal, her face dark and somber, headed for the family.

Andres raised his camera.

"No," I said quietly. "We don't need this."

I watched Detective Rosenthal reach Linda and her family. She spoke for several seconds, though I couldn't hear the words. I didn't need to. It was like watching a slow-motion film of a boxing match, frame by frame of a gloved hand moving toward the jaw of an opponent. It's going so slow you almost feel you can stop it. But you can't. The glove hits the jaw and it shatters. There's nothing you can do. Watching Rosenthal deliver her news was the emotional equivalent of glove hitting jaw. Linda's face was filled with hope, then twisted in tortured contortions as she began to scream uncontrollably.

It took only a minute for news to spread through the crowd and reach us. Remains of a human female had been found only twenty yards from the purse, buried in a shallow grave.

Forty-three

"We're wrapped for the day," I said to Andres.

He put his arm around my shoulder and gave it an approving squeeze.

"If Mike ever asks," I said, "tell him we hit overtime before the body was found. Tell him we'd left."

"You got it, boss."

I turned to Vera. "Andres and I have some stuff to shoot at a different location, so he's going to take me home. I don't need sound, Victor, so we'll drop you first."

"Vera can take me home," Victor jumped in. "We have to get into the whole Frank situation."

After we transferred Frank's things to Andres's van, I watched Vera and Victor head off to her car. I felt a little sorry for Vera having to endure Victor's questions about Frank, but it was her own fault for hanging out with us all day. Andres and I stood back and watched the rest of the crowd disperse.

Wyatt left quickly. Though his car was parked near ours, he walked past without a word. Julia and David left soon after. Instead of going directly to their car, Julia walked toward us, with David following.

"I can't believe this," she kept saying. "I figured she was dead, but knowing . . ." She started to cry.

David wrapped his arms around her. "It's better this way. Now we can put it all behind us."

"I don't think you can yet," I said. "There's still the matter of finding Theresa's killer."

"That doesn't have anything to do with us," he said.

"The police will want to talk with you."

"They can talk to us. We'll just keep saying what we've always said. Julia had no plans to see Theresa that day."

I looked at Julia, pressing her head against her husband's chest and crying into his shoulder.

"I'm sorry, Julia," I said. "I know you were hoping for a different outcome."

David answered for her. "We all were."

He led Julia to their car and helped her into the passenger seat. She was still crying when he pulled away.

Gray, Rosenthal, and Theresa's family were together at a spot in the clearing near the trees. I wanted to chat with Rosenthal but this wasn't the time. And unless Mike hired me for another day, it wasn't, technically, any of my business.

"What's this other shoot you want to do?" Andres asked.

I took a deep breath. "Oh, that. This is going to sound girly so I apologize in advance, but when I got home last night there was a package wrapped in brown paper on my doorstep. When I opened it, it was a shoe box with a dead bird in it."

"Someone sent you a dead bird?" Andres's voice had gotten so loud that Gray looked toward us.

"Sssh," I said. "It gets worse. The shoe box belonged to me. Someone got into my house, stole the box, put the bird in it, and left it on my porch."

"Did you call the police?"

I nodded. "Detective Podeski thinks I did it myself, so I would look like I'm being threatened. He thinks I'm trying to throw suspicion off me."

I could see Gray was still watching us, so I motioned for Andres to get in the van. Once we were inside, I told him the rest.

"The sun's about to set and I don't want to walk into a dark house by myself. I just need you to walk in with me."

"You can't stay there. I'll call my wife . . ."

"No, it's fine. I just need someone with me when I turn the lights on."

He nodded. "This is out of control, Kate."

"If it's about Frank, then it must be Vera who's doing it."

"That's the nicest woman I've met in my life." He paused. "Sorry. I mean, what she did was wrong, but she's no murderer."

"Then who?"

He shook his head. "Look, if Podeski won't help you maybe Rosenthal will. She seems like a good cop."

I looked at Rosenthal, still surrounded by the Morettis and their friends. "I think she has her hands full."

"All right," Andres said, "but if we get to your house and something's out of place, we start making calls until somebody puts an end to it."

As it turned out, there were no packages, no items in my house mysteriously straightened, no odd phone calls. Andres checked all the rooms, made me promise to call him if something happened, and left me alone with only ghosts to keep me company.

And although there were no bumps in the night, I did feel ghosts around me. I could still hear Linda's inconsolable weeping when she'd heard the news. She had so convinced herself that Theresa was alive and would now, in all likelihood, replace that certainty with the belief that she could have, should have, done something to keep her daughter safe.

I knew the feeling. My own "what ifs" about Frank had haunted me every day since his death. What if I'd been more supportive of his painting? What if I had stopped nagging him about earning a living and just accepted his love and support as enough of a contribution? What if I had tried harder or been nicer? And the biggest one—if he hadn't left, would he still be alive?

Andres had brought the three boxes of Frank's things into my bedroom: one contained items for his parents and me; the other two were filled with clothes for donation. I separated out what I was keeping and left them on top of the earlier pile of Frank's stuff, leaving the "family heirlooms" for Frank's parents. I put on Frank's Springsteen T-shirt and climbed into the queen bed we'd shared for most of our marriage.

For the last couple of years, as things had gotten colder between us, I'd found myself sleeping as far from him as possible. On a couple of occasions I nearly fell out of bed I was sleeping so close to the edge. When he left, I had the whole bed to myself for the first time in my adult life. It was odd at the beginning and then liberating. I loved being able to flop around, switching from pillow to pillow. And it was great to have both nightstands for my books, glasses, tissues, and whatever other items migrated to the room and stayed.

But once he died, the bed felt empty and cold. I'd gravitated back to my side as if I were leaving room for him. When he left me, there was the anger to fill the void. Now I felt myself actually missing him for the first time in a long time. I missed his breathing. I missed the way his big feet would cross mine or the way he would wrap his body around me, trapping me for the night. Crawling into bed knowing for certain we would never again share it made me feel completely alone.

Tonight it felt especially empty. In the old days, before we'd lost our way, when I'd had a hard day, I'd look forward to bedtime. I'd curl my body into Frank's, press my forehead into his neck, and tell him about the crying widow, the crazy crew, and all the other frustrations of my job. He'd wrap his long arms around me and squeeze me tight.

"It's all okay now," he'd say. "I'll take care of you."

Then he'd run his fingers through my hair and gently massage the back of my head until I fell asleep in the safety of his arms.

But that was all finished now. Tonight I had only his pillow for comfort. I placed it vertically and lay against it, looking for the same warmth that had once been there. I tried to remember what it felt like to have his arms around me, but it was no use. My mind could only think of twin images: Frank's body in the cold, hard ground and Theresa's tossed away in the woods.

Forty-four

"You're killing me, Kate!" Mike was screaming. "I mean what the fuck am I supposed to do with this?"

Mike was not a roll-with-the-punches kind of guy. He'd once yelled at me because a forensic expert had to leave our interview when he got called to the scene of a homicide. Then there was the time a tornado kept us from finishing some B-roll we needed from a DNA lab. Both of these occasions were, in Mike's mind, my fault. Today's screwup was finding Theresa's body.

"The show is called *Missing Persons*," he yelled. "Not *Dead Persons*. We already do a show about dead people. We want missing people. I sold this with the idea that the show would help find the person. How can that happen if they've already been found?"

I could have pointed out that I didn't actually cause Theresa's body to be discovered in the woods near Brookfield. But I hadn't caused the tornado or the homicide, and explaining those situations to Mike didn't seem to make a difference. My new tactic was silence. I just sat in my kitchen, held the phone away from me, and waited.

After ten more minutes of ranting, Mike finally ran out of energy and profanities. "We've put a lot of money into this. I can't just shelve it. Any chance they'll get the killer in the next two weeks?"

"I'm sure that's what they're hoping for, Mike. But if you're thinking of transferring this to a *Caught!* episode, you'll need a conviction or a plea before you can go on the air saying the case is solved. That could take years."

He grunted. "I'll call the network. Maybe I can fix this. Damn it, Kate, this is a huge problem." With that, he hung up.

What a lovely way to spend a Sunday morning.

My afternoon didn't get much better. I'd called Alex to let him know I had Frank's things back from Vera, but instead of picking them up at my place, he'd asked me over for lunch. I was hoping the invitation meant that Lynette wasn't home. I was wrong. When I arrived she greeted me with excessive, and suspicious, warmth.

"My poor Kate," she said. "I've missed you so much."

"Well, I'm here now."

She fussed over me, bringing me iced tea and complimenting the color of my T-shirt and generally making both Alex and me uncomfortable. By the time I stuck my fork into my pear and walnut salad, I was counting the minutes until my escape.

In the dining room, and on her best dishes, she'd laid out a spread of cold roast beef, homemade focaccia, and three-bean salad. On the sideboard was her specialty, a lemon layer cake with fresh strawberries and whipped cream. Say what you like about Lynette, and God knows I had, but she can cook. It was almost worth spending the afternoon with her. Almost, because it always came at a price. If Lynette had gone to all this trouble for me, she didn't just want something. She wanted something big.

"It was so nice of you to bring Frank's things home," Lynette said just as I'd finished my roast beef. "They're all we have of him now."

"I was happy to do it."

I looked toward Alex, who clearly had no more idea where this was going than I did. Lynette got up, took our plates, and in a move that was totally out of character, piled them on the sideboard next to the lemon cake. Lynette hated messes, actual and metaphorical. One small way to avoid them was to put the dinner dishes in the dishwasher before serving dessert. She'd done it that way for twenty years. The only reason I could think of that she'd break the habit now was because she didn't want to leave Alex and me alone.

I'd been at her house a thousand times and made the offer a thousand times, so I did it again. "Let me load the dishwasher for you, Lynette."

She'd never let me touch her dishes, concerned I might break them or maybe be better at dishwashing than she was, but today she looked up at me and said, "That would be so helpful, dear. You're so very thoughtful."

I carried the dishes to the kitchen, silently humming the theme to *The Twilight Zone*, and stacked them carefully in the dishwasher, As I loaded the last plate, I realized what this was about. Lynette wanted her hands on one more of Frank's belongings, the insurance money.

I'd been ambivalent about the money since the moment Alex told me. I needed it, and maybe I deserved it. But it wasn't really Frank's insurance policy. Alex had set it up and paid the premiums. Taking it seemed like taking money from Alex. But while *I* might feel that way, I wasn't prepared to be told that by my ex-mother-in-law. I debated whether I should beat her to the punch by turning down the money or whether I should storm off now. I chose the first. Storming off would only delay the inevitable and mean more visits with Lynette. Besides, if I left I'd miss dessert. And she did make a really good lemon cake.

"I've always wanted your recipe for this," I said as I returned to my seat and the slice of cake that was waiting for me.

"I'll make you copies of all my recipes," she said. "But this one can be a little tricky. Perhaps when you're not so busy, you can come over and we'll make it together."

"That would be great." I glanced toward Alex, who was now avoiding my eyes.

"I'm sorry, but I'll have to rush off after lunch. I've been working a lot and I've got so many errands to run. But there is something I wanted to talk—"

Lynette cut me off. "You do so much. I always said to Alex that you were run off your feet. Didn't I, Alex?"

"Well . . . ," he started.

"And I don't think Frank was as helpful to you as he should have been. That's why when Detective Podeski told me about Frank's insurance policy I was so glad it was going to you."

Alex leaned forward. "You knew Kate was the beneficiary?"

"Of course, dear. Though I have to admit I was a little annoyed you hadn't told me. But I suppose we're all a little preoccupied with our grief."

Alex turned white. He wasn't a shrinking violet but he did know how to keep the peace, and when it came to Frank, he generally let

Lynette have her way. I felt a little bad that he was in for whatever punishment Lynette had in store, but right now I was more concerned about me.

"It should help you fix up that house of yours. I know Frank did what he could but he's not around now, is he? And Kate . . ." She paused. "Maybe it would be a good idea for you to take a vacation. When's the last time you just relaxed on the beach?"

"I don't remember. I work a lot." I took a deep breath.

I felt like a rat in one of those laboratory mazes, desperately trying to find my way out but knowing that even if I succeeded my reward wouldn't be freedom, just a trip back to my cage.

"How's work going?" she asked.

"We're doing a show about a woman who went missing a year ago. The police just found her body yesterday."

"How sad. You do a lot of those investigative shows, don't you?"

"I do some."

"I'll bet you know a lot about how to catch a killer."

"I guess." I was sweating. In twenty years she hadn't once asked me about my work.

Lynette smiled. "Well, then, I need you to do me a favor."

Forty-five

"I think"—she leaned toward me—"you could find evidence about who killed Frank."

"Lynette!" Alex nearly shouted. "What are you talking about?"

"That detective was talking to me about Frank's death, and he seemed to think that Frank was murdered," she said.

I tried to sound calm. "Lynette, he seems to think I did it."

"Kate, I've known you most of your life. You don't have what it takes to kill someone."

She'd managed to make my lack of homicidal tendencies sound like an insult. I relaxed. I was back on familiar territory.

"Then what are you asking?" Alex demanded to know.

"Kate was obviously successful in getting Frank's things back from that woman. She's spoken to her. She's been to her house. All I'm asking is that she check her out a little. Use the skills she's gotten from working on those shows. Frank left her a tidy sum of money. How can she possibly enjoy it, knowing his killer is walking free?"

I took a bite of my lemon cake. I wasn't sure I wanted to say anything, but I knew I had no choice. Mike had a different style from Lynette's, but they were both bulldozers. I'd learned it was impossible to oppose either of them.

"In my own clumsy way," I admitted, "I've actually been trying to find out what really happened to Frank."

Lynette's eyes filled with tears. She jumped up and grabbed me, hugging me genuinely for the first time since I'd told her years ago that Frank and I were trying for a baby.

She insisted on moving the group into the living room and making fresh coffee before we discussed what I knew. Alex and I sat dumbfounded while Lynette put out cups and saucers and tiny pastel-colored mints. It was the sort of highly civilized discussion of murder that would normally require the presence of Miss Marple.

After the coffee had been poured, Lynette settled into the floral overstuffed chair that was her favorite and asked me what I thought of "her."

"She seems very nice," I said. "She seems to have loved him. If Frank was murdered, I suppose it makes sense that Vera did it but I don't see motive."

"She wanted his money," Lynette said. "He stood to inherit a neat sum from Alex and me."

I shook my head. "But only if they were married and they weren't yet. Besides, she's an heir to Knutson Foods."

"Well, maybe they're going bankrupt. Maybe she's cut from the will."

Alex put down his coffee. "Lynette, honey. I haven't read anything that would suggest Knutson's is anything but a profitable corporation."

"Well, maybe . . ."

"I guess I can check about her being in the will," I said, "but she doesn't seem motivated by money. And if she were, I would bet she has friends who have a lot more money than Alex and you, people with tens of millions of dollars in annual income. If she was looking for someone with money, I don't think she would have picked Frank."

Lynette seemed miffed at the suggestion that her upper-middle-class lifestyle wouldn't have impressed her son's new girlfriend. "Well, what then?"

"Did Frank mention getting engaged to her?" I asked.

"No!" Lynette seemed shocked at the very thought. "And he wouldn't have gotten engaged without telling us."

"Remember your heart, dear," Alex said, then he turned to me. "Did she say she was engaged to him?"

I nodded. "On the night Frank died. She told the doctor she was his fiancée. And later, I asked Neal about it and he confirmed it."

"Does she have a ring?" Lynette asked.

"Not that I know of."

Lynette pointed toward my hand and the wedding ring I was still wearing. "How can he be engaged to her when he's still married to you?"

"She must have thought they would marry when the divorce was final," Alex said flatly.

"That's the thing," I said. "According to Neal, Frank seemed to have changed his mind about the divorce. I don't know if it's true . . ."

"It is." Alex took a deep breath. "You know we were paying for Frank's divorce attorney." I nodded, and Alex smiled sadly. "I'm sorry about that, but what could we do?"

"It's okay."

It wasn't really. Frank's parents could afford a much better attorney than I could, and if the divorce had gone on much longer, Frank would probably have walked away with the house. But there was no point in bringing that up now.

"When I notified his attorney of Frank's death," Alex said, "I called him for a final bill. The amount I owed was next to nothing. When I asked why, he told me that Frank had put a halt to the divorce about two weeks before he died. I don't know the details, but I was hoping it was because he'd come to his senses."

"And that's why she killed him." Lynette sat back, satisfied that she had cracked the case. "He told her he was going back to you."

Forty-six

An hour later, I walked onto the beach at Montrose Avenue and looked for Vera. When people who have never been to Chicago talk about the city, they usually bring up Al Capone and deep-dish pizza. But when they visit, they are stunned to find out how beautiful my hometown is. One of the things that makes it so beautiful is Lake Michigan. We have beaches just a few blocks from skyscrapers. For those precious few months of warm weather, Chicagoans crowd onto those beaches and pretend that winter will never come.

Well, others crowd. My skin is too pale for the sun, and my disposition doesn't allow for much lying around doing nothing. But other Chicagoans love it. And if they have dogs they're usually at one of the few beaches with a dog park.

That was where I found Vera. I'd called her as I left Frank's parents, unsure of what to say but figuring that it was my next logical step if I was to fulfill my promise to Lynette. I didn't have an excuse for calling, but it turned out I didn't need one. Vera greeted me like an old friend and insisted I join her, Daisy, and Jay at Montrose Avenue Beach for an afternoon of catch.

To an outsider it looked like an innocent activity—two friends and two dogs spending the afternoon enjoying summer weather. But I was after something more significant than a day at the beach. I sat in the shade and watched Vera and the dogs play and wondered if Lynette was right. Did Vera kill Frank to keep him from coming home to me? It was certainly a logical theory. If Frank was hoping to reconcile, and if he'd told her his plan, Vera might have wanted to kill him. She'd admitted to being lonely, to having little luck with men. Maybe she'd pinned her last hopes for love on Frank and couldn't handle the rejection. Maybe. But it wasn't just my curiosity anymore; Lynette and Alex were now counting on me to find out.

The problem was how exactly was I supposed to find out when my entire skill as an interviewer was asking people questions I already had answers to?

"How did the rest of your shoot go?" Vera asked when she and the dogs sat down for a rest.

"Good. Andres and I got what we needed."

"They're both such nice people," she said. "Victor is hysterical. He actually hit on me on the drive home."

It's nice to be hit on by a younger man, so I could understand her giddiness at the thought. It's just that when the younger man is Victor it kind of takes the fun out of it.

"You certainly seemed to enjoy spending the day with us."

"I did. You're so lucky, Kate. You get to go to work every day, and on such interesting projects."

"I don't *get* to work, Vera. I have to work."

She nodded. "Being wealthy can be such a disadvantage. When I was just out of college some of my classmates took these awful entry-level jobs and worked twenty-hour days with mean bosses yelling at them—"

"It sounds like my life now."

"Well, I didn't. I didn't have to. My father paid for the house, for travel, for clothes, for anything I wanted."

"I'm not the best person if you're looking for sympathy for having too much money."

She smiled. "I know. It's not the worst problem to have. But those awful entry-level jobs my classmates had led to real careers. My father paying my way through life led to, well, it led to nothing. I dabble in things, but I've never really stuck with anything to get as good at it as you are at your job. And you are good, Kate. I was watching the way you handled yourself with everyone. It was really cool."

"Nothing stopped you from having a real career, Vera."

"You're probably right," she sighed. "I did try for a while. I got in business with several friends, opening shops and things. I thought something would click for me, but I never found my own passion. And once the businesses were on their feet, every one of my friends bought me out, and that was the end of the friendship." She turned to face me.

"Other than Frank, you may be the first person to like me regardless of the money."

"I don't really like you, Vera."

She playfully slapped my hand. "Then why are you here?"

That was a good question. To help a woman who had spent twenty years trying to get between me and Frank, I was spending time with another woman—who had actually succeeding in doing just that.

"I'm just trying to make sense of it, you know, everything that happened," I said. "I have so many questions."

"Like?"

"I don't know." I tried to think of a place to start. "Did he give you a ring?"

"What do you mean?"

"The night at the hospital you said you were engaged."

"Oh. No. He said he didn't have the money to buy one, and I didn't care one way or the other. I'm a little old for that sort of thing, don't you think?"

"I don't know. It's a nice tradition."

"You don't have one." She pointed to my wedding ring.

"I did. Lynette, Frank's mom, wanted it back once we separated. It was some kind of family heirloom. She's very into that stuff."

"That's a little pushy. It was your ring."

"It's easier not to argue with Lynette," I said. "Had you set a date?"

She seemed a little uncomfortable, but she smiled. "No. We were waiting until the divorce was final."

"And Frank had told you the divorce was on track?"

She stared at me. "Why?"

"I'm just curious about Frank's state of mind toward the end."

"You think it was suicide?"

"I think . . . we have to consider all the possibilities."

"He wouldn't have, Kate. Put that idea out of your mind. You have nothing to feel guilty about."

"I don't feel guilty."

"Of course you don't. Why should you?"

"Why would Frank commit suicide?"

"He wouldn't. I just said that."

I took a breath and started again. "Vera, according to Frank's attorney he stopped the divorce proceedings two weeks before he died. Did you know that?"

I watched for that telltale blush that appears across the faces of all liars when they're caught. All but the best liars. It wasn't there.

Vera turned her face from me and looked out at the water for a long time. She was breathing a little heavy.

"Are you okay?" I asked.

"I just don't get it."

"You don't get what?"

"Three days before he died he signed a lease on a space."

"For an art studio," I said.

"Frank told you." She seemed relieved. "He was nervous about that."

"It wasn't Frank. It was Podeski."

"That wasn't very nice of him. You didn't need that shoved in your face after everything you'd been through."

"Vera. Focus. Tell me about the lease."

"We'd been looking around and we finally found this place. It's actually not that far from your house. It was perfect for him to paint and to maybe have some students in and teach a few classes. That's what he wanted to do."

I'd heard all about Frank's plans over the years, but we'd never had the money to bankroll them, and after the first few years and the first half dozen plans, I'd given up listening. But now it looked like, with Vera's help, he was on the verge of making one idea actually come true.

"Do you have a lease or something?" I asked.

"Why? Don't you believe me?"

And in a move that was uncharacteristically open and honest, I said what I was thinking. "I don't know what to believe."

Forty-seven

After we'd brought the dogs back to her house, Vera showed me proof. Frank's signature was on the lease dated three days before he died. It was a year's lease on a small space just blocks from our—now my—house. It was an inexpensive place, which was getting harder to come by as Bucktown got trendier. I was surprised with Vera's money he hadn't gone for something more upscale.

"And, I don't know if you want to see this," Vera said, "but I have a video I made the day he signed the lease."

"Why wouldn't I want to see it?"

"I don't know. I just thought . . ." She took a deep breath. "I can't stop watching it myself."

Once it began to play, I understood what she meant. Frank was alive again. He was moving and talking and laughing. And he was happy, more than happy. He was practically giggling as he walked around the space, telling Vera where his easel would go. I wanted to reach out and touch the screen, somehow find a way to brush his hair out of his eyes and feel the warmth of his cheek, but I sat still and watched him.

"I can't wait to start painting again. I feel like I have so many ideas in my head just bursting to get out," he was saying.

"You're so talented." It was Vera's voice, from behind the camera.

"I just feel like it's finally my time to get everything going, you know," he said. "I've wasted a lot of years, but I'm really ready now."

"It's all going to be wonderful from here on out," Vera said.

"I love you," he said to her.

There it was. The punch in the gut I'd felt over and over since the first time I'd heard Vera's name. I turned the camera off.

If this really was one of my shows, I'd be in heaven: a video of a happy man on the verge of realizing his dream, who won't live to see the weekend. The point of using the videos on TV is to give some insight into the person, but after watching the video, I only had more questions. If Frank was a man desperate to come home to his wife, as Neal and Alex seemed to think, why was he telling another woman he loved her?

"Do you have a key to the place?" I asked.

"No. I looked for it a few days ago. I called the landlord to tell him about Frank and he asked for the key. It might have been among the things I gave you yesterday."

"I'll check."

"Why do you need it?"

"Just to make sure none of his possessions are there."

"They aren't. He kept everything here."

"What about his paintings? Because there are several that are actually mine. He painted them for me as gifts for our wedding and anniversaries."

She seemed confused. "You have his paintings. He said he left them in your garage."

"I don't have them, Vera."

"Of course you do," she said. "I told Frank he could bring them here. God knows there's plenty of room. But he didn't want to. He said that he had everything neatly stored away at the house, and since he was going to bring it to the art studio, he didn't think there was any point in moving it twice."

"But I don't have them," I said again.

"Well, go home and check, because you must have them." She seemed on the verge of hyperventilating. "Those paintings were everything to Frank. And if they're gone, if everything he created is gone . . ."

"Calm down. I'm sure they're somewhere. I'll look in the garage again. And I'll call his landlord. It's possible he had started to move some of his stuff there."

She took a deep breath. "It's stupid to get so upset. None of them were even mine."

"But they were Frank's, so they're important to you," I said, sounding kinder than I wanted to.

"He had planned this painting for me. He just didn't get around to it. He made a few sketches, so I know what it would have looked like, and it would have been really beautiful. It was going to be me in the garden with the flowers behind me and the sun hitting across my shoulder. Of course, he couldn't do it until he'd cleaned up the garden first."

I looked out the window to the overgrown bushes in her backyard. "It doesn't look like he got very far."

"He was working on it little by little. I suggested we just hire a gardener. I had one for years but I thought it was better for the environment if I just let it grow wild." She laughed. "Frank said a gardener was a waste of money. He said he would get it back under control, grow some vegetables and some fruits, and maybe someday cook me dinners from our very own garden."

That sounded familiar. I guess there was a certain comfort in knowing he was just reusing the old material—the misunderstood artist, the passionate cook—but it did make me wonder if there was a single moment of our marriage that belonged just to me and hadn't been warmed over for her.

I got up to leave. "You can always frame the sketches."

"You're right. I don't know what I'd do without you."

"I'm sure you'll figure it out. Why don't you call your friend Susan? Maybe go out and have a nice dinner."

I was getting anxious to get out of there. Vera was fine to be with, I was discovering, as long as Frank wasn't the subject.

"Susan is a little annoyed at me," she said. "But I will have a nice dinner. Just do me a favor and call me if you find the paintings."

"Who else would I call?"

I meant it to be sarcastic but as I walked out of her beautiful home I wondered, who else would I call? Vera thought her family fortune had kept her from real friendships but what was my excuse? My friends were really the wives of Frank's friends, and many of them had disappeared at the time of the separation. I had coworkers, like Andres and Victor, but I really only saw them when we were working together. And I had family, but we had nothing in common except a bloodline and a stubborn streak.

Depressing as it was, Vera might have been the closest thing to a friend I'd made in a while. And that would have been great, except for the pesky and uncomfortable reality that she was my husband's mistress, and possibly his killer.

For my entire career, I had scrupulously avoided working in the lowest forms of reality TV—the group of strangers who are forced together under the guise of finding true love, losing weight, or winning large sums of money. The real point of these shows, of course, is to watch people having highly amusing emotional breakdowns as they form temporary connections with people they secretly plan to betray.

Now I was doing the same thing as those awful contestants. I was going back and forth, shifting allegiances between Lynette and Vera. And for what? So I could uncover more of Frank's secrets, see him happy with someone else, and wonder what could have been?

Forty-eight

I went to bed late and didn't sleep. At seven I got up and made myself breakfast. As I sat on the front steps, drank coffee, and watched people rush to work, I tried to put myself in a good mood. One of the advantages of being freelance is that you often have Mondays off. Not that I had nothing to do. I had to do what I'd promised—figure out what had happened to Frank, and to his paintings. And it wasn't going to be easy.

One sweep of the garage that morning confirmed what I already knew. There were no paintings. All I discovered was that Frank had thoughtlessly rearranged some of the boxes on his last visit to the house, putting the box with fragile Christmas ornaments underneath the heavy one with mementos of happier days. I looked in the basement and attic and still found no paintings. If Frank had intended to keep them at the house, then he would have left the ones that were hanging exactly where they were. He had made a point of taking them and of telling me he was taking them. Why would he have done that if he were only going to store them in the garage?

But that wasn't what bothered me as I started my day. It was the sight of him yesterday, so happy and so ready to start a new life. It would have been easy to say that his beaming smile on that videotape was because Vera's money was buying him his dream, but it would have been a lie. Frank could have been painting these last few years. I hadn't been supportive but I hadn't stopped him. He didn't even need Vera for a space to paint. We had a basement, a garage, and a spare bedroom. All of which sat unused. And as Victor pointed out, a man in love can't be swayed by another woman's money.

There was the possibility that he'd gotten caught up in her image of him. Vera clearly believed in Frank with the same wide-eyed certainty that I'd had twenty years ago. That seemed a much more likely cause of his happiness. Maybe he just wanted that again—that fleeting moment when each person is perfect to the other—before it all returns to earth. Before she stops shaving her legs every day and he stops listening when she talks. That I could understand. And even envy.

But there was something more than that. Whenever I pictured him standing in that empty space, smiling and laughing and saying, "I love you," I was struck by the genuineness of his affection, the comfortable, easy way he had with her. There was nothing about him that seemed like a man looking for an escape. And if he was really in love with Vera, she had no motive to kill him.

Except—and it kept nagging at me—why did he stop the divorce? Why was he reading *Travels with Charley*? Why did he tell Neal he wanted to come back to me?

And if those things were true, why open an art studio with Vera?

I could have spent the whole day asking those questions and coming up with nothing. Lucky for me, Mike had other plans. I'd barely finished my coffee when he called.

"Talked to the network," he said without bothering to first say hello. "We figured it out. Two-part special. In the first part is the stuff we already have. Theresa is missing. Heartbroken mother, blah, blah, blah. Then we end with finding the purse at the scene. Second part is the discovery of the body, a second round of interviews. We still end the show with 'If you have information . . .' but instead of finding Theresa, it's about finding the killer. It will be the premiere episode of the series, so it makes us look like we helped crack the case. It'll be great. Three extra days of shooting, no overtime. Start making calls. We need this shit ASAP. And listen, Kate, no more slipups."

Then he hung up. In the entire call, the only word I'd said was "hello."

"She'd better not come back from the dead, or Mike will have my ass," I said, finally in the good mood I'd been searching for. Nothing like an insane boss to make me feel normal again.

"This is an ongoing police investigation, involving a number of departments," Detective Rosenthal told me when I called her about a second interview. "She was found in an unincorporated area of Cook County, so we're working with the sheriff's office. We are all focused on solving the case and bringing her killer to justice. That's all I can tell you, except that we won't be doing any additional interviews at this point. I'm sorry."

"Are you sure it's Theresa?"

"Off the record? Yes. There was jewelry found with the remains that were identified as belonging to Theresa. We're still waiting for dental records, though. Sorry, Kate, I wish I could help you more."

"I understand." I'd almost told her about the dead bird and all the other odd happenings in my life, but I just couldn't bring myself to go into the mess that was my life while she was immersed in Theresa's death. "If there is anything else . . ."

Instead of saying good-bye, Rosenthal hesitated. "Let me get back to you tomorrow." Then she hung up.

I called the others, asking for another interview. Gray and Wyatt, not surprisingly, agreed. Julia said she'd have to talk it over with David and get back to me. Linda kept me on the phone for nearly twenty minutes telling me, again, what a perfect daughter Theresa had been, before eventually agreeing to another interview. Jason didn't pick up any of the three times I called.

I got an e-mail from Mike telling me to expect a package with dubs, that is, copies of the tapes we'd already shot. He asked me to review them before shooting the next interviews. There were fifteen hours of tapes, and we were shooting again in a few days, but I replied with a simple "You bet" and made the necessary, but completely futile, middle-finger hand gesture.

Three hours later when the dubs arrived I made myself a large cup of coffee and popped the first DVD into my computer. It was the interview with Linda. I made notes of the best sound bites, the ones I would use for the final script.

Usually there are far too many good bites that end up cut from the show, but this time we had the luxury of a two-part special, which was especially good in this case because I could really go in so many directions. I had Linda and Gray telling me that Theresa was a saint. I had enough to create a Wyatt-Theresa-Jason love triangle, and bites from Julia suggesting a dark side.

And there was the money. I'd held back from telling Mike about it. He would have been proud of how I'd found out, and he would definitely want to play it up, but I wasn't sure I wanted to. Maybe Rosenthal had kept it a secret because something ought to be secret. Maybe finding out the entire truth wasn't as helpful as I'd once thought.

I watched Rosenthal's interview, which was, as I remembered, the standard police kind with succinct impersonal answers, but it would be a nice counterweight to the emotional stuff. I made a note of her best sound bites, then I popped in the DVD with Gray's interview on it.

There was something riveting about it, something behind all of that attractiveness and polish that I couldn't take my eyes off. Now that I had the chance to look without the need to be polite, I could study him. I noticed that a few times during the interview his eyes darted, just for a second, toward the camera. It was what people did when they were nervous. Why would a man who had been in front of the camera dozens of times, and who was just an acquaintance of the victim, be nervous? I made a note to push him more on his relationship with Theresa and was about to go on to Jason's tape when there was a knock at the door.

A few weeks ago that would have meant nothing to me, but since then I'd found homicide detectives and dead birds on my porch. I grabbed my cell phone, dialed a 9 and a 1, and kept my finger ready to push 1 again, just in case.

Forty-nine

Once I looked through the window, I put the phone down. It was a familiar, if not altogether happy, face.

"Neal?"

Neal blushed a little. "Sorry if I'm getting you in the middle of something."

"You're not. Come in. Shouldn't you be at work?"

"I took a long lunch." He walked in the house and looked around, as if he were unsure of what to do. "The place looks good," he said.

"The place looks exactly the same as the last time you were here, and the thousand times before." I gestured toward the couch.

Neal didn't move.

"Is everything okay?"

"Can I use your bathroom?"

"Of course. I have coffee that's still pretty fresh," I said and disappeared into the kitchen before he had a chance to protest. I poured two mugs of coffee and found some cookies. I put it all on a tray and headed back to the living room.

When I came back Neal was sitting on the couch, nervously folding and unfolding his hands. He stood up when he saw me.

"How chivalrous." I laughed.

"I don't know what you mean."

"Standing up when a lady walks in the room." I put the tray on the coffee table and handed him a mug. "Never mind. Obviously you have something you want to tell me, so why don't you?"

He sat down again and I sat on the chair facing him. I waited. Neal sipped his coffee and stared at the floor. "I've always liked this couch."

"Frank found it at some small shop about a block away," I said. "You know how he only liked buying things from small businesses. He said the quality was better and we were supporting real people, not corporations."

Neal smiled. "God, he would go on about that shit. He tore into me when he found out Beth and I had bought our bedroom set at Pottery Barn. I tried to tell him that real people worked for corporations but he wouldn't hear of it."

I looked at him. "But that's not why you're here. Another trip down memory lane."

"No." He cleared his throat. "I talked to Frank's dad. He told me you were looking into Vera as being the reason Frank died."

"Lynette asked me to."

"When have you cared what Lynette wants?"

I sighed. "Sadly, I have cared my entire marriage. But it's not just that, Neal. I want to know too."

"I think it's a bad idea."

"Why?"

"I just don't think Frank would want you and Vera spending time together."

"Frank doesn't get a vote. And if he did, I'd like to think he'd want his killer to be brought to justice."

"I think it's better to just leave things as they are. I know that's hard for you. It used to frustrate the hell out of Frank the way you were so . . ."

"Anal, pushy, annoyingly persistent?" I'd heard it a thousand times from Frank. "I know it drove Frank crazy. I used to bring this purple binder on our vacations with the plane, car, and hotel reservations printed out, plus a list of the hours and costs of all the sights we wanted to see."

"I remember," Neal said. "He threw it out the window when we all went to Key West."

"And when we got to the hotel, they didn't have our reservation, and we didn't have the confirmation number," I pointed out. "Don't you remember that we had to pay more for the rooms than we'd planned because I couldn't prove we had a reservation?"

He smiled. "Okay. You were right then, and you're probably right now, but there are police detectives involved in this. If Vera—if anyone— killed Frank, they will find out."

"You're forgetting they already have a suspect. Me. I'm not a big fan of their investigative skills so far."

"Just do me a favor, stay away from her." His voice had gotten insistent, even annoyed.

I stood up. What was up with him? "Is this about the fight you had with Frank?"

"Are you accusing me of something?" Neal stood up too and moved his six-foot, three-inch frame close to me. "I played basketball with him the day he died, if you're looking for another suspect."

"What was the fight about, Neal?"

"You. I told him to man up and go back to his wife and stop parading his girlfriend around town. He took her to a restaurant down the street from his dad's office. It was embarrassing."

"That was, what, three weeks before he died?"

"I guess so."

"So if he was anxious to come back to me, why did he take Vera to a restaurant where he could have run into his father?"

"Kate, I've never understood why Frank did the things he did any better than you have."

"And there's something else. Did you know just days before he died he signed a lease for an art space?"

"I don't know anything about that. He told me he was going to start teaching at the community center. I told you about that."

"He must have lied to you."

"He didn't."

"Then what did he say when you gave him that advice outside the restaurant?"

Neal turned white. "I don't know, Kate. Sometimes people make stupid decisions and they don't know how to turn back. Sometimes they need a friend to stop them before it gets out of control."

"Is that what you tried to do?"

"It's what I'm trying to do now."

His voice was getting angrier, and he was moving closer. I could feel my heart beating, my muscles tense. Though I'd known Neal since I was a junior in high school I was suddenly aware of how rarely we'd been alone together. I walked to the front door and opened it, relieved to see two of my neighbors chatting on the street.

"Thanks for the advice, Neal."

"That's exactly what Frank said. And obviously he didn't take it."

Neal slammed the screen door behind him and headed for his car at practically a run.

Fifty

The next morning Detective Rosenthal called. She wanted a favor.

"We often tape funerals when we're looking to see who comes, how people behave," she said. "It can make people nervous, the police taping them, even though we try to be discreet. I was thinking if you taped the funeral tomorrow, people would assume it was for the show and wouldn't think twice about it."

"Could we use the footage on the air?"

"I talked to Linda Moretti, and she was fine with it, so I suppose so. I just want to look at it too."

"It's okay with me," I said.

It wasn't really up to me to let the police look at the footage since I didn't actually own it. The network and Ripper Productions owned it. But I figured (and I was right) that Mike would be so excited to get an all-access pass to Theresa's funeral that he'd happily make dubs for the police. And more importantly, it was another line for the press release on how the show had helped the investigation.

The only problem was that it would make the three days of shooting a little tricky. No one wanted to be interviewed on the day of the funeral, so all the re-interviews would have to be crammed into the other two shoot days Mike had allowed. The only way to make that happen was to cut down on travel and setup time. And that meant finding a central location and having the interview subjects come to me.

I spent several hours hunting down an inexpensive conference room in the Loop, which would work well for Gray, Julia, and Wyatt. I could only book it for Thursday, which meant I had a day between the funeral and the interviews, For Linda and possibly Jason I found a small restaurant in Bridgeport that only opened for dinner. We could use the place Friday for a hundred bucks as long as we were out before five.

Then I went shopping for a new funeral outfit. I didn't really want to use the dress I wore for Frank's, which was all black and very widowy. I wanted something that would be practical enough to keep up with Andres and conservative enough to be appropriate for the occasion, but not all black since I wasn't really one of the mourners. It's a complicated thing to dress for the funeral of a woman whose death you are exploiting for ratings. I was just hoping that Victor put the same thought into it that I was.

Turned out I needn't have worried. Victor showed up in a dark navy suit with a white shirt and a gray tie. His hair was a normal brown, his nose ring had been removed, and even the tattoo that crept up the side of his neck seemed muted. Andres looked equally dapper in a charcoal suit and red tie.

"We clean up nice," I said.

"Are you going to be able to work in those?" Andres pointed to my shoes, dark gray pumps with three-inch heels that peeked out from my gray trousers. I'd found a black silk tank with a matching silk cardigan on sale, and I was feeling pretty for the first time in a while.

"No idea," I admitted as I looked down at my shoes. I normally dressed in practical flats or gym shoes. "I just thought they were cute."

"Now that we're all dressed up, what's the plan?" Andres asked.

"We hang back, shoot people as they go into the church, and shoot the funeral mass from the back. Then we go to the graveside ceremony. Obviously we want to focus on our interview subjects and Theresa's family, but we're here by the grace of Detective Rosenthal, so we have to shoot every face we can. That means sweeps of the crowd and anything that seems odd or out of place."

"Sounds easy. Unless you know something I don't."

"Not me. But someone coming today might."

We had been the first to arrive so we set up the camera a discreet distance from the Catholic church where the funeral mass would be held, but with a good view of the front door. Victor and I flanked Andres, as we had at the coffee shop. Within twenty minutes, people started to gather on the steps of the old church, hugging and offering comfort. It was a large crowd; probably much of the Bridgeport neighborhood had come to say good-bye. It was full of young faces who must have been friends of Theresa, but I didn't recognize any of them.

After a few minutes of shooting, I saw Detective Rosenthal in a dark-blue pantsuit talking with several men I assumed to be detectives. While two of the men stayed outside the church, Rosenthal and another man went inside.

I looked around. There were two uniformed officers a fair distance back, but they seemed to be more in charge of crowd control than looking for murder suspects. As the time for the funeral got closer, more and more people arrived and it was getting harder to find the people I knew in the growing crowd.

Then I spotted Julia and David. I watched them walk over to an older couple, greeting them warmly. Julia's parents, maybe. They were both touching Julia, who seemed inconsolable and only interested in leaning into her husband. David was looking around, seeing, I assumed, who else was there. When he spotted us, I thought he mouthed something but I couldn't tell what it was. I just hoped Andres had caught it on tape.

Gray came with his wife, an icy blonde I recognized immediately from the photograph in his office. He hugged Julia and the other couple and then spoke to David, who turned and pointed directly at us. Gray didn't seem surprised. He just nodded and seemed to be explaining the situation to David and the others. When he was done, he gestured toward the door of the church and the group moved inside.

After another few minutes of only seeing people I didn't recognize, I saw Wyatt, who seemed to be alone. He walked through the crowd and into the church without speaking to anyone. Given his description of his relationship with Theresa, it's possible he only knew a few of her friends.

Ten more minutes passed. The crowd had moved inside and only a handful of people were still outside the church. I saw Gray, Wyatt, and David reemerge and stand on the steps talking with a priest and two other men. Finally, a hearse pulled up in front of the church followed by a long black limousine.

Linda and Tom emerged from the limo and stood waiting by the hearse. They looked tired and vacant. I knew the feeling all too well. I felt intrusive for continuing to shoot, but it was what Mike wanted and what Rosenthal wanted, so I stood there and let Andres continue to roll tape.

The funeral director opened the doors of the hearse and began to slowly pull the casket out. Gray, Wyatt, Tom, David, and the two other men stepped forward to be Theresa's pallbearers. At the sight of her daughter's coffin, Linda collapsed.

Fifty-one

"Stop tape," I said to Andres.

"You sure?"

"Detective Rosenthal doesn't need this. And if Mike has this, he'll use it."

Victor gave me a look that said, "Isn't that the point?" but Andres put the camera down. Tom and Gray helped Linda over to a bench outside the church, where she sat sobbing for several minutes. The priest sat with her, offering whatever comfort you can in a situation like this, but it was obvious it meant nothing to Linda.

Andres let the camera rest on the hood of the van. "Where's Jason?"

"Is he here? I didn't see him arrive."

"Didn't you call him?"

"No." I looked over at Andres. "I'm not that much of a monster."

"Sorry. I just figured since you called him the day of the search . . ."

He didn't finish the sentence so it hung there. He just figured that I would place a good shot over my humanity, that's what he didn't say. Normally, of course, he was right but then I'd never had to attend the funeral of one of my stories.

"I am a little surprised Jason didn't just show up anyway," Victor threw in. "He seems the kind of guy who would want to pay his last respects."

"And get his ass kicked again?" Andres shook his head. "Not coming here today is the first thing that guy's done that makes any sense to me."

I saw Linda get up and walk back toward the hearse. She was still crying but she was holding tight to Wyatt's arm. Tom walked next to her but she seemed not to notice him.

"It's okay now," I said.

Andres began shooting again, got the casket as it came out of the hearse and as the six men accompanied it inside. Once they'd all gone in, we moved quickly to the back of the church for the mass.

While the words and songs were remarkably similar to Frank's funeral, the mood in the church was very different. With Frank we had all been in shock, but with Theresa this was, at least for some, an inevitable outcome. They had mourned her slowly, over more than a year. They were exhausted from mourning. I could feel a sad relief from some of them, but only some of them. Tom glared at everyone and everything, even his sister's casket. David pivoted toward us, scowling. Even Gray, who I could only see from the side, looked tense and irritated.

When the mass ended, we quickly darted outside and found a space at a respectful distance and waited for the mourners. As Andres got tape of every person who exited the church, Detective Rosenthal walked over.

"So far, so good," she said. "I was a little worried."

"Jason."

"Jason, Tom, Linda. There's a lot of emotion here today."

"Any leads?" I asked. "Off the record?"

She took a deep breath and seemed about to say something. I walked her away from the camera, and from the camera mic, which would have picked up our conversation. The sound wouldn't be great, which is why I'd never use it in an interview, but it would be there. And Mike might not be as picky about sound quality as I was.

Rosenthal looked around before speaking. "I heard something about a dead bird being found on your front porch."

I turned red. "From who?"

"Another detective."

"Podeski?"

She nodded. "He called me to get my take on it."

"There were some concerns about my husband's death." I was looking for an explanation that was simple and fast, though I was pretty sure she had already had the long version from Podeski.

"He told me what was going on. I'm so sorry, Kate, I had no idea."

"In case you're wondering, I didn't kill my husband." I figured it was better to just say it.

She waved me off. "Of course not. That's just Podeski playing all angles. And that's not what he wanted to talk to me about anyway. He called because he wanted to know if someone from this case could be threatening you."

"Seriously?"

"He's got a reputation for being very dogged. Which is a good thing for a homicide investigator, but I can see how he might get on people's nerves."

"You know him?"

She nodded. "I worked in major case with him briefly when I was just starting in that department. He's really a good guy. I know he doesn't have the best manners in the world, but he's got a good heart."

"What did you tell him?"

"To be honest I didn't have much to tell him. As far as I know there's no reason for any of these people to go after you. You're just filming a television show, not looking to solve the case, right?"

"I couldn't if I wanted to, and believe me I don't," I assured her. "I leave that sort of thing to you guys."

She seemed relieved. "Well, just be careful. And if anyone does strike you as acting strange . . ."

"They all strike me that way."

She laughed. "Well, dangerous strange. Let me know." She stopped and seemed to consider something. "You're re-interviewing everyone."

"Everyone we can."

"If I gave you a few questions to ask, would you ask them?"

"You can't ask questions?"

"I will. It's just that you might get more interesting answers."

"Sure," I said. "Speaking of questions, you haven't answered my question about any leads in the case."

"It's an open investigation."

"Detective, play fair. If you want to use me to conduct a police interview, that's fine. I just want to know why I'm asking."

"Okay. Theresa was wearing a silver chain bracelet the day she disappeared. According to Linda, there were two charms on it, a nurse's cap and the Daley Plaza Picasso," she said.

She was referring to the large sculpture Pablo Picasso made as a gift to the city in the late 1960s. It sits in front of the county court building where countless lawyers, people on their lunch hours, and tourists enjoy trying to figure out what it's meant to represent.

"She'd just gotten the bracelet a few weeks before and she'd had the charms reinforced so she wouldn't lose them. When we found her, she was still wearing the bracelet, but the charms were gone," Rosenthal said. "I don't think they just fell off. But just in case, we searched the area and couldn't find them. But we did find something else. There were five hairs caught in the bracelet."

"Left by her killer in a struggle?" I asked.

She shrugged. "We don't know. The hairs didn't have roots, so getting a DNA match is next to impossible, and anyway we don't have DNA samples from any of the possible suspects. I doubt the killer will offer it up at this stage. If I bring up the bracelet, the killer might clam up, but they might not be so careful around you."

"And the money? The ten thousand dollars. Do you want me to ask about that?"

"How do you know about that?"

I smiled.

"There's an explanation for it."

"And that is?"

She thought for a moment before speaking. "None of your business."

I couldn't argue with that, though I was about to try when I saw Andres packing up the camera. If we were going to the grave site, we had to leave.

"E-mail me your questions and I'll ask them," I said.

"Thanks. And seriously, Kate, if you feel nervous about any of these guys, let me know."

"It's fine," I said. "I'm really not that worried about it."

And I wasn't, at that moment. I was even relieved that Rosenthal knew my situation and was confident about my innocence. Until it occurred to me that Podeski might be playing the same game as Rosenthal—using a sympathetic substitute to get information he had failed to get.

Fifty-two

Only about thirty people attended the graveside ceremony to watch Theresa's body be lowered into the ground. Linda barely got through it, but other than that, it was a quiet, if sad, event.

I kept looking around for any sign of Jason watching from a distance, but there was none. Like Vera, he must have considered the feelings of the family and stayed away.

We had packed up the car and were in the midst of our daily argument about where to eat lunch when Gray approached.

"Kate, can I talk with you a moment?"

"A moment," I said. "My crew is on the clock and I need to get to another shoot." It was a lie. I had no idea how I was going to fill our afternoon. We already had all the B-roll we needed. It was just that the last time Gray had wanted to speak with me he'd told me about the results of Frank's autopsy. I wasn't ready for any more revelations.

He took my elbow and walked me several feet away from Andres and Victor. He handed me a pink pastry box tied with a ribbon.

"Linda asked me to give these cookies to you, as a thank-you for coming to the funeral," he said.

"She really doesn't need to keep thanking me. Especially now."

"I think it just gave her and Tom something to do these last couple of days. She gave me a box, and I think Detective Rosenthal got one too."

I held up the pastry box. "Please tell her thank you." I started to turn away, but Gray stopped me.

"That's not what I wanted to talk to you about. Not only that. I got a call right before the funeral. It was Vera. She's been pulled in for questioning about your husband's death."

"Why?"

"No idea. She asked me if I would come to the station and act as her lawyer."

"Then you should go."

"She wants you to come too."

It was very tempting to find out what the police had on Vera, but going was impossible. I pointed back to the crew.

"I'm working today. I can't just cancel a shoot midday. My boss would have to pay the crew for the whole day and I'd get killed for it."

"There's no way around that?"

"Kate." Andres called for me from the driver's seat of his van.

I walked over to him. "You'll never believe this."

"We heard." Andres pointed to the camera, which was rolling, and to Victor, who had the boom mic just peeking out from the window in the backseat. While a camera mic won't pick up much beyond a few feet, a boom mic could pick up every word Gray and I had said.

"You were listening to my private conversation."

Victor leaned forward. "I don't trust the guy. He did Theresa in and now he's going after you."

"It's sweet of you guys to be concerned, but you obviously know this isn't about me. It's about Vera."

Andres shut the camera off. "Don't you want to know what the police have on her?"

"Yeah," I admitted. "But Mike will want to see what else we shot today. What am I going to tell him?"

Andres looked back at Victor, who nodded. "Because we love you, and because this is a really weird situation . . ."

"And because I don't like working in a suit," Victor jumped in.

Andres rolled his eyes. "We were supposed to have tomorrow off, right? We're not doing the interviews until Thursday and Friday?"

"Right."

"We can do a half day tomorrow and shoot whatever you want. No extra charge. Mike will never know the difference."

To people like Andres, Victor, and me, time really is money. We usually get paid by the day. As a producer my day can be three hours or fifteen and I get paid the same amount, but a camera crew usually has ten hours at the normal rate and then time and a half after that. If the day ends early, there is no discount. Which is why guys like Mike make sure I pack every day with enough shooting to last ten hours but not a minute more. To give me a half day is an act of exceptional generosity.

I squeezed Andres's hand. "We can start the day with lunch. Wherever you want."

After they pulled away, I got into Gray's Porsche for the half-hour drive from Bridgeport to Area 3 headquarters.

"You and Vera must be very close," I said as Gray sped through a red light.

"Not really. We've just known each other a long time."

"Is she a friend of your wife's?"

He looked at me, puzzled. "No. They wouldn't have much in common."

"What does that mean?"

"My wife likes to shop. Vera likes to . . ."

I almost said, "break up people's marriages," but I refrained. "She seems very into her dogs," I said instead.

"Does she still live in that town house her dad bought?"

"It's quite beautiful."

"So you've been inside?"

"Yes. Does that surprise you?"

"Considering she's your husband's mistress, it kind of does." He pressed the accelerator and I could see we were now going close to seventy on a street with a posted limit of forty-five.

"Are you training for the Indianapolis 500 or something?" I asked.

Gray put his foot on the brake, bringing the car to the posted speed. "Sorry. One of my vices."

I smiled. "So you have vices? You present yourself as such a do-gooder."

"Sorry to hear that. I just like to do the right thing."

"Except when it comes to traffic laws."

He laughed. "I never say I'm perfect. I say I try. That's it. If there's one thing I've learned from politics it's you can survive anything but hypocrisy. It's why Bill Clinton kept high approval ratings during the whole Monica Lewinsky scandal, while at the same time two Republican House leaders resigned after their affairs became public. Clinton never pretended to be a perfect husband so no one blamed him when he wasn't."

"Are you a perfect husband?"

"What's that got to do with anything?"

"Well, it's part of your image, isn't it? Adoring husband."

"Given your recent experience I can understand your attitude, but not all husbands cheat, Kate."

"Not even with Theresa?"

Gray glanced toward me for a moment and then pointed toward the nondescript police building on the corner of Belmont and Western.

"I have to make a call so I'll drop you off and park in the lot," he said. "Just wait for me inside. Don't ask for Podeski until I get there. Understand?"

"Perfectly."

As I reached for the door handle, Gray touched my arm. "Not even with Theresa."

I nodded and got out of the car. Gray hit the gas and sped off toward the parking lot.

Fifty-three

I did as I was told and waited for Gray to arrive, which he did a few minutes later. He knew the desk sergeant, as well as many of the detectives, and even greeted Podeski like an old friend.

"I'd like to see my client," he said once the friendly chitchat had ended. "I assume she's been read her rights."

"She's not under arrest," Podeski said. "We're just asking questions."

"Not since she asked to speak to me, I hope."

"We explained that she should wait for you, but she has been talking. We couldn't actually get her to stop. But you'll be happy to know she hasn't said anything about the death of her boyfriend." Podeski glanced toward me. "She's been telling us about her visit to the Brookfield forest preserve with Mrs. Conway. She seemed very interested in how we investigate a homicide. Fact is, she's been asking us more questions than we've been asking her."

"She's like that," I said. "She likes to get involved." Once again I was defending Vera to Podeski, with no reason why I should.

"You two have become quite chummy, haven't you?"

"I wouldn't say that. I'd say, given the circumstances, we're both just trying to make the best of it until we can put this behind us and get on with our lives."

"So why is Vera being questioned?" Gray asked, bringing the conversation back to the reason why we were here.

Podeski turned his large body toward Gray. "I went by her place this morning for a chat. I had a few questions to ask her about the situation at Mrs. Conway's house. The dead bird and the break-in. I just wanted to make sure it wasn't coming from her."

"What break-in?" Gray looked toward me.

"Long story," I said.

"We had a nice conversation," Podeski continued. "She even showed me around the place after I told her I loved the old houses."

"You searched her house," Gray said.

"With her permission."

The two men stared at each other, both jaws tensed. I sensed a pissing contest about to begin. I inched between them. "What did you find?"

"She has a foxglove plant in her backyard," Podeski said. "And it's missing some of its leaves near the top."

"And those are the best leaves for extracting digitalis." I finished his thought.

Gray snorted. "That's crazy. You're saying she killed someone by poisoning him with the leaves of a plant in her own backyard?"

"It is a little Sherlock Holmes, I know, but it happens. Some people like to get creative with their murders."

"Vera doesn't know anything about that garden," I said. "She had a gardener and then let it grow wild. I don't think she's ever pulled up a weed back there."

Podeski looked at me, an amused expression spreading across his face. "How do you know about foxglove, Mrs. Conway?"

"I looked it up on the Internet."

"Well, there you see. I'll bet Ms. Brigham could have done that too." He turned back to Gray. "Mr. Meyer, you can talk to your client if you like while I get Mrs. Conway some coffee."

Gray stood squarely in front of Podeski, his three-thousand-dollar suit within inches of Podeski's Salvation Army castoffs. "You said my client wasn't under arrest, so why don't you bring her to me, and I'll take both women somewhere else for coffee."

Podeski stood toe-to-toe with Gray for a moment then backed away. "Mrs. Conway, you can sit at my desk over there. Your friend left her sweater and tote bag on the chair, but I'm sure you can look after them while Mr. Meyer and I retrieve Ms. Bingham."

I picked up Vera's sweater, a bright-pink cotton cardigan with a designer label, and rested it on my lap. I looked around and saw that no one was paying attention to me, so I reached into her tote bag. There was the usual stuff. Her driver's license placed her age at forty-one, four years older than me, which I had pretty much guessed. She'd put her weight at one twenty-five, which made me smile. Not because it was probably thirty pounds off the truth, which was also the case on my license, but because Vera didn't strike me as being particularly vain.

The rest of her wallet contained a half dozen credit cards, a photo of Frank, and a voter's registration card. She had a dog-eared paperback of *Anna Karenina* with a bookmark at the halfway point and a cell phone.

It probably didn't mean anything but she had said her friend Susan was upset with her. I scrolled through the address book of her phone and found Susan's number. I'd barely copied it onto a scrap of paper from Podeski's desk when Gray and Vera emerged from a back room.

Vera came toward me, arms outstretched.

"No hugging," I said.

"Right. I keep forgetting you hate that."

Fifty-four

"What about the break-in?" Gray asked once we had settled into a booth at an upscale European-style coffeehouse near Vera's home.

We'd ordered cappuccinos and apple torte and I was enjoying the aroma while I waited. The surroundings were elegant enough to make me almost forget that I was with two people I didn't really want to spend time with, discussing a topic I didn't want to discuss.

"Vera is your client," I reminded Gray. "And she's a suspect in the crazy stuff that's been going on at my house, and my husband's death. I'm not really sure we're on the same side."

"I didn't do either of those things," Vera chimed in.

As she spoke, the coffee and food arrived. Vera and I dug in, but Gray pushed his coffee aside.

"Do you honestly think Vera killed your husband?"

"Do you have anyone better in mind?"

"No," he admitted. "I just know that Vera isn't capable of that. What about Frank? Could he have taken the leaves and, I don't know, mistaken them for something else?"

"The leaves do look similar to another plant called comfrey. I found a few sites that sell it for medicinal purposes," I said.

"They also look like salad greens," Vera offered. "You know, the kind you find in fancy salads."

Gray shot Vera a look. Her helpfulness would make her a difficult client if it ever came to an actual arrest. He turned his eyes to me. "Maybe Frank made some kind of salad or something and used the leaves."

"I don't think so," I said. "It would be like Frank to grab stuff from the garden, but I don't see him mistaking it for salad greens or comfrey. He went through this phase where he was really into gardening. He read a ton of books and took a few classes at the Botanic Garden.

I looked at photos of both plants. The leaves look the same to me. But for someone like Frank, I just don't see it."

"That leads us back to Vera," Gray said. "At the moment I don't know how I'm going to explain it."

Vera smiled. "Guys, I'm not a child. I don't need either of you fussing over me. I didn't kill Frank. Maybe my word doesn't mean anything. Probably it shouldn't. But the reason I let Podeski wander through my house is because I had nothing to hide. And as far as Kate's break-in goes . . ."

I waved her off. "I don't know about Frank, but I don't see you killing a bird and then coming back three days later, putting him in a shoe box, and leaving him on my porch."

"It is a bit macabre, isn't it," she said.

Gray sipped his coffee, then sighed. "Whoever it is has a flair for the dramatic."

"That could be a few people," I said. That list included Wyatt, Linda, and even, on occasion, me. But it wasn't what I wanted to think about. I sat back against the leather seat and bit into my dessert.

An hour later, despite Gray's persistence, I begged off getting a ride home, claiming I had errands to run. Vera wanted to walk home, and Gray said something about going to his office downtown.

"Are you sure I can't drop you off on my way?" he said, once we'd said good-bye to Vera.

"No. I've got to pick up groceries and make a few other stops. But I'll see you the day after tomorrow."

"Another interview. I really hate interviews but it's for a good cause." He paused. "You're very nice to her, Kate. I know Vera's a good person, but under the circumstances no one would blame you if you hated her."

"It wasn't all her fault."

"You can't blame yourself."

"I meant Frank."

He nodded. "It's hard, isn't it? Marriage, I mean. You make a promise to one person and then you meet someone else, someone you might like more, might be more suited to, and there's nothing you can do about it."

His eyes, his startlingly green eyes, were staring into mine. Suddenly I was aware of the way his crisp white shirt accentuated the muscle on his arm and the casual way he held his suit coat. It was the way he got to people, I realized. People not used to having the attentions of someone with his charm and good looks.

"I don't know if Frank was suited to Vera." My voice was harder than it needed to be.

"I didn't mean . . . ," he started. "I just really admire the way you've handled this. I don't think everyone would be as generous as you."

"Thank you." As much as I was trying not to be won over, I found myself grateful for the compliment.

"You sure I can't give you a ride?"

"Errands," I reminded him.

"Okay." He touched my shoulder lightly and then headed off toward his car.

I'd lied about the errands. I just didn't want to talk about Frank or Vera anymore. As soon as I walked away, though, my phone rang and I knew Frank would be back in the conversation.

"Hi, Lynette," I said.

"Kate, dear, I'm so glad I caught you. How has your day gone?"

I hesitated but I found myself telling her anyway. Not about the funeral, but about being called to the police station and about the plant in Vera's backyard.

"That's wonderful, Kate. It sounds like the police are going to arrest her soon. I'm so proud of you."

My feet, which had been in three-inch pumps all day, were finally beginning to hurt. I found a nearby bench and sat.

"The thing is, Lynette, I don't think she did it." There was a pause.

"Based on what?"

That was a good question. "Based on gut instinct, I guess. I know how difficult this has been for you. It's been hard on me too . . ."

"On you?" Her voice was shrill and uncompromising.

What followed was the "talking-to" I'd been getting from my mother-in-law since my wedding. Something about how I needed to remember where my loyalties were, especially after everything Frank's family had done for me. She was about two minutes into her tirade when I heard a scuffle and Alex came on the line.

"Hey, kiddo," he said with forced casualness. "The reason Lynette was calling is that we can't find the cuff links we gave Frank for his wedding. For your wedding."

"It might have gotten mixed up with some of the stuff I took back from Vera," I said. "I'll check when I get home."

"Listen, they were a wedding present, so they're really yours, but we were thinking of giving them to Henry. He just got tenure."

Henry was Frank's younger brother and a history professor at Northwestern University. It wasn't the U.S. Senate seat they wanted for Frank, but at least it gave them bragging rights.

"You can have the cuff links," I said. This whole thing was getting exhausting. I would have given them anything just to be left alone. "Let me check when I get home," I said again. "I'll call you tomorrow."

"Thanks, dear. And don't worry about Lynette. You just do what you think is right, and we'll be one hundred percent behind you."

"I know, Alex, thanks," I said. "Listen, while we're on the subject of Frank's belongings, did he happen to store his paintings at your house?"

"No. Doesn't that woman have them?"

"She said she doesn't. That's okay. Don't worry about it. I'll find them."

I hung up before Lynette could get back on the phone and yell at me about losing her son's legacy or some such nonsense.

I took a cab to my neighborhood then picked up some pasta for dinner. The apple torte was great, but since it was the only thing I'd eaten since breakfast, it was hardly going to keep me going into the evening. I passed a drugstore and remembered I was out of shampoo. After I got that, I stopped at the bank to withdraw some money for the next day's lunch.

"I'm doing errands after all," I said, smiling. A man walked past me but didn't even look. That's the great thing about city living. You can talk to yourself and no one bothers to notice.

I walked the two blocks to the house, grabbed the mail, and went inside. I was looking forward to a relaxing evening and a good night's sleep. But it only took a moment to know my plans had changed.

Fifty-five

All the wedding photos of Frank and me, the ones I'd packed up and stored in the garage months before, were displayed in the living room. They were on shelves, the coffee table, even the couch. There were other photos of us when we were dating, when we first married, when we bought the house, took vacations, celebrated anniversaries, even one taken the week before we split up. Everywhere I looked were images of Frank and me from every part of our life together. Maybe three or four dozen of them. Many of them were in the frames I'd put them in, and stored them in, but some were taken out of the photo albums that had been in the kitchen. And even those were open and propped up against the coffee table. It was as if someone wanted my whole life to flash before my eyes.

I didn't take another step inside. I turned and ran down the steps and down the block until I came to a major street with people and traffic and noise. My feet were pounding in shoes not meant for running, but I would have gone another ten miles if I had to.

I grabbed my cell phone and dialed 911.

"Hello. My name is Kate Conway. There's been a break-in at my house. I need someone to come quickly, and call Detective Podeski of the Area 3 homicide division."

Within minutes two squad cars were on my street. I'd waited at the end of the block until I saw the flashing blue lights and then went running toward them. Podeski arrived just seconds later. He and two other officers went into my house while I waited with a third uniformed officer outside.

It was several minutes before they came out and when they did, Podeski was shaking his head.

"Do you have a place to spend the night?" he asked me.

"Yes, I guess. Is there anybody in there?"

"No. The place is clear. The only area that's been disturbed is the living room. Whoever did it designed it to scare the hell out of you the moment you walked in the door."

"It worked."

"Listen, Mrs. Conway, this is getting serious."

"I didn't do this."

He nodded. "I believe you. I know this is hard and I know you're scared, but you have to think about who might want to do this to you."

"I don't know." I threw up my arms. "You're the one investigating Frank's death. Shouldn't someone be trying to come after you?"

"And you're sure this is about your husband?"

"I don't know. You obviously know about the show I'm working on. I talked with Detective Rosenthal. She told me you called her."

"She didn't think anyone you've interviewed would do this."

"There's nothing else going on in my life. There's Frank and there's the show. That's it."

My voice was getting loud. I was sounding hysterical. I could see a few neighbors standing on their porches, using me for their evening's entertainment. I took a deep breath and leaned against one of the police cars.

Podeski watched me quietly. Then, when I was calm, he said softly, "Whoever did this is trying to send you a message."

"Well, he's doing a terrible job because I have no idea what the message is."

"The good news is that this sicko hasn't tried to hurt you so far."

"I liked every part of that sentence except for the last two words."

I took another deep breath. I tried to think. I knew I was shaking and my heart was pounding, but I had to focus. Podeski was right. Someone was trying to scare me. The only control I had over the situation was not to let myself be scared. I took a third deep breath and looked toward the house.

"I'll need clothes and some toiletries. I just need to go in for ten minutes."

He sent me inside. I walked quickly past the living room, trying not to look at the pictures still displayed there or at the officers who were photographing the display while commenting about how weird it all was.

I went into the bedroom, where everything still looked normal. I grabbed some pajamas, Frank's Springsteen T-shirt, jeans, a white short-sleeved shirt, and some gym shoes. I stuffed them in an overnight bag, slipped off my pumps, put on a pair of sandals, and sat on the bed. Facing me on the dresser was the stuff I'd brought back from Vera's on Saturday, which had been piled on the stuff she'd brought to me before that.

I'd promised Alex I'd look for the cuff links when I got home, and if I didn't I'd have to explain why or face another dressing-down from Lynette. Neither option seemed very attractive.

I got up and carefully searched through the things, moving one piece at a time. There were no cuff links. But they weren't the only thing that wasn't there. Frank's wedding ring was gone.

I opened up the boxes of Frank's old clothes that I'd promised to donate but hadn't yet. I went through each piece but still no cuff links. In the pocket of his favorite jeans I did find what had happened to them, though. There was a receipt for a pair of diamond cuff links from a local pawnshop.

"What the hell did you do that for, Frank?" I asked no one.

"Mrs. Conway, are you okay?" Podeski was at the door to my bedroom.

"I can't find my husband's wedding ring. It was in this pile of his things that I'd left on my dresser. And now it's gone."

"You sure?"

He didn't wait for a response. He strode into the room and went searching through the pile himself. He came up just as empty as I had. We searched the floor around the dressers, the drawers, and finally the whole room. Nothing.

For the next hour I went room by room checking everything, with Podeski standing next to me. We looked for anything else that might be missing. There were a few sauté pans, a large plastic pitcher we used to take on picnics, and a paring knife that I couldn't find, but I figured Frank had taken those, especially since Vera seemed to have revived his love of cooking. Everything of value was still there. Everything but the ring.

Fifty-six

I showed up on Ellen's doorstep with an overnight bag and a stupid story about finding rats in my house.

"This is about that detective," she said before I'd even sat down. "Are you trying to avoid him or something?"

"If I were, I wouldn't have come here," I pointed out. "He knows where you live."

"You didn't come here because you found rats, Kate. So if it isn't the detective, what is it? And I think we both know I will not let up until you tell me."

I took a moment and came up with a plausible story. I hinted that the *Missing Persons* episode I was working on brought me in contact with some drug dealer who didn't like that I might mention his name in the story. I didn't want to be home alone in case he came by to convince me not to include him. It was more interesting and less personal than the truth.

Ellen leaned back, obviously sure she had gotten the full story. "You can have the guest room for as long as you want, but I'm surprised at you, letting some jerk scare you out of your own house."

"I'm a little surprised too," I admitted.

Andres and Victor picked me up at my sister's house at eleven thirty the next morning and we drove south. On the way I told them about my latest adventure and was chewed out for not being more careful.

"I think you should call Mike and tell him that we're canceling the rest of the shoot," Andres said.

"This might not have anything to do with the shoot. It might be about Frank."

"If we cancel the shoot, you'll know for sure."

"That still doesn't tell me who it is or guarantee it will stop," I said. "We'll miss two days' pay for nothing. I can't afford that, can you?"

Andres shook his head. "There has to be a better way to make a living than this."

We stopped first at the clinic that Theresa had saved from closing down. I didn't see it making the finished piece; we had photos of Theresa with the mayor that would cover the voice-over about her award, but it was something to shoot. I left the guys to get the exterior while I went looking for permission to film interiors.

I didn't get it.

"We have patient privacy to consider," the administrator told me. She was a formidable-looking woman, a Sherman tank in pumps, but when I told her why I was getting footage, she melted. "Theresa was a lovely girl, so giving."

"Do you know how she got the money for the clinic? I heard it was a hundred thousand dollars."

"It was. Kept us going until the grant came through. She made some calls. She knew people."

"How? She was a nursing student from a working-class family."

She shrugged. "I don't know. When someone works miracles, you don't ask for details."

"Did you contact the mayor's office? Is that how she got the award?"

"Oh, no. Gray Meyer did that. Have you met him?"

"I have."

"That is a beautiful man," she said, flashing a smile. "He called the mayor, I think. Pretty much set the whole thing up. She was Volunteer of the Year before we'd even received all the money she'd raised."

"How did he do that?"

She laughed. "When Gray Meyer wants something, he gets it. Haven't you figured that out yet?"

I came back out to the van, annoyed. If Gray Meyer had suggested Theresa for the award, why not just say it? It was my job to manipulate people, but ever since I'd started on this story I'd felt like the puppet instead of the puppeteer.

"What's next?" Andres asked as we drove away from the clinic.

I thought about it for a moment. "Let's go back to the coffee shop where Theresa was last seen."

"We already have that," Victor said.

"Not inside."

"Do we need it?" Andres asked.

"Someone is trying to scare the hell out of me," I said. "If it has to do with Frank then it can only be Vera, but if it's got something to do with Theresa's death, then I'm going to find out everything I can about her. And while I'm doing that, you can grab some B-roll. It's perfect." Before he could respond, I got out of the van and walked across the street to Hank's.

Hank's Restaurant was every bit as depressing on the inside as it looked on the outside. The booths were old and worn, as were the waitresses. The menus were laminated but still managed to have stains all over them, and there was a cigarette burn in the No Smoking sign.

"Can I speak to the manager?" I asked a man behind the cash register.

"Why?"

I pointed toward Andres, holding his camera, and Victor, standing behind him, yawning. "We're a camera crew hoping to shoot some footage inside the restaurant."

"I'm the manager. What's it for?"

"A show on Crime TV called *Missing Persons*. It's about Theresa Moretti."

"I remember her."

That surprised me. "You do?"

"Not her," he corrected himself. "I remember the police bringing around her picture."

"Had you ever seen her in here?"

"What did I tell the police?"

"I don't know," I lied. "Let me show you a picture and see if it jogs your memory." I pulled out my laptop and set it up at one of the tables. "Is it okay if they get some shots of the place while we chat?"

The manager looked at Andres. "No customers without their permission," he said.

Andres nodded and he and Victor walked toward the booths.

I pulled up one of the photos of Theresa I'd gotten on disc from Linda. "Does she look familiar?"

"No. Not that it means anything. I don't memorize the customers."

I was about to close my laptop when I got an idea. Rosenthal had said the police had shown Theresa's photos after her disappearance, but she never mentioned whether anyone had passed around pictures of Julia. I grabbed the DVD that had the B-roll we'd taken of Julia and popped it in. On it, she and David were laughing and giggling as they ate cupcakes at the bakery near their apartment.

"Do you recognize her?" I pointed toward Julia. "She might have been the one to suggest this place to meet Theresa."

"She's a pretty woman," he said as he leaned down, resting his hand next to my computer. I could smell the grease from his clothes. "But I don't know her either. I know him, though."

"David?"

"I don't know his name." He leaned closer and studied the images. "Yeah. I know him. He used to come in here pretty frequently. Always ordered the same thing." He straightened up and turned toward the kitchen. "Stacy!"

A waitress turned from a table. "What?"

He pointed to the computer. "You know this guy?"

She took one look. "BLT no mayo, slice of chocolate cream pie."

"When's the last time he was here?" I asked her.

"Is he in trouble?"

"It's about that missing girl," the manager told her.

"Dead girl," I corrected him. "They found her body Saturday."

"Oh, my God," Stacy said. "He looks so nice. He always tipped well too."

"When was the last time he was here?" I asked again.

"You know, it's weird because he stopped coming around about the time that girl disappeared last summer."

I looked back at the smiling image of David as he looked lovingly at his wife. Maybe he knew more about what happened to Theresa than he'd let on. Maybe he knew more about me too.

Fifty-seven

"We call Rosenthal and turn the creep in," Andres said as we drove away from the coffee shop with both the footage and the information we needed.

"For what?"

Victor leaned forward and practically shouted in my ear. "For killing Theresa. For messing with you. And for being an ass wipe."

"All we know," I said, "was that he used to go to that restaurant. That's hardly an arrestable offense. What it could mean is that he told Julia about it. She doesn't have an alibi for the day Theresa disappeared. She said she was shopping alone all day."

Andres pulled the van over. "You think Julia is strong enough to drag Theresa's body to those woods and dig a hole?"

"Properly motivated I think people can do pretty much anything. Besides, she didn't have to park where we did. She could have driven her car into the clearing just outside the wooded area. The body wasn't really that far from there."

"So that's what we tell Rosenthal," Andres said. "This isn't something for us to get in the middle of."

"Somebody is putting me in the middle of it, Andres. I'm not going to just sit on the sidelines."

"But you said that Podeski believes you now. Just tell him, if you don't want to go to Rosenthal."

"He says he believes me. Rosenthal says she believes me. But really what does that mean?" I asked. "I say that all the time. I tell people I'm their friend, that I understand what they're going through, that I care. I've sat across from people in prison for first-degree murder and pretended to like them. Two experienced detectives could be pretending to be on my side because they hope it will lead to evidence that I killed Frank." I was practically shouting.

Andres stared out the car's window. "I think you're getting paranoid."

From the backseat, Victor cleared his throat. "I think she's right."

When the tenseness of the moment had passed, I told them about the pawn ticket I'd found in Frank's jeans and they insisted on coming with me to find out what it meant.

Having never been in one, I'd pictured pawnshops as seedy places operated by guys in wife-beater T-shirts. The pawnshop where Frank had left his cuff links was more like a Walmart for used merchandise with bright lighting, clean floors, and neat displays of jewelry, electronics, and decorative items.

A man in a golf shirt and khaki pants came toward us. "Can I help you?"

I handed him the receipt. "My husband brought these in. Are they still here?"

"They should be," he said after studying the receipt for a moment. "This item was used as collateral for a loan." After a quick search on the computer he confirmed it. "I have them in back. Would you like to claim them?"

"How much?"

"We gave your husband three thousand dollars, so we would need that plus the interest. If you give me a moment I can get you the figure."

"Did he bring any other items in?" I asked. "A wedding ring?"

He glanced down at the computer. "No. Sorry."

I tried again. "What about paintings?"

"From an estate?"

"No. He would have painted them."

He smiled. "I support the arts by going to the ballet, not by buying the work of aspiring artists."

"Of course." I took back the receipt. "I can't get these now but someone will claim them in the next few days."

"That's fine. Just be aware the interest will keep accumulating until the loan is paid. And if the loan is not paid in ninety days, the item is put up for sale."

With that, the man turned toward another customer, an older woman with a plastic bag full of jewelry. Judging by the smile on the man's face as he walked to her, she was a regular customer.

Andres and Victor, who had been lurking in the background, came toward me.

"Aren't you going to get his cuff links?" Victor asked.

"Not me. I'll call his father. Three thousand dollars will mean nothing to him as long as it gets his wife off his back."

Andres held the door open for me as we walked out. "Where now?"

I thought about it for a moment. There were so many places we could go, but I needed time to organize my thoughts. There was no point in running around if I didn't know what exactly I was looking for.

"Can you bring me by the house so I can get clothes for tomorrow? I can't wear jeans to an interview."

Victor and Andres exchanged a look. "Twenty minutes, Kate. And we go in first," Andres said.

When we got to the house, the guys did a sweep before Victor came out to the car to get me.

"It's freaky in there," Victor said.

And he was right. The photos were still on display, or at least half of them were. Andres was piling them in one corner of the living room.

"Get clothes," he barked at me. "And let's get out of here."

I packed a small suitcase with enough clothes to last several days and then rejoined the guys in the living room, which Andres had returned to normal. Victor brought me a pot of hot water with a selection of herbal teas and the cookies Linda had given me at the funeral. He made such a lovely display of the tea bags and cookies that I almost made a joke about what a great wife he'd make someone, but I knew he'd be hurt. So I chose one of the tea bags and dunked it in the hot water while the guys sat, fidgeting.

"What are those?" Victor pointed to the tin of butterscotch candies I'd left on the coffee table.

"They're Scottish," I said. "Vera gave them to me."

"Are they good?"

"I don't know." I grabbed one and popped it in my mouth. They were good. When it was finished I reflexively grabbed another. The three of us sat and chatted as if everything was fine. But none of us took our eyes off the neat pile of photos Andres had made.

"It's so weird," Victor said eventually.

"Told ya." I looked toward Andres, who seemed to be getting comfortable on the leather chair. "I thought you were in a hurry to get out of here."

"It's okay as long as we're with you," Victor said.

"And we were thinking," Andres added, "you need to talk this out. Like, what was Frank up to? He stops the divorce, tells his best friend he's going back to you—"

"Not that you would have taken him back," Victor jumped in. "You could do much better."

Every once in a while, Victor could surprise you.

Andres nodded. "He rents a space with Vera, but he also puts his cuff links up as collateral on a loan. Why? I thought Vera was his sugar mama."

"Maybe he was doing something he didn't want Vera to know about," Victor offered.

That made sense. "Like what?"

Victor pursed his lips. "The guy did seem to play things close to the vest. I get that. I'm a little like that myself. Mysterious, you know. The ladies like that." Andres and I both tried not to smile, as Victor continued talking. "But even a guy like that tells his secrets to someone. So if it wasn't you, and it wasn't Vera, I'd start looking for door number three."

Fifty-eight

Assuming there wasn't another woman, there could be only one other person Frank would have trusted with his secrets. I had the guys drop me off at my sister's and promised to spend the evening resting and watching TV. But I didn't even go inside. Instead I got in my car and drove straight to Neal's house.

As usual, the door to his garage was open, with kids' toys and bicycles littering the driveway. There was one car in the driveway but it didn't look like Neal or Beth was inside the house. Just in case, I parked my car down the street. I wasn't sure what I was going to do, but I had a hunch about something and I wanted to check it out.

I walked into the garage, past the reclining chairs and the mini-fridge and toward the boxes and other junk covered with a tarp. We all have a lot of extra stuff lying around. The storage industry is built on it. But it seemed like too much stuff and too unattractively hidden for a garage with so much on decoration.

And there was something else nagging at me. I hadn't stayed long enough inside my house to really look at what photos were displayed. Some of them were certainly mine, and Neal would have known they were in the garage. But if Neal were looking to make a really big point, and do it quickly, he could have added to the scene with his own photos of Frank and me. He had nearly as many as I did and about half as many as Frank's mother.

I glanced out on to the street to see if any of the neighbors were watching, but it was still early. The kids were at day care or summer camp and the parents at work. I grabbed the edge of the tarp and pulled.

It was a crib. It had been disassembled and placed against the wall. An infant car seat, bassinet, and stroller were pushed up against it.

"We're not planning on having any more kids."

I turned around and saw Neal. The sun was behind him, putting his body in near darkness.

"I thought you had Frank's paintings."

"You have my phone number. If you wanted to find out you could have called." He stepped inside the garage and pressed a button on the side. The door started to lower.

"What's going on, Neal?"

"What's going on is that you are getting out of control. This whole situation is getting out of control. It has to stop, Kate."

He took a few steps toward me. I saw that the side door, the one that led to his kitchen, was within a few feet of me. I saw him walking toward me. More out of instinct than logic, I picked up the car seat and threw it at him.

"What the hell?"

As he was yelling I ran for the door, turned the knob, and found myself in his kitchen, just a few feet from his wife, Beth.

"Kate? What are you doing here? Is something wrong?" she asked.

I turned and saw their three children in the family room just as Neal walked into the house.

"She came to ask me something about Frank," Neal said. "About his paintings."

I tried to sound relaxed, as if everything were normal. "They're missing."

Beth walked over to me and hugged me. "I'm so sorry. I didn't know that. But I guess I haven't been a very good friend to you. Everything has just been so crazy."

She grabbed my arm and moved me to the kitchen counter. As I sat down, Beth put a plate of fruit in front of me. "Neal, get her some lemonade. And a glass for me. We'll sit here and catch up. I feel so bad that I haven't called you."

Neal put our drinks in front of us and stood behind his wife. He glared at me. I ignored him and drank my lemonade. The incident in the garage had left my throat dry and I finished it in two gulps.

"That's okay, Beth. I've been working anyway," I said. "Speaking of which, shouldn't you both be at work?"

"Family vacation." Neal glared at me. "We went to Traverse City. We took the kids to the cherry festival."

Beth smiled. "It was so fun when the four of us went years ago. You remember, Kate." I nodded. "But three kids in a car for six hours each way. Two days in one room of a motel. I don't know what I was thinking. Plus, we missed my nephew's birthday party, so my sister is ready to kill me."

Neal put his arm around his wife, and as he did, he moved her slightly away from me. "Sometimes you have to think about yourself, and the people you love most," he said. "And everyone else can go to hell."

I looked up at the best friend Frank had in the world. "Problem is, it can be tricky to figure out who fits into the category of people you love most and who you'd toss into hell."

I stayed only another five minutes, making some excuse about having to work early. If nothing else, I felt I'd stood my ground with Neal. But it was little comfort. I didn't get any information and by the time I got back to the car, I felt sick. He'd always been my favorite of Frank's friends, right from the beginning. Though he was every bit as popular as Frank in high school, and was known for dating the school A-list, Neal had encouraged our romance. He'd called me Frank's other half because, he said, Frank was the dreamer and I the realist. Together we'd be able to go further than either of us could alone. Except, of course, it turned out that we just got in each other's way. But even when it went bad, Neal was one of the few people to call and offer me support. His hostility now didn't make sense.

By the time I got into the bed in my sister's guest room, my head was spinning. At first, I didn't know if it was stress or something else, but as I was about to turn off the lights I realized that either my sister had repainted the blue room a sickly shade of green, or I was seeing the world with a yellow tinge.

Fifty-nine

The next morning I felt fine. I told myself it was just my imagination, that fear and confusion and the grief that surrounded me, for both Frank and Theresa, were making me sick. Or that the lights were playing tricks on me. I'd been tired and stressed, sleeping in an unfamiliar bed. If it was anything else, I didn't have time to think about it anyway. I had three interviews to conduct and they would, thankfully, take me away from my own problems for the day.

I didn't bother to say anything to the guys. I didn't need another round of warnings. I'd booked a conference room in a Loop hotel, and I arrived determined to focus on the shoot. While Andres and Victor set up, I ordered fruit and bagels along with strong, hot coffee. I hoped the food and caffeine would cure the last of my stomach pains. While we ate, we waited for Gray, who was late once again.

I used the time to prep for the interviews. Rosenthal had e-mailed me a set of questions to ask everyone I interviewed, though I assumed she was interested in the answers of only a few people. I just didn't know which ones. The questions were mostly about the bracelet, though there were some pointed questions about everyone's whereabouts on the day of Theresa's disappearance. And of course I had a few questions of my own I was dying to get answered.

"Sorry. Really sorry." Gray entered the room as if he owned it, shaking hands with Andres and Victor before coming over to me. "Another bad habit, Kate. Habitual lateness."

"You're a busy man," I said and motioned for him to sit in one of the seats we had set out for the interview. "Unless you want coffee first?"

He shook his head. "Wired enough as it is. Thanks. How are things?"

"Fine."

"No more strange happenings at your house?"

Both Andres and Victor stopped what they were doing and turned to Gray.

"Podeski told him," I said. "About the bird and the first break-in."

"The first break-in?" Gray looked at me. "There's been another one?"

"No big deal. The police are getting to the bottom of it." I turned to Victor. "Can you mic him, please?"

"You got it, Kate." Victor made a point of flexing what little muscle he had as he put the mic on Gray's shirt. "We really like working with Kate, you know."

"She seems great," Gray said.

"We're very protective of her."

"It's good she has people looking out for her."

I just shook my head and smiled. "If you're ready, Victor."

"I'm right where you need me." He looked toward Gray. "Inches away."

Gray nodded solemnly, but I could see he was more amused than threatened.

Unfortunately, it was probably the best part of the interview. Gray didn't offer much more about Theresa's disappearance than he had before. He gave me good, if somewhat canned, sound bites about the tragedy of such a young death, but he didn't offer much in the way of insight. It was only when I got to Rosenthal's questions that things got interesting.

"Do you remember where you were the day she disappeared?"

"No. It was over a year ago. Do you remember where you were a year ago?"

I didn't, actually, but that wasn't the point. "Did the police ever ask you about it?"

"No. There was no reason to."

"Do you know anything about a charm bracelet she was wearing?"

Gray sat up. "Yes. I gave it to her."

I wasn't expecting that. "You gave her jewelry?"

"I wouldn't call it jewelry exactly. It probably cost fifty dollars."

"But you're a married man giving a young woman jewelry."

"I thought we'd been over that, Kate."

The tone in his voice was Dean Martin smooth and the same green eyes were staring into mine, but this time I wasn't going to fall for it.

"Let's go over it again."

"Theresa was a friend of Julia Kenny. Julia's dad is a business associate of mine and a friend. That's how I met Theresa. She came to a party my wife and I threw, and she helped me with some research for a case I was working on two years ago."

"You didn't mention that before."

"Didn't I? She needed a summer job and I was doing a pro bono case, so I couldn't really afford to hire too many legal assistants. Theresa was willing to work for what I could pay, and the case involved some medical issues, so her training was very valuable. I didn't see her much. There were thirty young people just like her working on the case."

"So the bracelet was a thank-you gift?"

"No. It was a birthday gift. I put a charm from the Picasso outside Daley Plaza on it. She spent a lot of time going in and out of those courtrooms for me, so it seemed like a nice gift."

"What about the nurse's cap?"

"I think she got that for her graduation. I didn't give it to her."

"Did she tell people about it?"

"I wouldn't have any idea if she did or didn't, Kate. It wasn't a secret."

"Do you know the charms were missing when her body was found?"

"I didn't know she was even wearing the bracelet." His voice was strong and authoritative. Dean Martin had been replaced by Perry Mason.

"It must have meant a lot to her if she continued to wear it," I said.

"I'm glad that it did."

"Why are you only telling me this now?"

"You're only asking me about this now."

"Or maybe now that I've found out, you have to give me some version of the truth. That's what politicians do, isn't it?"

"Maybe it's the lawyer in me, but I don't answer questions that haven't been asked." He tried to sound relaxed, but I could see his jaw tense up.

"Okay, then let me ask you about the award you arranged for Theresa."

"I think that's a bit strongly put. I nominated her for the Volunteer of the Year Award and was thrilled when she was chosen."

"Why nominate her?" I asked. "And don't tell me what a wonderful person she was. I'm sure you know lots of wonderful people. Why Theresa?"

He glanced toward his shoes then looked up at me. "Her mother asked me to. She felt it would help Theresa get a job and some much-deserved recognition."

"And how does Linda Moretti get you to do her a favor? It's not like she's got any political clout. What's in it for you?"

"She does make great butter cookies." He smiled, but it quickly faded when I didn't respond. "Linda Moretti is very persistent. As I'm sure you've seen. She wanted her daughter's name in the paper and Theresa really was a wonderful person, so why not?"

"Where did she get the donations?"

"I gave her my address book. Nothing sinister, Kate. Just good old Chicago politicking the way it's always been done."

"So why keep it a secret?"

"Just because I didn't tell you doesn't mean it was a secret."

He reached into his pants pocket and pulled out his cell phone. "Can you excuse me for a moment? I had the phone on vibrate because I was expecting a call."

Without waiting for Victor, he disconnected the mic and left the room.

"Kate is the man," Victor said. "You had that guy sweating."

"Give me a minute," I said. "I have a little surprise for act two."

I went into the hallway. Gray was on the phone at one end, so I walked to the other and into the ladies' room. I searched through the list of recent calls on my cell phone. There were four 312 area codes I'd dialed in the last few days. I knew one of them was Vera but I couldn't remember which one. I took a guess and pressed the "call" button.

"You know Gray well," I said when she answered the phone.

"Pretty well. Why?"

"Frank's dad mentioned to me that Gray had planned to run for the state senate but changed his mind because of some rumors of infidelity. Do you know anything about that?"

"Yeah. But I think that's all behind them."

"What do you know about it?"

"Why? Aren't you interviewing him about Theresa today? You're not going to ask about his marriage, are you?"

"Vera, I just have one question and I would really appreciate it if you would help me out on this. Okay? It's for Theresa that I'm asking."

I could hear a loud sigh from her end of the phone. "Okay."

"Do you know the name of the woman he slept with?"

"Woman? You've got it wrong, Kate. It wasn't Gray who cheated. It was his wife."

When I got back to the conference room, Gray was seated in his chair and Victor was once again putting the mic on him. Andres gave me a wink as I entered and it was clear that Victor too was ready for the big reveal. I, on the other hand, was deflated.

I sat across from Gray, a charming, handsome, rich, successful man, and felt as sorry for him as I had been feeling for myself all these months. I reminded myself I didn't care who had actually killed Theresa, only who I was going to make *look* guilty, and I no longer had the heart to fit Gray for the part.

"Let me ask you about Wyatt," I said.

Gray seemed puzzled. "What about him?"

"You helped him get an agent. Why?"

"I gave him the name of an agent. I just thought it would help."

"Back to helping everybody."

"That really bothers you, doesn't it?"

"It's a little too good to be true."

"I know that in the fields of politics and entertainment this doesn't always apply, but some people are who they say they are."

"Are you who you say you are?"

"It depends on who's asking."

"I'm asking."

He smiled a little then fidgeted with his tie before looking back at me. "Probably not. But then, you have a camera in my face."

"What about with Theresa? Did she see the real you?"

He leaned forward, well out of the shot. "Theresa was just a young woman I knew. And I did not . . ." He glanced over at Victor, obviously aware that, whether his face was on camera or not, he was being recorded. "Theresa was the best friend of my friend's daughter. And she did a little work for me. That's all."

"Okay. You can lean back," I said. Gray nodded and readjusted his position. "Let's get back to Wyatt. Do you think he is who he says he is?"

"I don't know. Did you ever check out that bar he worked at?"

"He and Theresa had a big fight a few days before she disappeared. But you knew that when you sent me there. Do you think Wyatt did it?"

He glanced toward Andres. "Can you stop the tape?"

Andres turned to me and I nodded. I heard the camera click off.

Gray returned his eyes to me. "It was only three days after Theresa went missing. We were all at a call center that had been set up in the basement of a church. The same church she was just buried from. Everyone was in shock, as you can imagine. Theresa's family was falling apart. Jason was hovering around outside, just trying to be a part of the whole thing. Julia was calling everyone she could think of, trying to find Theresa. And Wyatt was asking me if I knew the name of an agent. Seventy-two hours after his girlfriend vanishes and he's worried about his career. Honestly, Kate. What's that about?"

Sixty

An hour later, Wyatt sat in the same chair Gray had occupied. I didn't bother with lead-ins. I just went straight to the question Gray had wanted an answer to.

"Why, in the midst of a search for Theresa, were you hitting Gray Meyer up for the name of an agent?"

Wyatt was caught off guard. "I don't think it was in the midst of anything."

"At the call center, less than seventy-two hours after Theresa went missing. Seems an odd time to be worried about your career."

"I was just making small talk. I'd never met Gray before. Theresa had talked about him. She said he was all connected and stuff. I was just curious if he knew. I didn't expect him to give me a name. When he did, what was I supposed to do?"

"You started dating your current girlfriend before Theresa was even gone, didn't you? You met your current girlfriend in April; Theresa disappeared in late May."

"I met her. I didn't date her." He shifted in his chair.

"But you were ready to move on."

"I suppose. What's going on here? I thought we were going to talk about how sad we all are that Theresa's dead."

"Theresa's dead because somebody killed her," I said. "That's not conjecture anymore. That's fact. Now we have to ask who."

"Well, it wasn't me." He laughed a nervous laugh. "What about that ex-boyfriend of hers? The stalker."

"You told me he was harmless."

"That was before."

"Before what?"

"Before, you know, her body was found." He took a breath. "But now that we know for sure that she's dead, he seems like the best suspect, doesn't he?"

"Because she dumped him for you?"

"That's exactly why. He couldn't handle being rejected. Theresa didn't want anything more to do with him. She was scared of him."

"You didn't say that before. Did you tell the police?"

"I didn't want to ruin the guy's life."

"Your girlfriend was missing and you didn't tell anyone you thought Jason had something to do with it because you didn't want to ruin his life?"

"I didn't really care."

The words came out like bullets, and when he was finished he looked as shocked as I was. I wasn't surprised that he didn't care about Theresa. That much was obvious from the beginning. But it was astounding that he would say it. On camera.

After Wyatt left, Andres placed his finger on the rewind button. "Are we keeping that?"

"Why wouldn't we?"

"I don't know. That's going to be really hard for Linda to hear, don't you think?"

"I haven't gone that soft. That will be the best moment of the show, especially with Linda's buildup of him being Mr. Wonderful. I'll try to prepare her, though."

I wasn't really sure how I would do that. I called Linda to confirm our interview for the next day, hoping to softly broach the subject. I was expecting a tearful conversation, but Linda was quite upbeat.

"I'm really looking forward to it," she said. "I'm going to bring lunch, so don't eat before the interview. And we might actually have some other people join us."

"Other people?"

"I talked to Gray Meyer at the funeral about putting together a nursing scholarship in Theresa's name and he's going to help arrange a benefit to get it started. He's going to meet me at the restaurant where we are doing the interview. We're going to brainstorm ways to raise funds. Maybe you can put something about the scholarship on the show."

"Yeah, sure. I just interviewed him today and he didn't mention it."

"Oh, he's so modest," she gushed.

"Did you know he gave Theresa a bracelet?"

"The charm bracelet? She loved it. I showed you the photo of her with the nurse's cap, didn't I?"

I remembered that she had. "Did Gray give her that charm?"

"I did. What's a charm bracelet with just one charm on it?" She seemed almost playful. "By the way, I've told Tom to be with me just in case I need him. I've also left a message for Julia to meet up with us for lunch. And of course Wyatt. I'm really hoping to see him."

I took a deep breath, ready to tell her about his comments during the interview. Then I chickened out. "We should talk about him tomorrow."

"Okay, Kate. I'll see you at one o'clock. And thanks so much. I know you're going to do everything you can to honor Theresa's memory."

I didn't respond to that. I just said good-bye and hung up. There was one other call I needed to make before Julia, and probably David, showed up for the final interview of the day.

"Jason?" He had, much to my surprise, picked up.

"Hi, Kate. Look, I'm sorry I haven't gotten back to you. It's just, well, now that we know what happened, this whole thing seems really creepy."

"I know you haven't been comfortable with this from the beginning, Jason, but it's even more important now that you get your side of things out there. More and more people are pointing their finger at you. And that's easy to do if you're not there to defend yourself. I'd like you to have a chance to talk about how you feel knowing that Theresa is dead and her killer is still out there."

"Maybe next week."

"I need to do this tomorrow," I said.

He spoke so softly that I almost couldn't hear him. "Is eleven okay?"

As soon as I agreed, he hung up, leaving me wondering if he would be able to go through with it. Jason struck me as a little fragile, and maybe talking about Theresa's death on a television show was the last thing he needed to do. But it was my job, and if he wanted to say no he would have, I told myself. Except I knew I wasn't letting him say no. I was pushing, and maybe I was pushing too hard.

Sixty-one

I turned to see Julia and David come into the room. David immediately went over to Andres and Victor to say hello but seemed to be avoiding me. Or maybe I was just reading into things, because of what had happened at Hank's Restaurant.

"How are you doing?" I asked Julia.

"I feel like it happened all over again. Like it's the first day and she's missing and we're all in shock." She hesitated. "But now, you know, it's over and we can move on without any more interruptions."

"Interruptions?"

"David and I had been planning to look at houses this week. He just got a promotion at work and we thought it would be a good time. But we had to spend the weekend at the search, and then the wake and funeral, and now this interview," she said. "I don't mind doing it . . ."

"Of course not," I agreed. "It's just that all this stuff that's happened with Theresa is sort of overshadowing what's happening with you."

"Exactly. It's happened our whole lives. Did you know that my birthday is three days after hers?"

"I didn't."

"When we were growing up, her mother would throw this huge birthday party for her, and by my birthday everyone was sort of over it. My getting married was the first time I was going to have all the attention."

"And then she had to disappear and throw the dimmer switch on your spotlight."

Julia froze. I probably shouldn't have said it. Well, actually, I know I shouldn't have said it, since I was supposed to be her friend until I got the final interview on tape. But I was getting tired of Theresa's death having been either an inconvenience or an opportunity for these people. Vera, Frank, and I might have made for a screwed-up threesome, but at least we hadn't entirely lost perspective on which of us had the worst end of the deal.

My big mouth had exactly the impact I'd expected on Julia's interview. For the entire time, I got "Theresa was amazing and we all miss her" as the answer to nearly every question I asked. Even when I brought out Rosenthal's questions, Julia used the subject of the missing charms as an opportunity to praise her dead friend, and she repeated, almost in the same words, where she'd been on the day Theresa disappeared. For a nice added touch, she named the stores where she'd been shopping for bridesmaids' gifts.

"You must have shown the police receipts," I said.

"I didn't buy anything. I was just looking. I ended up getting all the gifts online a few weeks later."

That was convenient. I asked a few more questions but the interview was going nowhere. Rather than continue past the first tape, I turned to David, who was hovering at the back of the room.

"Why don't we get you in here?" I asked. "I think you would have an interesting, more objective opinion about her."

He shook his head. "Camera shy."

"You weren't the other day at the bakery," I reminded him. "Look, David, I have Theresa's friends and family and I think they're all in such shock that it's difficult for any of them to give me what I need for this to be a good story. But a man in your field is used to being objective, to setting aside your own emotions and opinions and just looking at things as they are. I really need that."

He nodded. It's amazing how people can be so easily stroked. Once he sat down, my attitude changed.

"One thing that's interested me as I've done these interviews," I said, "is that everyone describes Theresa as a nice girl, a good girl. Maybe she enjoyed a drink or two, but what twenty-two-year-old doesn't. How is it that the only people to hint at a dark side are you and Julia?"

"We knew her better than the others."

"Okay. So what is the dark side? Who is it that she was involved with?"

"I never got a name."

"What did Theresa say that made you think there was someone?"

"I don't know. She just said there was someone."

"She told you."

"Yes."

"You must have been close, if she was confiding in her friend's fiancé about behavior that everyone else has described as outside her character."

"I guess."

"So what did she tell you?"

He squirmed a little. "Maybe it wasn't anything specific. I just got a feeling that she was stepping out on Wyatt."

"Did she give you any details?"

He looked around. His neck was getting red and he was looking down at his hands. I waited but he didn't answer.

"You really have no idea whether Theresa was actually involved with anyone other than Wyatt, do you?" I said. "You just made it up."

"I don't know." I started to have the distinct impression that I'd been duped. Had I really been manipulated by this dull-as-toast husband?

"Why would you tell me that Theresa had a dark side? Were you trying to get me to look somewhere else? Not to look at you and Julia?"

He looked up at me. "Why would you look at us? We didn't do anything."

"Did you know Hank's Restaurant, where Theresa said she was going?"

"No. Never been there."

"You've never walked inside that place? Not once in your life?"

"Yeah. I mean, I know it now. But I assumed you were asking about before."

"So you go there now. Do you go frequently?"

"No. I think you misunderstood. Because of Theresa's disappearance I've certainly heard of it. I may have gone there once or twice."

"That's all?"

"Yes."

"Then how come the manager and a waitress recognized you from footage I showed them? In fact, the waitress even knew you ordered a BLT no mayo and chocolate cream pie. She said they were your favorites."

I heard Julia gasp. She almost got to her feet but Victor motioned for her to stay where she was.

David looked at me. There was defiance and anger. "You are mistaken."

"Is that what you're going to tell the police?"

The defiance last only a second longer. "It's not what it looks like."

Sixty-two

"So what does it look like?"

"Theresa and I met up at the coffee shop that morning. I used to work near there and I'd go at lunch, so I never took Julia there. It was the perfect place to meet and not run into anybody."

Julia ignored Victor's warnings and walked over to her husband. "For what?"

"Don't freak out. We were planning a surprise for the wedding. That's all. We were going to put together this video with pictures of you growing up, your favorite songs, and stuff like that. Theresa and I were just figuring out what we needed to do to pull it off. That's all we were doing." He looked over at me. "I swear."

I nodded. "But you didn't tell the police."

"No. I knew how it would look. I knew that it would mean I was the last person to see her alive. And I was meeting her in secret. I lied to Julia. Theresa lied to her mom. I didn't want people looking at me as having done something wrong. I didn't want Julia thinking that."

The suspicion drained from Julia's face as she wrapped her arms around David. Andres kept shooting the whole time, but once the hug lasted past thirty seconds, he looked over and me and shrugged. I motioned for him to keep rolling.

"I hate to break this up," I said, "but why did Theresa lie to her mother?"

Julia wiped away some tears. "Because she was so weird about my getting married first and I'll bet she would have given Theresa a hard time about spending time on a video when she could have been cozying up to Mr. Smooth." I assumed she meant Wyatt.

David nodded. "She'd gotten a lot of grief from her mom about spending money on gifts and the bridesmaid's dress. Money she had to borrow from her mom. She just didn't want to deal with any more crap."

"Okay. I can see that. But you've been holding on to some valuable

information for over a year. Did Theresa say she was meeting somebody or going somewhere after she left the coffee shop?"

He shook his head. "I know I look like an asshole, but if I knew
anything I thought would help the police, I would have come forward.
All she said was that she was going home. But I don't know if that's
true. She could have been lying to me."

"And the other man?"

Julia looked sheepish. "She'd talk about guys that she met once in a
while, and after she broke up with Jason, she had a couple of one-night
stands. She was just blowing off some steam, that's all, after how claus-
trophobic it had been with Jason. But when she met Wyatt she seemed
really into him. It's just that . . ." She paused then decided to tell me.
"There was something she was hiding. I assumed it was another man,
but I don't know."

"David, you're not the other man?" I asked.

"God, no. I was just trying to do something nice for Julia."

"Can you prove that? Maybe show me a copy of the tape you made
for Julia?"

David turned white. "After Theresa went missing, I just dropped
it. We were all so focused on finding her. And then on just getting
through the wedding."

"I believe him," Julia said. "Isn't that all that matters?"

"Women in love believe a lot of things, Julia," I said. "I don't think
that's enough proof for the police."

Sixty-three

I reminded myself of that when the guys finally dropped me off at Ellen's house after the shoot. Women believe a lot of things when they're in love. They believe that it will last forever, that it will fill all the gaps in their self-worth, that it will be enough to overcome any obstacle. And they believe that he is just as much in love.

Vera and I, at one point or another, had both believed all those things about Frank. But he was keeping secrets from both of us. As I had the night before, I pretended to enter my sister's house but jumped in my car as soon as Andres's van pulled around the corner.

I didn't have the key to Frank's art space, but I did have the address that had been written on the lease. I passed my house on the way, and though it looked dark and empty, it wasn't showing any obvious spooky signs, which, considering the state of things, was an improvement. Whoever had been harassing me had either changed his mind or knew that I wasn't there.

I parked in front of the art space and saw a big "For Rent" sign out front. The landlord had obviously lost no time in putting it back on the market, which made me wonder if Vera had gotten her deposit back.

"Not my problem," I said to myself.

The space had floor-to-ceiling windows and from what I could see from the outside it looked as it had in the videos. It was a large empty room with two closets at the back, a cement floor, dirty white walls, and exposed pipes. I could picture Frank happy in the space. But I couldn't see any paintings that Frank might have stored there.

There was nothing to be gained by staring in windows, but I did write down the phone number on the rental sign in hopes of getting access to check for Frank's paintings. If they weren't stored in some back room, then I had run out of places to look. I felt as though I'd let him down. Somehow I'd let the things that mattered most to him slip away, and I had no idea how to get them back.

As I walked back to my car, I had another idea. I didn't know if it was worth believing, but Neal had said Frank was planning to work at the community art center, just a block away. I walked over and saw the center, the same kind of urban space as Frank's rental but larger and full of life.

"Excuse me," I said to a woman setting out flyers for an upcoming class. "I need to ask about someone who might have been planning to teach here. His name was Frank Conway."

Her face lit up. "Frank. Yeah. He was supposed to start a week ago. What happened to him?"

"He died."

After the initial shock wore off, we sat at a desk in the corner and I filled her in on some of the details of Frank's death.

"So he was supposed to teach here?" I asked. "It's kind of confusing because he had also planned to rent his own studio."

"We've been growing faster than we anticipated. Frank was going to teach a class or two here and we'd promised him overflow students for his place. And we were helping him apply for a grant."

"What did he need that for?"

"For rent and supplies, operating costs. I think he had a few thousand dollars for start-up expenses, but he was worried about how he would pay for things after that. It takes time to build up a reputation."

"Wouldn't he end up being your competition?"

She smiled. "We're all artists. It's more a community than a competition. And Frank was really talented. His work is amazing."

A lump caught in my throat. "You've seen his work?"

"They're here." She pointed toward a stack of canvases in the corner. "He's been using our space to paint, and he stored his stuff here."

I walked over to the paintings and looked through them. They were all there. The painting he'd made me of the couple walking down Michigan Avenue, the one of me sleeping, the scenes of Chicago, the still lifes, the sketches. They were all safe.

I bent down and touched one of my favorites, a painting he'd done years ago of a tree in our backyard. It had been a beautiful afternoon, and I sat on a lounge chair and read while he painted. Every once in a while I'd look up from my book and watch him. I'd loved the way his eyes squinted as he studied the tree, and the way his fingers wrapped around his brush when he painted. When he saw me watching, he smiled.

"You're in love with me," he said.

"Every day," I told him.

And now he was gone. It hit me again as it had a thousand times, but this time, before I could stop myself, tears rolled down my face. I could feel sobs moving up from my chest and I could hear the sound of my own cries. It was the first time I'd cried since Frank died, and once I started, I couldn't stop. By finding the paintings I had found the one thing I was certain Frank loved and it was like finding Frank alive again.

The woman, in her kindness, simply waited. When I was calm again, she brought me tissues and water.

"I'm sorry."

She shook her head. "He must have meant a lot to you."

"He did."

She gave me the paintings and sketches and helped me pile them in my car. As she was about to go back into the center, I stopped her.

"Why did he keep them here? He had several places to store them."

"He said the person who had them was really pissed at him. He was worried they would end up in the trash."

I smiled. "He might have been right about that." I hesitated to ask, but I asked anyway. "It's probably a dumb question, but did he ever mention a wife or a fiancée?"

"Not specifically. Not that I remember. He did say once his personal life was pretty complicated, but he was hoping to get it straightened out soon."

I'd promised Vera I'd call her when I found the paintings, and I almost did, but something stopped me. Frank wasn't using her money to open the studio. He'd obviously pawned the cuff links to get himself started and had been working on a plan to find financial backing elsewhere. It had taken me all this time to realize it was only Frank's name on the lease. Not Frank and Vera. Did that mean he was coming back to me? He was finally becoming the man I'd always wanted him to be: focused and practical, while also following his own passion. I was excited at the idea even as I reminded myself it would never happen.

But another thought pushed its way in. What if Frank was doing this for Vera? She'd said that everyone she had helped before had pushed her aside once they no longer needed her help financially. Maybe Frank was proving he didn't love Vera for her money but for herself.

I searched through my purse for another phone number. Susan's number. At Frank's wake she'd said Vera doesn't always see what's obvious to other people. Maybe there was something obvious about Vera's relationship to Frank that even Vera hadn't seen. If there was, maybe Susan could tell me what neither Vera nor I seemed to know for sure.

Sixty-four

We met for coffee at a chain place with little atmosphere but a good selection of beverages and music loud enough to keep our conversation from anyone who wanted to listen.

Susan was nervous. She'd ordered a complicated drink with half of this and a dusting of that, and while she waited for it she tapped her fingers on the counter. I just smiled warmly and found us a table.

"I'll just get straight to the point," I said but she waved me off.

"Look, I get that in your situation you might think you have the right to lecture me, but it's totally different from you and Frank."

I had no idea what she was talking about, but I played along. "Why is it different?"

"Neal couldn't leave his wife because of the kids."

I'm sure my eyes got wide and my face red. Neal had been having an affair. He'd been hiding an affair. He hadn't wanted me to talk to Vera because she knew about it and might tell me. And I might tell Beth.

"Is that how you met Neal?" I asked. "Did Vera and Frank introduce you?"

"No, the other way around."

"Frank told me he met Vera in a grocery store."

She laughed. "I think he was just being funny. You know, she's a grocery heiress."

Another joke on me. "Are you and Neal still . . ."

"We broke up. Neal had some come-to-Jesus moment when his daughter got hurt riding her bike."

"I remember that. She needed stitches. It was nothing but it scared the hell out of both Neal and Beth."

"It obviously scared him straight."

I took a moment to collect myself. Susan seemed like a nice person, not masochistic in any way. "Why did you come to Frank's funeral? You had to know Neal would be there."

"I wanted to support Vera. She was determined to go, and I knew she'd be alone in there. But I guess I also wanted Neal to see me. We were together for eighteen months. Eighteen months of him telling me how much he loved me, how he was waiting for the right time to tell his wife. And then one tiny crisis and poof! He's father of the year." She blushed a little. "Sorry. I know you're not the best audience for this."

"It's okay."

She took a deep breath. "When you called and said you wanted to talk, I thought this was going to be hell. Like a confrontation with Neal's wife by proxy. But you seem really understanding. Just like you were at the wake. You were so nice to Vera. I was shocked by how cool you were about her being there."

I laughed. "I'm not cool about it, Susan. I just find Vera hard to dislike."

"She said the same thing about you. I thought it was a little weird how friendly you two were getting. We even got into a couple of arguments about it. But she said it made her feel closer to Frank. And it made her mad at him too."

"Mad?"

"I think she's been seeing him from your point of view. That maybe he wasn't Prince Charming. That he had a nice wife and a good marriage and he screwed it up."

"We both screwed it up, but it's nice to know my husband's mistress is on my side."

I got up from the table, but Susan grabbed my hand. "Is Neal's wife nice?"

"Yeah. She's very nice."

She smiled, but her eyes were filling with tears. "I guess that's good then."

I was barely in my car when I dialed Neal's number. I told him to meet me in the parking lot of the church where Frank and I had married, just three years before Neal and Beth walked down that same aisle.

He pulled up twenty minutes later, stopping his car a couple of feet and almost perpendicular to mine in the empty lot.

"What's this about?" he asked as he got out of his car. "You sounded so weird on the phone."

I rushed him. I pounded his chest and slapped him across the face in a mad fury. At first he tried to protect himself, but after a minute he just stood there and let me hit him. Finally I wore myself out.

"You are a good-for-nothing son of a bitch," I screamed.

"I know." His voice was quiet, sad. "Vera finally told you."

"Susan told me."

He turned white. "Are you going to tell Beth?"

"I don't know." I spat out the words. "What is wrong with you? Why would you screw up your marriage like this?"

It was a question I'd asked Frank once, and he hadn't answered. Now I saw Neal avoid it too. He just sighed. "It was a mistake."

"Was Frank going to tell Beth?" I asked. "Was that what the fight was about?"

Neal shook his head. "He would never tell Beth. He was better at keeping secrets than anybody."

"I'm finding that out."

"Yeah, I guess you are. The fight was what I said it was about. I told Frank that he should go home to you. And he told me that I wasn't in a position to lecture. We went a few rounds, but it didn't mean anything. We were both just a little ashamed of ourselves, that's all."

"I'm glad at least you both had the decency for that."

"Kate, I know this is a crappy question, but if Frank had broken up with Vera before you knew anything about it, would you have wanted to know?"

My head was spinning. For nearly three weeks I'd been discovering all the hidden half-truths of Frank's life and it exhausted me. I felt like I'd never known him. If I could go back six months, to my unhappy marriage and blissful ignorance, would I?

"I don't know," I finally said.

He grabbed my arm and pulled me down, sitting next to me on a parking lot bumper. "It happened. It was a mistake. And it's over. I don't want to hurt Beth and I don't want to end my marriage. I'm asking you, if you can, to please forget you have this information."

I couldn't make that promise, but I also wasn't sure that I wouldn't. Maybe it was better for Beth and their children if she didn't know. It wasn't a decision I would make tonight. I changed the subject.

"Do you remember the day Frank and I got married?"

He smiled. "It was supposed to be this perfect September day and instead it was a huge downpour."

"Yeah, I remember. But I wasn't talking about that. When I was walking down the aisle, Frank leaned over and whispered something to you. I've always wondered what he said, but I never asked him. I was worried he was getting cold feet."

"He wasn't." Neal took my hand. "He said, 'I'm not good enough for her.' And I said, 'As long as she never finds that out, you're fine.'"

He laughed at the memory. But I cried. After weeks of not being able to push the tears out from behind my eyes, I was now unable to stop. Neal and I sat in the parking lot for more than an hour with my head on his shoulder, both of us crying for what had been irrecoverably lost.

Sixty-five

"You said you played basketball with him on the day he died." Neal and I had finally composed ourselves enough to move from the parking lot to his car, where we listened to a CD and talked about better days. Evening was turning into night, but I didn't want to leave until I knew everything he could tell me.

"We played basketball. Over there." He pointed to a corner of the parking lot that served as a basketball court when the spaces weren't needed for the cars of churchgoers.

"What was his mood?"

He shrugged. "He was Frank. He was upbeat and happy."

"What did you talk about?"

"Basketball."

"Other than basketball."

"Nothing. It wasn't a therapy session, Kate. It was just two middle-aged guys reliving their glory days and getting ready for a reunion of the team."

"It sounds fun."

"It was fun." He laughed. "But man, were we out of shape. I thought I was going to have a heart attack and Frank drank a two-liter pitcher of iced tea and he was still dehydrated."

"Do you know where he went after the game?"

"He went to his mom's house. She'd called him about some problem he needed to rush over and fix. Knowing Lynette, she probably broke a nail."

We laughed and started on a roll of Lynette stories, each crazier than the last. It felt good to laugh and not worry, at least for a while, about any of the darker aspects of the whole experience. Sitting with him now, I realized it was crazy to think he had ever hurt Frank. He had loved him nearly as much as I did.

After a while, I got out of Neal's passenger seat. Rather than just saying good-bye and driving off, he walked me the three feet to my car. We hugged, and for a long time we wouldn't let each other go. But I had one more question.

"I want the truth, Neal. Was Frank really coming home?"

He paused. "I don't know," he said, almost in a whisper. "He talked about it. He didn't know if you would take him back. He talked about that a lot. But he also talked about Vera. I think he loved you both."

"So when you said he thought his engagement to Vera was a mistake . . ."

"He said it was. He said they were moving too fast."

"Had he told her that?"

"I don't know."

"And you don't know if he was ending it or just slowing things down?"

"To tell you the truth, Kate, I'd say on the day he died, it could have gone either way."

I kissed Neal on the cheek and got into my car. I was supposed to go back to Ellen's but I just wanted to go home. If there was some crazed killer waiting for me, so be it. I wanted to sleep in my own bed.

Sixty-six

Unfortunately the person waiting for me at my house wasn't a crazed killer. I wasn't that lucky.

"Hi, Lynette," I said as I got out of my car.

She and Alex were standing on my front step.

"We called you and you didn't answer, so we came over," Lynette said. Then she looked me over. "Is everything all right? You look like you've been dragged through an alley."

Instinctively, I wiped my face. The streaks from crying were, I was sure, still visible but there was nothing that could be done about that at the moment.

"Come inside," I said. Then I held my breath, prayed that there were no surprises waiting for me, and opened the door.

"Look at all the photos," Lynette said.

"Where?"

Then I realized she was walking over to the pile of photos that Andres had made.

"I've been organizing them," I said. "I'll get you something to drink. Sit down."

I walked through the rest of the rooms to make sure they were empty, which they were, then I went into the bathroom and washed my face. I put on a little concealer and some lipstick to make myself look less horrible but gave up when it only seemed to make me even more hollow and pale.

I went into the kitchen and put the kettle on. Out of the corner of my eye I saw a shadow. I took a breath and turned.

"Alex! You really shouldn't sneak up behind me."

"Sorry, kiddo. I just wanted to let you know that the insurance check is being released. You should have it in a week or so."

"I thought it was being held up pending cause of death. Did the coroner change it from undetermined to something else?" That something else could, I knew, only be accident, suicide, or homicide. Since there was a large amount of digitalis found in Frank's system he could not have died of natural causes.

"I don't think so. I was told that your Detective Podeski notified the company that you were not a suspect in your husband's death, so they released the check."

"I feel a little weird about taking it, though."

He walked toward me and put his hands on my shoulders. "You are my daughter, Kate. I'm going to take care of you. It's what Frank would have wanted. It's what I want."

And, for the third time that day, I burst into tears.

"What's going on in here? What have you done to that girl?" Lynette had entered the kitchen.

"Nothing, Lynette," I said. "I'm just doing this a lot."

"Of course you are, dear. And I haven't helped." She glanced toward her husband. "Alex and I came here to sit down with you and find out why you think that woman isn't responsible for Frank's death. And then we'll figure out where we go from there." She pushed me toward the living room. "Now go sit down and I'll make you a cup of tea. Just tell me where you keep it."

I walked over to the cabinet and opened it, showing her the dozen or so varieties I had.

"Honestly, Kate, why do you need all these teas? All you need is one good brand of coffee and one good brand of tea. Why do you overcomplicate things?"

"Most of them are Frank's."

She blushed. For the first time I had actually won an argument. An argument so small that no one but me would have noticed. But I did notice and it was all that mattered.

"Here," I said, pulling down a bright blue tin. "I had this yesterday. It was good."

"I don't want that. It's one of those teas that's full of a lot of silly flowers," Lynette said.

"It's not." I turned the tin around until I saw the list of ingredients.

It was a blend of different herbs and leaves—among them comfrey. The tin showed that it had been produced and packaged by a small specialty tea shop just blocks from the house. I searched the cabinet next to the sink. I'd known it was missing since the day Podeski and I had gone through the house. The two-liter pitcher. On that last day when he'd stopped by, Frank must have used it to make himself iced tea.

I reached the store just as it was closing.

"Did you sell this?" I said to the woman who was trying to close up.

She took one look and turned white. It was all the proof I needed.

"We used to. We don't anymore. Did you drink that? Please tell me you didn't."

"It's not comfrey in there, is it?"

She buried her face in her hands. "No. It's a very dangerous plant. A foxglove. But you must know that if you're asking. It can cause illness and some heart issues if taken internally."

"I know."

"There was an inexperienced person that worked with me. It was a really popular tea in our shop for a while. And then about six months ago, we were running out of comfrey and she picked some leaves from a plant that grew in her mother's backyard. She thought it was the same. She even showed me the leaves. Without the flowers to compare, they look really similar."

"So without knowing what it was, you put it in a tin and sold it as comfrey just to make a few bucks? You couldn't have just been sold out and waited for a source you could trust?"

She looked defeated and even trembled a little. "We sold maybe five tins of that batch before we realized the problem. We got all but one back. We sent out e-mails to everyone on our mailing list. I guess that's the one we missed."

"I guess."

"It's only really dangerous, I mean really dangerous, if you drink a ton of it. We say on the tin that you should only have one or two cups a day. Some of the herbs have great healing properties if used in moderation but they can cause some issues if you use a lot at one time." Now she was talking fast and getting defensive. "We're very clear about that on the label."

I opened the tin and revealed the three tea bags that were left of the original thirty. "Do you know what happens if a thirty-seven-year-old man drinks a two-liter pitcher of iced tea made with this? I'll tell you what happens. He dies."

"Oh, my God" was all she got out.

I walked a few steps away from her to a bench by a waterfall that took up one wall of the small store. I grabbed my cell phone, dialed, and waited for the answer.

"Detective Podeski, I know how Frank died."

When he arrived he was alone. He walked into the store and took one look at the terror-stricken shop owner who was watching me from behind the counter.

"We're closed," she said.

"That's an understatement." He walked over to me and sat beside me on the bench. "I'm so sorry, Kate."

I leaned into his brown polyester suit jacket, and he put his arm around me.

"I thought it was his fault, somehow," I said. "If Vera had killed him, if he had died of a heart attack because he wasn't taking care of himself. Or he'd taken some drug or some pill he shouldn't have. I thought he had done it to himself."

"He didn't do anything wrong," Podeski said quietly. "Neither of you did."

I'd called Alex and Lynette after I'd phoned Podeski. I'd scared the hell out of both of them by running out of the house with the tea, so I explained what I'd found out. They walked into the shop as I sat and stared into space.

Alex talked of lawsuits and Lynette screamed. Podeski called to get warrants and told the woman a criminal investigation would now take place. I just left. I had asked myself once if knowing how Frank had died would really make a difference. And now I knew. It did. Whatever adrenaline had kept me going for the last three weeks was gone. I was too exhausted even to cry.

Sixty-seven

The next morning came too soon. I dragged myself from bed, made a pathetic attempt to ready myself for the day, and met Andres and Victor outside my house. It was a dreary, gray day and we were promised thunderstorms. At least Mother Nature knew how I was feeling.

And I knew Andres did too. I'd called him the night before to explain what I'd found out and to tell him to pick me up at my house rather than my sister's. I'd also told him I wouldn't be able to get through the last day of shooting if we talked about it. Andres said there wouldn't be a word about it, and I knew that if he said it, it would be true. There were, as Gray had said, some people in the world who are who they say they are, and Andres was one of them.

Work had always been my distraction but I wasn't looking forward to being a witness to more grief. I told myself to remember that this wasn't personal, that I didn't care, and that these people were just a collection of sound bites to be used for entertainment. I just wasn't sure I believed it anymore.

First up was Jason. The restaurant I'd rented for the day had let us in an hour before he was scheduled to arrive, and we set up the camera and lights. I got the guys breakfast and went through my notes. Jason was supposed to arrive at eleven, but when he hadn't shown up at eleven forty-five, I assumed he wasn't coming. I dialed his number but only got voice mail.

At twelve thirty, Andres and I started talking about Linda's interview, scheduled for one o'clock. As we talked, Jason walked into the restaurant. He seemed almost as tired as I was, so I got coffee for us and we sat in a corner while Andres and Victor hung back and pretended to be setting up. I could tell that Jason needed a few minutes before he was in front of the camera to relax and prepare himself. I didn't want to waste time with a useless interview and I was beginning to think that was what it would be. Jason was distracted, unfocused, and fidgeting with something in the pocket of his windbreaker.

"Have you been to her grave?" I asked.

"No. I figured I'd wait until things quieted down. I don't really want to run into her family."

"It's a shame that all of this hasn't brought you closer to them. You're all suffering the same loss."

Even through the pockets of his windbreaker I could see he was clenching his fist. "They didn't understand what I'd lost."

Andres looked over at me. "We're ready."

I got up. "Do you need a few more minutes?"

He shook his head and got up from the chair. As he did he took something out of his pocket. He saw me notice.

"My good-luck charm," he said.

"Can I see it?" It didn't look like the saint's medal he'd held at the earlier interview and, just to be sure, I wanted to see it up close. He was hesitant to let it go, but I smiled at him. "I need to get a good-luck charm. Something that will keep me safe when I'm nervous."

"You get nervous? You seem like you're always in control."

"I need help too. Everyone does. I just haven't found myself the right charm."

"Yeah. Okay. I thought you were just using me, but you've turned out to be the one person I could trust."

I held out my hand and he placed the object in it. A sadness I hadn't expected washed over me when I looked at the tiny silver jewelry. It was a nurse's cap. "This was Theresa's."

He glanced at the charm. "Yeah. It's something she gave me."

I shook my head. "It was a charm her mother had given her for graduation. Why would she give that to you?"

"She left it at my apartment."

"No, Jason," I said quietly. "You said she'd never been at your apartment."

He tried to be casual, but I could see red blotches begin to appear on his neck and face. He was nervous. And when he spoke, he stammered. "Then it must have been somewhere else."

"She only had it a few weeks before she died. She broke up with you before that."

I started to walk away but Jason grabbed me, pulling me to him so that he was behind me with his arm wrapped around my waist.

"You of all people should understand what it feels like when the person you were supposed to spend the rest of your life with gets stolen from you."

I struggled but couldn't get away. Andres and Victor started to run toward us but stopped suddenly. As I turned my head to the right, I could see what had stopped them. Jason had a gun. It hadn't been a fist he'd been making earlier. He'd been wrapping his hand around the gun in his pocket.

"Come on, Jason," I said. "I was really on your side. I was going to make you look innocent. You were the one person in a really long time I actually believed."

"That's because we're the same."

I looked at Andres and made the eye gesture I'd made a thousand times before. He moved his head slightly back and forth. He was saying no. I squelched the urge to remind him that I was the boss on this crew and made the eye gesture a second time. Andres backed up, moving toward the camera.

"What are you doing?" Jason screamed.

"The camera's been on," Andres said. "I'm turning it off. I assume you wouldn't want this on television."

"Whatever. Just don't come closer."

Andres looked toward me one more time, then pressed the "on" button on the camera and walked a few steps away. For once I wasn't thinking of a great shot. I was thinking that if Andres, Victor, and I died in this room I wanted to provide the police with irrefutable proof of our killer's identity.

Then I took a deep breath and tried to pretend this was an interview. "You killed Theresa by accident. You loved her and you didn't want to hurt her. Is that what happened? Because I think everyone would understand that."

"They hate me."

"No. They just don't know how much you loved each other and how much it hurt to lose her. But I do, Jason. I loved my husband very much." My voice was shaking and I could feel myself starting to cry but this was not the time. I tried to focus. "If you kill me it won't be an accident. It will be on purpose. And that would make you a murderer. And you're not, Jason. You're a nice guy who loved someone and got hurt."

I could feel his grip tighten.

"I'm sorry," he said softly.

I felt him raise the gun and I closed my eyes in preparation, wondering how long it would take for the bullet to hit, and how long after my death it would be before Mike tried to air the tape.

But Jason let go. I was almost too shocked to run, but Victor yelled at me and brought me to my senses. I ran to Andres, who pushed me behind him. I thought it was over but it wasn't.

"Don't do that, man," I heard Victor say. "Over a chick? That's such a waste."

I looked out from behind Andres and saw that Jason had put the gun against his own temple. "I can't live without her," he said.

"Yes, you can." We all turned to see Linda. She was carrying a big metal catering tray. She walked into the room, put the tray on a table, and headed for Jason.

"He killed Theresa," I said.

She walked closer. "Is this what you are going to do in my daughter's memory? Is this what you think she would want? She planned to save lives, Jason. Do you think she would want you to take your own because of what happened? If you do then you didn't love my daughter."

Jason stared at her in disbelief then started to shake. He lowered the gun and let it fall on the floor. As soon as the gun hit the floor, he collapsed in a heap.

Sixty-eight

J ason sat handcuffed at one of the restaurant tables. There were half a dozen detectives and at least twice as many uniformed officers walking in and out of the building. Detective Rosenthal was finally sitting with the man who had killed Theresa.

"What happened, Jason?" she asked.

"I saw her the day before. She told me to leave her alone. She told me she wanted to be with that actor, who was cheating on her. I tried to tell her. She wouldn't listen. I told her I'd followed him and I saw him with another woman. I never cheated on her. I loved her. Even after we broke up. She slept with other guys. She did things she shouldn't have, but I forgave her. I deserved her."

"Okay," Rosenthal said softly. "Then what happened?"

"She told me she knew exactly who I was. She said I didn't surprise her. Like it was a bad thing."

"And on the day she died?"

"I followed her. I saw her with Julia's fiancé. She didn't want me, but she did want some guy who was already getting married. I grabbed her when she came out of the restaurant. I asked her what kind of a slut strings me along, sleeps with some good-for-nothing actor, and then goes after the fiancé of her best friend. She told me to leave her alone. She said her friends said she was crazy for talking to me. That she'd had to hide it from them. She said she felt sorry for me. But she didn't anymore. She was going to tell everyone I was bothering her. She was going to stop talking to me."

"Did you take her somewhere?"

He nodded. "I made her get in my car and we went for a drive. I didn't really pay attention to where I was going, so we ended up out in the suburbs. I saw the signs for the forest preserve and I figured it would be a quiet place to talk. That's all I wanted to do—talk. I don't know what happened next."

"Yes, you do, Jason."

I looked at Rosenthal. She was sitting inches from him. She was calm and understanding: his best friend. She was me, with no camera and a far better reason for pretending to care.

Jason sighed. "She got really mad at me. She said her mother would wonder where she was. She said she had to get home. She told me she never wanted to see me again." He clenched his jaw, but as he got to the moment of Theresa's death, his voice was emotionless. It was like he was describing something he'd seen on television. "I hit her. And I just kept hitting her until she stopped moving. Then I put her in the ground and went home."

"How could you do that?" The words just came out of my mouth. Everyone, including Jason, turned to look at me.

Jason shook his head. "I thought you would understand. That's why I put the pictures out to remind you of what you had lost."

"You left a dead bird on my porch and broke into my house because you thought I understood you?"

"I got that letter saying your show was going to find out the truth about what happened to Theresa. And then you told me that I would end up looking guilty, that people would think I didn't love her. You were going to tell everyone that I was a bad guy. I tried to warn you off. You wouldn't listen. Then I tried to remind you of what it felt like to be thrown away by the person who was supposed to love you. You still didn't listen. But then I thought . . . I thought you finally knew how I felt. I thought you understood that you don't stop loving someone just because they hurt you."

I did. That's why, even though everything had pointed to Jason, I hadn't believed it. I hadn't wanted to believe it.

"I just wanted a good story," I said.

"Well, you got it. Just make sure you say that I loved Theresa."

He was staring right through me. I thought of what it must have been like for Jason's eyes to be the last thing Theresa saw. Then I remembered something else. "Where's my husband's ring?"

Jason nodded toward an evidence bag that contained items one of the uniformed officers had collected from Jason's pockets. The officer was just about to seal the bag, putting Frank's ring into judicial limbo, when Rosenthal stopped him. She took out the ring and handed it back to me.

"It was one of my good-luck charms," Jason said. "To remind me of what Theresa and I were meant to have if she would only have come back to me."

We watched as Jason was put into the back of a squad car. Then Andres, Victor, Linda, and I gave our statements to Rosenthal. As soon as that was done, I handed her the shot tape of Jason holding me at gunpoint. I knew Mike would give me grief about it later, but he could wait until the trial was over to get it back.

Tom had been just behind Linda with a large plate of desserts that were now sitting untouched on a table. Gray, Wyatt, David, and Julia had arrived after Jason's arrest for what was supposed to be another thank-you lunch and their meeting about a scholarship fund. Instead it was a bunch of shell-shocked people sitting around with Tom telling us he knew all along.

"Why did you know?" I asked him.

"She was my sister," he said. "I could tell whenever his name came up she was scared. She wouldn't get specific, but I knew." I could hear the catch in his throat. "I've always been the problem child and Theresa was always the saint. I guess she figured I'd beat him up or something. She wouldn't have wanted that. She hated violence." He paused. "It killed me knowing that he must have done something to her but not being able to do anything about it. I never knew I could feel so much anger. I take it out on everyone, even my mom. Even you."

"I wouldn't worry about it, Tom," I said. "I think we all grieve in our own way."

I watched David put his arm around his wife. I still didn't like the guy exactly, but he did love Julia, and she loved him. She looked up at me, her face streaked with tears.

"We all were so sick of hearing about Jason that I think she felt she couldn't admit she still talked to him," Julia said. "I think she must have felt she had to handle it on her own."

"It may give you some comfort to know that she was reaching out," Rosenthal said. "We found a slip of paper in her purse with three numbers on it."

"Four, three, seven," I said. "I remember seeing them in the evidence bag."

"The last three numbers of a stalker hotline. We were able to confirm she'd called to get advice."

Gray sat down next to me. "Are you okay?"

"No." I laughed. "Thirty-seven years of the dullest life you could possibly imagine, but the last few weeks have certainly made up for it."

"You want to go back to dull?"

"I want the new *TV Guide* arriving in my mailbox to be the most exciting part of my week."

"I can't picture you enjoying that. You're too smart. And you read people really well."

"I had you figured for Theresa's lover."

He smiled. "Okay, you read most people well. I was just . . ."

"Me. Some poor unhappily married sap who found out your spouse preferred someone else."

"Worse. I didn't know I was unhappily married. But as it's been pointed out to me, I wasn't really around enough to know." He stared at the floor. "And I guess I've always felt a little smug that my wife and I never found anyone else we liked more than each other." He paused, seeming for the first time uncertain. "I guess I was more wrong than I thought."

"You'll make it work."

"Is that what you would have done?"

"I don't know if I would have had the chance. Vera makes for pretty stiff competition."

He smiled, then seemed to weigh whether he should say something. "I have a beach house in St. Joe's, right on Lake Michigan," he said finally. "I'm not going to be using it, so if you want a place to go for a while and just hang out . . ."

"You have a real knight-in-shining-armor complex, don't you?" I said. "Thanks, but I'll be okay."

"I know I can be pushy. But I've seen too many people like Theresa. They don't ask for help until it's too late, so I offer even when it's none of my business. I'm sorry, if it's too—"

I stopped him. "It's very kind of you. Thank you."

He smiled. "And listen, I heard about what happened at the tea shop. I'm really sorry about your husband."

"Tell me, Gray, do you also know where they buried Hoffa?"

He laughed. "That was Detroit. I don't have a lot of connections in Detroit."

We stayed together in the restaurant for several hours. Eventually we did get hungry, and the food was amazing. When I was ready to leave I saw Linda sitting with Tom and went over to say good-bye.

"I have a feeling my boss will want some comments from you," I said, "but not today."

She hugged me, and I hugged back. I could feel tears rolling down my cheeks. It was annoying. I couldn't seem to stop.

"Thank you, Kate. Thank you so much."

"I think you're the one who at the very least stopped a suicide from happening, so I should be thanking you. How did you know what to say?"

"I knew my daughter. I knew what she would have said if she were here."

I smiled. "I know what she'd say now. She'd say she was very proud of you."

"She'd say I was always interfering, and I was too pushy and I liked being the center of attention too much. And she'd be right. It breaks my heart we'll never argue about those things again, but at least I know she's not in pain."

"I don't know how you manage to be so at peace about it."

She leaned in. "Believing she was alive kept me alive, and now keeping her memory alive will get me up in the morning. If I think about what I've lost, I'll lose my mind. So I've decided to focus on what

Theresa brought to my life while she was with me." She took my hand. "And who she has brought to my life even after she was gone."

We hugged again and I promised to keep in touch. I say that to nearly all the people I interview, but this time I meant it.

I moved over to Tom and hugged him as well. "I have to ask you," I said quietly, "if you know anything about some money Theresa had in her account. I didn't want to ask your mom, in case . . ."

"It was mine. I was saving it to go to New York for school."

"Why not put it in your own account?"

He looked sheepish. "I had some trouble a while ago. Writing bad checks. It was stupid but it's sort of followed me. I couldn't get a bank account. But I've been doing catering jobs on the side, fancy weddings and shit. I gave the money to Theresa to keep so I wouldn't do something stupid, like spend it." He glanced at his mother, talking with Gray. "My mom didn't know at the time that I was thinking of moving. She's a little overprotective."

"And then you withdrew the money after she disappeared?"

"I told my mom when Theresa went missing. She was on Theresa's account so she took the money out. We needed it to put together a reward for information . . . It's a little embarrassing so I hope you won't use it."

"I won't."

An innocent explanation. I could have pretended not to understand why Rosenthal had blacked it out, but I knew. If I had been doing my job properly, I would have played that up. I would have turned a nothing trip to a strip club, a few too many drinks in a bar, and some large bank deposits into a potential secret life. By the end of the show, the truth would have been revealed, but by then the damage would have been done. Rosenthal had tried to protect Theresa and her family from me. And I was glad that she had.

As I was about to leave, I thought of another question for Tom. "Not that it's any of my business, but why did you gouge out Julia's eyes in those photos?"

Tom and I looked over at Julia, who had joined Linda and Gray.

"She told me a few weeks before her wedding that Theresa's disappearance was upstaging her big day. I took my revenge on her photos."

"Is that why she and David said you had issues? They made kind of a deal out of it."

He laughed. "Well, the photos weren't my only revenge. They wanted chocolate cake with vanilla icing for their wedding cake. I made banana. Julia breaks out in a rash when she eats bananas. She itched all day."

Sixty-nine

I t took me almost a week, but eventually I drove out to the graveyard. The stone was new and the grass beneath it freshly cut.

"Hi, Theresa," I said. "We didn't meet, but I know a lot about you."

I laid a bouquet of fresh flowers at the edge of the stone. I wasn't the only one who'd been there. Ribbons, photos, and other bouquets nearly covered the grave.

"I just wanted to say I hope that I do your story justice. I want you to know I'll try to keep it respectful and honest." I paused. "You never worked in television, so you probably don't realize just how hard that's going to be."

An hour later, I was in another graveyard. This time there was a bench facing a large headstone. It said, "Francis John Conway. Loving Husband. Adored Son. Devoted Friend."

If Frank's death had been an episode of one of my true-crime shows, it would have ended here. We always take the loved ones to the grave, often providing the flowers and balloons they leave there, so we can get that nice end shot of them mourning their loss.

Instead of flowers, I laid one of those kid's paint sets at his grave, with a new paintbrush, and sat on the bench.

"I love you. I just want you to know that."

The tears came easily, as they'd done all week. I'd been through three boxes of tissues and two rolls of toilet paper in just the last few days. It was getting to the point where I was thinking of buying in bulk.

"Mike—you remember Mike, don't you, Frank? He was really happy with the footage we shot. And we even got Linda to do another interview. She said that *Missing Persons* had helped solve her daughter's murder. She said it on tape. Mike is going to use that to promote the show. He'll probably be sending me a lot more work, which is kind of a mixed blessing if you know what I mean."

I looked at the grass beneath my feet.

"I had lunch with your parents. I've promised to come by once a month for lunch. Also a mixed blessing. But I told them about Theresa and they've contributed to the fund for a nursing scholarship and we're even going to set up an art scholarship in your name at the community center. Some of your insurance money will go toward that and some of it has to go to getting a new roof. Remember how I used to nag you about how we need a new roof? Well, it's leaking." I smiled. "I guess that's not very important. It's just something that's going on.

"The woman from the store where you bought the tea, she's facing charges of involuntary manslaughter. I know she didn't do it on purpose, but I'm helping Detective Podeski with all the information I can. It was just so careless. Right when you were finally coming into your own. I know there might be some people who think that you would have been all gung ho for a while and then lost interest in it. But I don't think you would have, this time. I think you would have stuck with it, Frank. You would have made a success of it."

I looked at the marble with his name carved in it. He would have thought it was too stuffy and formal, but it looked strong. Like it could withstand anything.

"I'm really proud of you, Frank."

There was of course only silence in response. I didn't want to, but I laughed. For so much of our marriage, when I talked, Frank ignored me. Especially when there was a basketball game on TV. I guess from now on whenever we had these little chats it would be just like Frank was watching a game.

After I left the cemetery, I drove to her house and sat in my car. I'd already told her I was coming but for some reason I was reluctant to go inside. But I saw Vera and her dogs watching me out the front window, so I had no choice. I grabbed the painting and met her at the front door.

I handed her a painting Frank had made about five years before. It was of the Montrose Avenue Beach dog park. It had been a beautiful summer day and Frank had perfectly captured the carefree fun of a summer afternoon.

"I know it was before he met you," I said, "but you said Frank hadn't painted anything for you yet, so I thought this might be something you would like."

Her eyes widened and her hands came to her heart. "But are you sure? It belongs to you."

"I have about thirty of Frank's paintings. I gave several to his parents. Neal took one. The painting of the couple on Michigan Avenue is back over the fireplace, and I've put two in the bedroom, one in the kitchen, and one in the guest room. There's plenty to go around."

She started to tear up. "I'm sorry, Kate. For everything. I don't know if I really said that before."

"It's okay," I said. We sat in her kitchen and watched as a gardener worked out back, getting her garden into the kind of shape that Frank had planned to do. Or had said he planned to do. Of all the answers I'd found over the last few weeks, in both Frank's and Theresa's death, the one question that remained was whether Frank had intended to stay with Vera or come home to me.

And it was a question that would never be answered.

After about an hour I let Vera walk me to my car.

"I almost forgot," she said as she took a key from her pocket. "Gray stopped by the other day. He asked me to give this to you. It's a spare key to his house in Michigan. He said you might want to go there for a rest."

I laughed. "He never stops trying."

"No, he never gives up. He told me he and his wife are going to Europe for the entire month of August. Second honeymoon kind of thing. He said you inspired it so he wanted you to have the house."

"I'm not going to use it. You go, Vera."

"My family has three houses on Lake Michigan, two on Martha's Vineyard, a place in the south of France, and a small estate in Scotland.

And I think we still have a place somewhere in the Caribbean. I can't remember where."

"So you're saying you have somewhere to go if you need to get away."

She laughed. "I'm good, yeah."

I took the key. Maybe a few weeks dangling my feet into one of the Great Lakes wasn't a bad idea.

"I've got a million errands to run today," she said. "But normally I'm around. If you ever want to talk. Or just anything."

"I'll keep that in mind."

"And Victor's band is playing Friday. He called and invited me to come, so if you want to have a night out . . . "

"Maybe."

"I think Andres and his wife are going so it would be a bunch of friends."

I got in my car. "I'll see you around, Vera."

As I drove away, I saw Vera talking to an elderly neighbor. They sat on her front steps and were laughing. It was just like something Frank would have done. A million errands to run, and yet he'd get distracted by a friend.

I had gone only three blocks when I pulled over and looked at my cell phone. Her number was the last I'd dialed. I could delete it, or I could just do nothing. Within days, as I made and received new calls, it would disappear from my phone, and I could let go of Vera forever.

I hesitated, then pressed "Add to my address book" and typed in her name. I hesitated again before pressing "Save."